Raw Voices:

Tales From East-Central Arizona

by

The Cedar Hills Writers Group

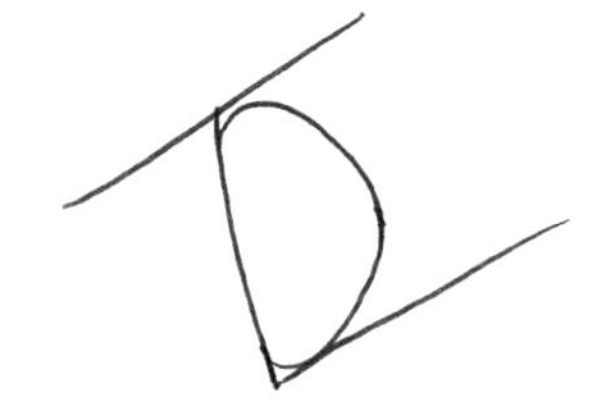

Cover photo by Orina Hodgson

Format Editing by Paula F Winskye

ISBN: 978-1979137980

Contents

Introduction

The high desert.

Such a term invokes many images in peoples' minds, from the moonlit silhouette of a baying coyote, to the tranquil peace of the Petrified Forest, to the lone juniper tree standing vigil over a windswept land. The land is a study in contrasts. It burns with the heat of an Arizona summer but the winters, surprisingly enough, can be bitterly cold. It is a land of stark and rugged mountains, yet contains the gentle beauty of summer sunflowers and crystal blue skies. It is inhospitable to those who do not respect it and welcomes those who do. Above all that, it is a land of both dark and delightful treasures, secreted away from the rest of the world.

In these pages, you will discover these secrets.

It takes a special soul to seek out east-central Arizona. The lifestyle can be unforgiving and harsh and yet the residents persevere. They find new and better ways to live with nature or grapple to defeat it. These are the modern pioneers, the adventurers, the brave and the bold. Faced with common struggle, they develop their own shared heritage. No matter where you go, you can speak to the locals about the strong spring winds, or dealing with a herd of stubborn cattle blocking their path, or that one visit downstate that reminded them why they preferred the smaller remote towns. Similar themes...and yet, no two stories are exactly the same. Everyone living here has a unique saga to tell, or a vision of what could come.

Walk with the authors and you will discover tales of heartbreak and murderous passion; of evil lurking beneath the boughs of ruined forests; of animals and humans that save each other; of humanity's struggle against the very elements, and of the resiliency of the residents after the fall of society. You will read of life journeys spent taming their own slice of heaven, and others as they cope with the difficulties of rural distance and isolation.

And in the end? Whether a longtime resident or as someone just passing through, you will come to know the spirit of the high desert, and take it with you no matter where you roam.

Thank you for reading.

The Cedar Hills Writers Group

Bad Residue

by

Jonathan S. Pembroke

Twigs crunched under the tires as the truck shuddered to a stop. Andy killed the engine and sipped his coffee. "Told you the snow wouldn't amount to much. Even if had, old Alice here can get us through anything." He tapped the dashboard.

I nodded. The thin blanket of white was broken by clumps of tall grass and mossy rocks. I glanced out the side window. Swaths of both charred and bare wood stared back at me. I shook my head.

Andy glanced my way. "You all right?"

"Yeah. Just never fails. Every time we come up here, I feel like I'm staring at a corpse."

"Well, you are. The forest used to be alive. Now, it's not." Andy produced a cardboard pack from the console and banged it against the heel of his fist. He extracted a cigarette and lit it with practiced ease.

I wrinkled my nose but said nothing. It was his truck.

I unbuckled myself from the seat and pushed open the door. The old metal creaked and I wondered if Andy was ever going to fix Alice's door hinges.

I paused for a moment and stared at the burnt trunks and leafless limbs. "Good to see you boys again."

Andy came around the front of the truck. "Talking to the trees now, Ryan? You're losing it, bud."

"Yeah, maybe."

I took a deep breath, conscious of how loud it was. There was no twitter of birdsong. There was no breeze. It was as quiet as an open grave, giving mute testimony to the extent of the destruction.

I felt a sharp rap on my shoulder, shaking me from my reverie. Andy jerked his head at the truck. "Okay, dude. Enough spacing out. Let's get cutting."

We dragged the chainsaws from the back of the cab, along with our safety gear. It took a few minutes to get our kevlar chaps attached, the saws fueled and our helmets strapped on...and then it was to business. I selected a Douglas Fir with a thick bole, about fourteen inches across. Our cutting permits prohibited cutting tress with trunks wider than sixteen inches. Andy said the Forestry Service reserved the bigger, better trees for commercial cutters.

Andy was a cynic. He was also probably right.

I cut a shallow notch, pulled the saw, and made an angled cut from the other side. Before I got through, I glanced up to check Andy's position. He was a hundred yards away, off to the side. I made the last cut and gave the trunk a good shove. It splintered and the whole thing toppled.

A heavy blow struck my helmet and I staggered. A short, thick branch lay on the ground. "Widowmakers," they called them; detached branches that got dislodged and struck from above when the tree was jostled. For what undoubtedly would not be the last time, I was glad my wife insisted I wear the helmet.

We paused after an hour. I sat on the trailer and surveyed the carnage. Downed firs littered the area in front of Andy's truck. I sighed. Cutting them down was the easy part. There was still the limbing, sectioning, and loading the rounds onto the flatbed.

I palmed a handful of peanuts and popped them in my mouth. There were more than three cords already down. Even after setting aside money for gas and to replace our chains, we'd probably clear three hundred dollars on this trip.

Andy flopped down next to me, gnawing on a green apple. His mind must have been working in the same direction. "I make it about three and half cords."

"Yep, I'd guess we're looking at three, three-fifty after costs."

He smiled. "Not bad for a day's work, especially when 'The Man' isn't taking half."

I affected a shocked look. "You mean you don't report your earnings come tax time? You crook. I can't hang with you any more."

"Ryan, Lynette would kick your ass if you reported this on yours."

I laughed. "You're probably right."

"Did you get a kitchen pass to come up tomorrow too?"

"Yeah, she's cool with it as long as I get some rest before I go back on shift. We can keep doing this unless we run out of trees."

Andy snorted. "The fire burned over half a million acres. Just up here around Terry Flat there must be tens of thousands of standing dead fir. No, my friend, we'll be doing this for a while."

I took a swig of water. "It's the biggest one, isn't it?"

"What's that?"

"The Wallow Fire. It's the biggest one in state history."

Andy nodded. "Yeah, it passed up Rodeo-Chideski."

I glanced at the trees again. "What a waste. All that life,

just...extinguished."

"Forest fires are just part of nature, Ryan." Andy shrugged. "It happens, right?"

We were silent for a moment. My eyes drifted to the trees. A vague sense of unease crept into my mind. It didn't feel as if something was watching us but more that the forest itself was tense with anticipation.

What the hell is going on?

“Andy, does it feel like it is a little...*too* quiet to you?"

"You sound like a bad movie."

"No, I'm serious."

Andy paused and cocked his head. "No, it sounds like it always does. You're not going soft on me, are you, Dude? I told you becoming a nurse would take away your balls."

"Well, there was that couple who got mauled over on Escudilla."

Campers, vacationing from Los Angeles, just a few weeks ago. They were up on Mt. Escudilla, not too far from a burn zone, and not too far from where we now stood. Both of them ended up in the hospital. I was in the ER the night they were brought in. Those marks on the campers' bodies. I would have called them burns but we got shoved aside before I got a good look.

Rangers from the Spingerville district said the two were attacked by a bear--insisted on it, in fact. The officer that came in that night stuck to that story but couldn't look anyone in the eye. Maybe she was unnerved by the campers' injuries. Or maybe it had something to do with the government spook who stayed glued to her side and drove away curious inquiry with a mere flick of his icy gaze.

Neither of the campers argued with the story. Neither said much at all and as soon as they were released, they hightailed it home.

Andy scoffed. "Ryan, that was just a bear. The Forest Service already put it down."

The haunted terror in their eyes was etched in my brain. It wasn't a bear.

Andy stood, chucking his apple core aside. "Okay, break's over. I got a date with Alicia if we can get off this mountain in time. You ready?"

I nodded with more conviction than I felt. "Yeah."

"Good, let's get these logs chopped."

We picked out the nearest tree and started measuring six foot sections. I tried to concentrate. Hell, I fought to concentrate, since letting your mind wander while swinging a chainsaw is a good way to end up missing a leg. My thoughts and eyes kept wandering back to the sense of menace hanging over our heads. I released the switch, flipped up the helmet mask, and looked around.

Andy straightened and stopped his saw. "What?"

"I don't know. Something's not right here."

"Ryan," Andy said, his voice serious, "I don't know what's into you today but you need to snap out of it."

"Listen, man, I--"

A sharp crack sounded behind us. This time, there was no mistaking it for our imaginations. We both pivoted to our rear. Andy dropped his saw. His hand reached for the .357 tucked in his rear waistband. I reached for mine--a twin revolver to Andy's--only to remember that I had left it on my dresser.

"You heard it too, right?" My voice was just a whisper.

"Yeah."

I squinted into the woods. Nothing moved.

After a long moment, Andy relaxed. "Jesus, Ryan, you've got me all jumpy now."

"Sorry, man, but I can't shake it."

"What?"

"This weird feeling we're being watched." My eyes kept scanning the woods. "You know, every culture has myths and legends to explain the random bumps in the night."

"It's daytime, you clown."

"Maybe they have some root in the truth. Maybe something *is* out there."

"Yeah, that's it." He chuckled.

"I'm serious."

"Ryan, come on, man, it was just a branch falling or something."

I kept going as if he hadn't spoken. "Vampires, ghosts, bogeymen. The form is different but the idea is the same, all over the world. The stories tell of a sense of foreboding, of evil, that they just can't describe. That's what I feel."

"But--"

"Even the Navajo have tales of *chindi*--spirits that were nothing but the lingering bad residue of those who had died. Most of the Navajo I've spoken to didn't care to discuss it. They may not believe all of it but they've seen enough to not look too deeply."

Andy looked like he'd bitten into a lemon. "I can't believe we're having this conversation."

"Look, man, I know it sounds strange but there is something off today. I admit, I'm more than a little scared."

The words felt funny coming from my mouth but I *was* scared.

There was a menace in the air. I couldn't see anything but my instincts screamed at me to run, as though some visceral hatred had wafted past my nose on invisible vapor trails--just enough to smell the danger but not enough to pinpoint it. Despite the mild temperature, fresh beads of sweat formed on my forehead.

Andy was incredulous. "You want to leave?"

"I think so, yes."

"Unbelievable." He waved his hands in the air. "Un-freaking-believable."

I opened my mouth to reply when another snap echoed through the treeline. Again, Andy reacted. He spun and dropped to one knee. His revolver was in his hands, his gaze on the treeline.

A steady wind picked up, whistling through the bare treetops. Even though the cold wasn't intense, I shivered.

I reached for my revolver again, and again remembered I didn't have it.

My lever-action 30-30 lay in the back seat. I had taken my first step for the truck when I heard Andy. His voice trembled with disbelief. "What. The. Hell?"

I turned towards him. For the rest of my life, I would wish I hadn't.

It was approximatley the size and shape of a smal whitetail--but there any similarity ended. If it was once alive, it was long past decay. Sticks poked through muddy skin. Its face was a blank slate. Viscous black slime dribbled from its body; where the ooze fell, the grass curled and withered as if aflame. It lurched towards us on four stiff legs.

Icy numbness descended over my mind.

Am I really seeing this?

Andy knelt, frozen. The...thing shambled his direction. I saw the blood drain from his face. Smoking plants crumbled in the thing's wake and the idea of what it might do to flesh shook the lethargy from my mind. "Andy!"

He blinked and opened fire.

One hundred twenty-five grain hollow point bullets, traveling at fourteen hundred feet per second...that should have been enough to put anything down. Instead, the bullets splatted through the thing without so much as slowing it. It came onward. Andy emptied his cylinder and rose, stumbling backwards.

I didn't have my gun but I did have my knife. The Marines called it a fighting knife. Seven inches of tempered, serrated steel. It was out of its sheath and in my hand before I realized it.

Andy took a step back and his boot heel snagged on an enormous root. He tripped back and landed hard on his hip.

I felt faint. That root hadn't been there a moment before.

The thing stepped over the root and bent its neck towards Andy. A gaping maw opened where the mouth on a deer would be. It hadn't uttered so much as a whisper.

I lunged across the space and planted my knife in the thing's shoulder. I ripped the blade sideways, expecting to meet resistance. I sliced through rotted wood but met nothing solid. It was mostly mud.

The thing wheeled with sudden speed, wrenching the knife from my hands. I backpedalled, scouring the ground for a makeshift weapon.

Andy scrambled to his feet, a heavy branch in his hand. He swung. The thing's head went tumbling away, splatting against nearby trunk. My short-lived relief vanished as the creature, though staggered, renewed its attack.

"Ryan, go left!"

I dodged to my left as Andy swung again, this time in a heavy overhead blow. The branch severed one of the creature's legs. The leg fell to the forest floor, where it lay twitching.

The beast reared up and jabbed at Andy with its remaining foreleg. Primordial fingers appeared where the foot should have been.

My friend wasn't fast enough; the thing clamped down on his wrist. Andy's eyes bulged and he screamed.

If I hadn't taken a whiz an hour before, I would have pissed my pants on the spot. Last year, I saw Andy stab through his hand with a screwdriver, and I had never heard him cry out in such pain.

Focusing on Andy, the creature turned its back to me. My knife was still lodged in the monster. I yanked it out and hacked at the leg gripping Andy. It separated at once. I slashed again, separating a chunk of mud and wood. A searing pain lanced through my hand--so strong it almost caused me to drop my weapon. It had to have been a drop of the slime. I attacked with renewed desperation.

Andy grabbed the bottom of his flannel shirt, covered his free hand and pried loose the detached limb locked about his wrist. He raised the branch and joined my attack with fury and tears in his eyes.

For several long seconds, there was no sound save the wet *splutch* of metal and wood striking mud. We kept swinging until the creature was nothing but a pile of mud and sticks. Even then, it quivered as if straining to reach us. I nudged the pile and realized the "sticks" were actually rotted bone. My stomach churned.

The wind howled louder, then fell still.

Andy slumped against a tree.

"Andy, lemme see your wrist." I raised his arm, ignoring his whimper. The skin was blackened, though it did not appear deep. In a flash, I knew where I had seen such burns before.

"We need to get you to the hospital, right this second."

He smiled, in spite of the pain. "That's going to leave a hell of a scar, isn't it?"

"Most likely."

"Ryan, what the hell just happened?"

"I don't know. All I know is that I need to get you to the ER."

"Can't you do patch it up?"

I shook my head. "Not out here. This is beyond first aid and--"

Andy stiffened. "Oh shit."

I followed his gaze.

More of the abominations lurched from the trees. Some were the same size and shape as before. Others were smaller, reminding me of foxes or rabbits. One massive one shambled forward, its rounded head topped by two bear-like ears.

"Get in the truck, Andy."

He looked at our fallen chainsaws, half-submerged in the thin snow cover. "But--"

"Get in the goddamn truck!"

I all but tossed him in the passenger seat and darted around to the driver side. Andy had, as usual, left the keys in the ignition while we were cutting. I used to chide him for it but this one time, I was relieved. The big diesel engine roared to life.

Even in the midst of his pain, Andy grinned. "Alice never lets me down."

"Alice can have all the oil changes she wants if she gets us out of this."

I slammed the truck into gear and crunched down on the accelerator. The wheels spun; I kicked it to four-wheel drive and forced myself to go slowly. The truck crawled to speed just as the first creature reached the rear trailer. It clung to the rail but the powerful truck yanked away and then we were past them, bursting through the ring and down the mountain trail.

I glanced in the rearview mirror just as Andy screamed, "Ryan, look out!"

A lone creature advanced down the road towards us. Unlike the others, this one walked on two legs and staggered towards the truck, arms outstretched. Its fingers opened and closed as it reached for us. A blood-curdling scream reverberated through the trees and a fresh chill bolted down my spine as I realized the howl emanted from the demon before us.

Andy's voice was full of panic and fear. "Don't stop!"

It had no fear of the truck, never altering its path even as I plowed the grill straight into it. Black mud and dirt splattered over the windshield. I hit the wipers, which cleaned the debris away. Within seconds, the bare blades scraped against glass. The rubber had been eaten away.

We reached a spot where the land fell away from the road and I I slowed, making sure we didn't go careening off the side. Andy kept glancing back but I focused on the road. There just wasn't much room for error, between the rock wall on the right and a long drop to the left. I drove as fast as I dared, my knuckles white on the wheel.

At last, we reached a lower meadow and the paved road appeared in front of us. I hit the brakes and we skidded to a stop.

Andy and I sat there for a moment, breathing hard, neither of us saying a word. I got out and inspected the trailer. Ugly streaks of melted metal scarred the rails but the bed appeared intact and amazingly, our helmets had survived the whole trip down the mountain, remaining in the bed. I didn't even remember tossing them in there.

Andy got down and came back, holding his wrist. His voice trembled. "Our saws?"

"No. Plus my knife and whatever damage your truck has. Damage to the trailer looks superficial but I won't know 'til I get it home and look closer."

"We have to go back and get them."

Andy's eyes were wide and his face was pale. His breath came in short, shallow gasps. My training kicked in; he was going into shock.

I put my arm around his shoulders and guided him back to the truck. He moved his wrist and winced. I got him in the seat and pulled a blanket from the roadside emergency kit he kept in the truck's tool chest. I wrapped it around him, reclined his seat, and said, "Okay, let's get up to Show Low, and get you looked at."

A few moments later, we turned onto US 191 and headed for the hospital. I pondered what had happened. Nothing I had ever heard about in myths or legends matched what we had seen. The things seemed intent on burning us with their acidic grips. Burning....

"Andy?"

"What?"

"Have you ever seen a wounded animal? Sometimes, they attack any and everything that gets close."

"Yeah."

I took a deep breath. "I think that's what was happening. The earth was still in pain from the fire. The earth, nature, whatever you want to call it. It was lashing out at us, like a pain-maddened animal. I'm guessing all those muddy piles of bones were the forest creatures that died in the fire."

He didn't say anything for a few moments. I kept stealing glances at Andy, making sure he was still breathing, but he seemed to have calmed a little. When he did speak, his voice was thick and distant. "And the last one?"

"What about it?"

"It looked like a man."

My throat felt dry. I mustered as much optimism as I could. "Couldn't have been."

Andy didn't answer.

Out of the vaults of my mind came my previous words: *even the Navajo have tales of chindi--spirits that were nothing but the lingering bad residue of those who had died.*

I swallowed hard.

"Ryan?"

"Yeah, buddy?"

"What are we going to tell Lynn and Alicia?"

I didn't say anything. Like the rest, I knew a good answer to that question was something I just didn't really have.

Alice's tires *thrummed* over the pavement as we drove away from the mountain, each of us lost in our own impossible thoughts.

###

Deanna's Story

by

Trish Zaabel

The late June morning started with bright sunshine and no clouds, but still, heavy air. There was little hint of the storm that would strike later, just an uneasy feeling in my gut. I wondered if we were in for the first monsoon of the season.

Usually, I would try to get my work done by late morning and take the afternoon off. But today wasn't my usual day. I finished feeding the twenty seven horses in my care and headed for the house, mentally scheduling my day.

My husband Jerry snapped me back into the present as I entered the kitchen. "Remember Deanna and her husband are coming for a BBQ. They are up from Queen Creek to look for property. I invited Ed and Carol also. Make sure you're done with everything by 4:30."

They're your guests, not mine, flashed across my mind.

I knew Jerry was under a lot of stress, not only from work but also physical pain. A back injury had crippled a vibrant man in his late 50's into one who relied on a cane to walk.

Jerry's frustration at the inactivity was tangible - almost like the heavy feeling permeating the air. I understood his pain. I had once been unable to do what I loved too. If having some friends over for an evening helped, I would support him with that.

"What is Deanna's husband's name? I can never remember it."

Jerry kept following to me as I paced through the house.

I felt trapped. "Richard I think."

"You're right. What do you have planned for the day? Do you think you can clean the house a bit before they get here?"

I glanced around for anything untidy. For a ranch house in the middle of nowhere, Arizona, it looked pretty good to me. Sure I could dust and vacuum but that was a daily ritual if not hourly when the wind was blowing.

I chose to respond to the first question. "Erin should be here by 10:30, I need to go to town to buy hay, Kristin is coming to work on Blaise and watch me work Sophie."

"Just how are you going to do all that and have the horses fed by 4:30?"

Jerry's question was the thunder to my lightening. The building storm in my gut had nothing to do with the weather. Taking a deep breath, I shrugged. "I'll be done."

My client, Erin, and her friend Mary arrived by 10:30. Hopefully, I could stay on my timeline.

The universe seemed to have other plans for me though. Erin, who was pregnant, had an emotional breakdown. I spent time settling her before we could work with her horse. Then she needed to eat so we went to Show low for lunch. That worked because I needed to get hay. On the drive home I felt pretty good about getting everything done on schedule until my left back tire blew.

"Great, just great."

That heavy, icky sensation was back. It felt sinister and I just wanted to shake it off. Now I was behind again with Kristin waiting for us back at the ranch.

I was back on the road within a half hour now imaging what would not get done today.

Thankfully, the afternoon went smoothly with horses getting

worked and clients happy with progress. We actually had some time to sit under a tree by the arena and talk. Jerry, who is always a favorite of my lady clients, joined us. Deanna and Richard arrived. The ugliness seemed to dissipate.

Then Carol and Ed drove in and suddenly Jerry realized what time it was.

"It's after 5, you better hurry up with feeding." His words replaced the calm with an impending storm.

We scattered. Erin and Mary headed out first. Kristin said she would feed her horse before she left.

Jerry and Richard walked to the house to start the grill and visit with Carol and Ed. Deanna offered to help me so I would get done faster.

I sent her out with feed buckets to the different pens. Deanna was a horse person so I was not worried about her walking among my animals. If there was a horse to be careful of I warned her how to handle the situation.

Deanna was in the pen with JD and Coppertone, the last two horses at the end of driveway. They were both even minded and quiet. I started toward her to let her know that I could feed hay myself.

A crack of noise shattered the peaceful scene. The atmosphere was ripped apart. Later I would be the only one who could attest to hearing the mysterious sound.

JD spooked into Coppertone. Athletic Coppertone jumped away from Deanna but JD pushed right over the top of her, knocking her to the ground.

I didn't move, waiting for the horses to settle before I approached. Then I walked up quickly, calling her name. As I knelt beside her, Deanna turned towards me and tried to sit up. She grimaced.

"How much do you hurt?"

"I'm okay. Let me just sit here."

Blood trickled from her mouth. She coughed and spit red. I saw bubbles in the blood by her lips. Not a good sign. My first aid training kicked in. A college professor drilled calm reaction for a semester.

I tried to call Jerry's phone. No answer. I could not leave her lying on the ground in a pen with two horses.

Deanna's phone, Richard's number.

"Hey Love" Richard answered.

"Richard it's me, Trish. Deanna's been hurt. Come quick."

"What, where?" He was breathless.

I looked up the driveway toward the house. I could see him in the distance.

"Just come straight down the driveway towards the road."

Richard started to run towards me. Jerry and Ed followed in confusion.

Meanwhile, I called 911. Again I explained what happened and told them to send a helicopter because she was bleeding internally. They asked my address, said they would call back and hung up.

"911 hung up on me!"

"WHAT?" Richard was frantic.

A former police officer, Jerry recognized the volatile situation. He moved to calm Richard and protect Deanna from the horses.

Ed limped to his home across the street. He was an old man suffering with many health issues. "When they call back, tell them to send the helicopter towards the light. I'll go home and turn on the spotlight on my windmill right now."

Minutes passed. No 911 call. I moved the horses from the pen so paramedics could get to Deanna safely. Richard fumed, then yelled, finally storming off to get his truck, determine to drive his wife to the hospital himself. 911 was taking too long.

I motioned Jerry away from Deanna. I didn't want to scare her.

"You can't let him move her. She's bleeding internally."

"I can't physically fight him right now. He may be smaller than me but I can barely move. It's his wife, I won't stop him."

"This is a bad idea."

Richard drove his truck up to the gate. He tried to lift Deanna but she screamed. Jerry spotted one of the chairs by the tree. They eased her into the chair, then carried her by chair to the truck. Adrenaline must have made Jerry stronger.

With Deanna in the truck, Richard backed out, determine to get her to the hospital, barely stopping for directions.

"That was a bad idea." Doom filled my words.

"It's his wife."

We heard shouts on the road. Jerry and I walked out of the driveway to find Richard had not gotten far. Ed was blocking the road with his other car. The two men were in each other's faces, ready to come to blows. Jerry moved to break up the fight.

I walked around to the passenger side of Richard's truck. A young woman had a blood pressure cuff on Deanna. In the truck, a wild looking man with unkempt hair, unshaven, and dressed in cut off jean shorts was stabilizing Deanna. He relayed medical information rapidly to the girl. She conveyed the message by cellphone.

Jerry put his hand on Richard's shoulder. "Walk with me."

I looked at Ed with questions in my eyes.

"This is Flint and his daughter Ashley. Flint is a retired paramedic. I went to get him after I turned the light on."

"911 never called me back."

"That's because we called and told them we're on scene," Ashley said as she left the truck. "I just hung up."

Ashley looked at Richard arguing with Jerry. She got in Richard's face. "Listen to me. Your wife has a punctured lung. If you would have driven the 5 miles of dirt road, every bump would make it worse. By the time you got to pavement, she would have bled out and died."

Quietly, Jerry said “Let them take care of her.”

Richard shrank back in horror as the realization hit him.

Ed disappeared for a short time then came back with an oxygen tank and mask. “Will these help?”

Ashley took them with a grateful look. “Ed, you’re a hero.”

Flint stayed in the truck, holding Deanna’s neck and monitoring vital signs. We waited and waited and waited some more.

Finally, in the distance we heard sirens, then saw EMS from Concho making its way toward us. Over an hour since I first made the call.

Two old men and a younger woman climbed out. They took one look at Flint and Ashley and backed off. About 10 minutes later, Vernon EMS arrived. Again, they deferred to Flint and Ashley.

The St. Johns ambulance reached us about 5 minutes after Vernon. When they arrived you could almost hear the collective sigh of relief. Finally, we had the real medical people.

Until then, I think Flint and Ashely had been protecting “their” patient. They turned Deanna over to St Johns.

A man from the St. Johns crew called out “ETA helicopter, 5 minutes.”

About 30 seconds later a light in the dark sky came zooming towards us. They hovered, looking for a clear place to land. Our property is covered in juniper and pinon pine but Ed had a large open pasture across the street.

“Can we land there?” the man coordinating the landing asked Ed.

“My horses are by the barn. Let me close the gate and it’s all yours.”

Vernon EMS brought out the wire cutters, cut the fence, and pulled it back.

After the helicopter landed, the pilot talked with us while the paramedics prepared Deanna for transport. When I had made the first call, they told him to get ready. The pilot started to fly towards Concho without a specific location. When he saw the light on Ed's windmill, he knew that was the place.

They took Deanna to Scottsdale Osborn hospital. The ER doctors said whoever first assisted her did exactly the right thing. Her injuries could have killed her with a wrong move.

I was right about the storm brewing that day. I just had no idea the kind of storm it would be. When it finally broke over us, strangers worked to save a life. Somehow, together we made decisions in a crisis. Jerry and I were just learning how to live in this remote area. That night we made lasting new friends while saving old relationships.

###

Entitlement

By

Kaye Phelps

Carl Donne slapped the pen on the offending document, stood so fast that he knocked over the heavy conference room chair, and fled the room.

Winded by the time he reached his old truck, he yanked open the door and plopped himself on the driver's seat.

He realized that the Navajo County Courthouse parking lot was not an auspicious place for a meltdown. He forced himself to drive carefully across Holbrook and under the I-40 overpass, then ordered an undesired cup of coffee at the McDonald's drive-in window.

While he sat in the parking lot, a couple of big drops landed on his dirty windshield, creating circles of red mud. He looked at the dark clouds to the north. *Maybe the Navajo and Hopi are getting some rain.* He wasn't too impressed with monsoon season, either the one he'd experienced in Phoenix or last year in Snowflake.

Carl set the cup in a holder, thinking back almost a year and a half as he pulled down the shift lever.

Spring. He'd answered a Craigslist personal ad from a middle-aged woman seeking companionship in the White Mountains. One Saturday morning he drove to Snowflake from Phoenix to meet Liz Merriwether.

Liz seemed older than middle-aged – fifty-three. She was a soft-looking woman with gray eyes, graying hair and not much fashion sense, but she could cook like an angel. And she owned her spotless, modest home on a quiet side street.

He had been disappointed that she didn't welcome him into her bed right away. But she did offer him a meal of ribs and au gratin potatoes from scratch. And the use of her guest room since it was too late to drive back to Phoenix.

By Sunday night he wondered if he could find work in the Show Low/Snowflake area. As a metalworker, he kept his toolbox and welder bolted to the bed of his old truck.

Liz was a retired teacher and knew the area well. Throughout that summer they visited small museums in tiny, dusty towns and attended festivals all over the state. She drove him through the Petrified Forest and along the trail of the Mogollon Rim. She taught him Arizona history, he who grew up in the Midwest and moved to Phoenix to escape winter.

Once she sent him out to get an ingredient and he found out the only real grocery in Snowflake was closed on Sunday, as were most businesses except gas stations and fast food joints. He tried to tease her about the heavy Mormon influence in the town and she blinked back owlishly – how the woman didn't need glasses when she read so much, he had no clue – and informed him that Latter Day Saints made good neighbors. "Just for the record, I'm Baptist!"

She did attend church every Sunday, dressed even more conservatively than usual. At first she invited him along but gave up after he refused every time. When they decided to get married in the fall, he talked her out of a church wedding. "Costs a lot, and we're not going to have kids or anything," he reasoned. They stood up before the local judge.

They had a quiet Christmas and he even got her to drink a glass of wine on New Year's Eve. Their joining that evening was a little more lively than usual and Carl reminded her that his birthday was in January. He mentioned that his name should be on the deed to her house, "Just in case."

In late January he came home with a new, red Ram truck. "How do you intend to pay for this?" Liz demanded, arms crossed over her chest.

"It's my birthday!" he protested, not understanding why she wouldn't be happy to pay for his birthday present. In truth, he'd worked little since he'd come to Snowflake. Didn't even look. Life with Liz was just too comfortable.

"Your old truck runs just fine. Take the new one back!"

He realized later that was probably the end of his marriage. Their joinings dwindled to none and they stopped playing tourist. She sent him to live on a desolate piece of property east of Snowflake and refused to purchase one of those tiny houses. That would require a septic system and a well, or at least a way to haul water. She did buy him a used travel trailer and paid to have it hauled to the site, but he had to drag it into town frequently to empty its holding tanks, buy propane and fill it with water.

As he turned onto Concho Highway from State 77, he snorted. They had been required to talk to an arbitrator about dividing the marital assets. He rejected the first arbitrator, a woman, believing she would not favor him because he was male. He also rejected the second, a Mormon fellow who asked where he had served his mission. The third, another woman, had informed him smugly that he had no more choices. If he and Liz could not reach an agreement, the judge would decide, and that would not likely be advantageous to him.

So he and Liz stayed in the conference room. Liz's lawyer presented the case that her home, her car and her retirement income were hers alone since she owned them as well as the piece of desert he was living on before the marriage.

She would allow him to live there and he could keep the trailer since she purchased it during their marriage. But if he left it, the land returned to her. He got his truck and personal belongings.

He was tempted to take his chances with the judge, but the look on Liz's face – matching those of her lawyer and the arbitrator – brought him up short. He couldn't believe that someone as nice as Liz would know how to play hardball. So he signed the agreement and left the building.

He must have passed the Country Store – did he need gas? Propane? He didn't have much cash. So he drove on past Hay Hollow Wash and turned north on the rutted road to his small home. The clouds had turned gunmetal gray and a few more drops decorated his windshield.

Five miles in, as the rain increased, he found the road blocked by cattle, a truck and trailer, and several mounted cowboys in yellow slickers trying to make order out of the mess. One of them rode up to his truck. "We'll get them out of here in about twenty minutes."

Angry now, he cranked the wheel and drove back to the place where a side wash crossed. He knew he could bypass a stretch of the blocked road by driving east on the wash and coming up behind his place. He hoped to get home before he had to walk much in the rain, but at least it was warm and he didn't have to shovel it.

He shifted the transmission into low four-wheel-drive and turned onto the wash. His truck growled in the muddy sand but kept going. The wash grew deeper and narrower when he came upon a tangle of junipers jammed tightly in the wash. He had no choice but to back out.

His right rear wheel ran up the bank and stuck on a basketball-sized rock. When he gunned the engine his truck lurched and fell slowly onto its driver's side, leaving him looking through the window at the sandy bottom of the wash. "F***!" he swore.

Would Liz spring for the tow bill? Not likely. He climbed out of the passenger window and jumped over the cab, twisting his ankle on a jagged rock as he landed, sending him to his knees.

Before he could stand, a big slab of the muddy bank collapsed and buried him.

***

The local cowboys found him several days later when they spotted his truck in the wash. They helped the responding deputy dig his body out.

"Isn't that the guy who married your sister-in-law's neighbor?" one of them asked.

"Guess so," the other replied. "She's a nice lady. Helped get Marianne to the hospital when my nephew got hurt at school."

The first man nodded. "For a gentile, she's a good neighbor."

###

A Family Mystery

by

Conni de Wolfe

MEMORIES

I was born in Portland, Oregon in October, 1937. My mother had birth problems, so the doctors decided she shouldn't have any more children. Because of this decision, and being first born, I became an only child.

Some of us remember, or learned in American history, the beginning of World War II, on December 7, 1941. I was four so I didn't notice.

Early in December of 1942, my father and I traveled to Vale, Oregon where my grandparents lived. He worked for the IRS and had been traveling his district, when he received notice to take a call at his parents' house.

I met him in Lakeview, Oregon. I rode -alone- on a bus from Klamath Falls, Oregon, where we lived. Mother put a very nice bus driver in charge of me. I think I slept most of the short trip.

We then traveled on to Vale in our 1940 Plymouth Coupe. When we arrived I remember my grandparents were packing their pickup truck and trailer for a road trip to Florida. My Dad and I were alone at the house.

My Dad told me he was waiting for a phone-call, several days later he received it. The phone call woke me from a nap and I heard my Dad's low voice, but I didn't understand his end of the conversation

After the call, Dad took me back to my mother in Klamath Falls, packed up and left. This was just before Christmas. He had joined the Army Air Corps. And so the Mystery began.

My next clear memory is boarding a train in Ontario, Oregon. We were going to meet my Dad in Amarillo, Texas. We then would travel on to Hobbs, New Mexico, where he was stationed.

When we boarded the train we realized that our transport was a troop train, filled with military men returning from the South Pacific. They treated my mother and me like a long lost family. My mother was a good looking blonde and I, at the time, had long blonde curls. They hadn't seen a 'round eyed' woman in a long time.

My mother told the marine and sailor sitting across from us that I knew how to sing *Mairzey Doats*. They proceeded to tell the whole car I could sing it, stood me up in a seat in the middle of the car, and encouraged me sing.

I think I looked out at the sea of men and women's faces in confusion and turned to my Mother, with my finger in my mouth. She and the two men kept urging me on, so I sang it. I know it was applauded well. I think some of them sang along with me.

The marine had made a bracelet out of scraps of a Jap Zero airplane. He teased me about my curls and said he would give it to me if I'd give him one of my curls. Of course I wouldn't do it, because I had earlier taken scissors to my front curl and cut it off, but he gave it to me anyway. I still have it.

***

We lived in Hobbs twice. The first time I got the "big measles." The second time I started first grade, a scary day in my memory as I didn't know anybody. We lived the usual military life but were housed off-base because housing on base was limited to officers and their families.

I remember the B-17's -Flying Fortress bombers- flying over our house day and night, rattling our tin roof. I learned later they were practicing how to fly low take-offs and landings before heading overseas. It was a prerequisite for low-altitude bombing runs, also known as hedge-hopping.

***

The day came when Dad received new orders. We, all three, packed up and returned to Portland, via Vale, where my Mother left me with my grandparents to finish the school year. I had a neat teacher.

Mother got a teaching job in Gilchrist, Oregon that fall and I only saw my Dad one more time before he shipped out. He only had a three or four day leave. I later learned from letters he went to India.

I also made a seven-year-old *faux pas*. We had received one of the few letters we got from Dad, telling us that he had flown over "The Hump" into China. I, being so proud, spread it all over school that my daddy had flown over the *hill.* A definite no-no in military language. My Mother was horrified when she learned it was going around town that he had *deserted.*

After the school year ended, my mother and I returned to Portland. With the shortage of teachers, my mother had no trouble finding another job.

***

One afternoon, I went out to the paper box and got the *Portland Oregonian* paper. As I unfolded it I saw a picture of my Dad sitting on a roof, binoculars in hand, watching a Chinese civil war battle. It said he was in Kunming, China. I was so excited to show my mother I ran for the house tripping over my own feet. Later we heard he ended up in a firefight with a Chinese general, was wounded, and received a Purple Heart.

Dad arrived home from the Orient in January, 1946. Mother met him in Seattle. Unfortunately he brought a case of malaria with him. His first bout scared my eight-year-old self to death. The shaking, sweating and shivering, plus incoherent talking wasn't like my tall and strong daddy.

He returned to Klamath Falls and started to remodel our house, while Mother and I stayed in Portland to finish out the school year. He also went back to work for the IRS.

CONTEMPLATIONS AND QUESTIONS

When Mother and I returned to Klamath Falls, I promptly got the mumps. Naturally I was confined to the bedroom when my uncle, aunt and younger cousin came to visit. It ruined the whole summer for me because I couldn't play with my cousin and they confined me to my room while they were there.

Dad continued to work on the house before we got there and finished it about the time school started. The house was completed with the addition of a bedroom over the garage for me and a den. And my mother became a stay-at-home mom. The school year ran smoothly until May of 1947. Then our life changed…drastically.

My dad was fisherman/hunter. He and his Navy recruiter buddy from work planned a weekend fishing trip. Dad had promised me once before that the next time he went fishing I could go with him. He told me I couldn't go on this two-day trip to Odell Lake, north of Crater Lake, either. I remember crying and begging to go. He promised, again, I could go next time.

It was a bright and sunny day on May 24, 1947, when a man that my mother knew, came to our house bringing the news that my Dad and his friend had disappeared from the lake. My mother, in shock, stumbled into the house. She then collapsed on the couch, where she stayed and cried off and on for days. Who notified the rest of the family, I don't know. I only remember going to my room upstairs -that my Dad had built- confused and wondering if I should cry too.

Evidence in their cabin showed that the men had eaten breakfast that morning. They had apparently taken the boat out to fish. All the authorities could find was the boat bobbing on the lake, with the paraphernalia, including my Dad's wallet, floating on the water. The chain was also hanging loose on the front of the boat.

Navy Seabees scoured the lake, considered one of the coldest in the world, and was one of the bottomless lakes in the area. No bodies were ever found. Dad was declared dead by the authorities seven months later.

Over the years speculations within the family, along with much guessing about my Dad have come forth. However, no conclusive evidence has ever been found or supplied to us.

I theorized that Dad had been an OSS (predecessor to the CIA) operative in China. He was considered a Sergeant in the Army Air Corps to everyone; I found out in his separation papers years later that he was discharged as a Captain. Only his father knew for sure and he never told my mother or anyone else.

When he had come home from the war he returned to work for the IRS. At the time of his disappearance he was supposedly investigating a mob boss in the area.

My mother tried to check into his military files with the government but was told they couldn't be opened under secrecy laws. This was 40 years after his disappearance.

The question is, did he really die? Was he killed by the mob? Or was he whisked away by the government and put in hiding? If so, why did he leave us behind? It's been 70 years ago this last May 24, 2017. Should I try to open his file, again?

The mystery of his disappearance still –bum-fuzzles- and intrigues he family. Several of my children have researched this, but so far no evidence could be located. Why is the information still restricted? The mystery will probably never be solved. But we still wonder.

###

First Sighting

by

Orina Hodgson

"This is the most amazing sunset I've ever seen! Just when I think it's peaked, wham! The colors are more intense than ever." Maggie took a hit and passed the doobie to Keith. He was almost asleep, stretched out on a blanket spread across stubby grass and red clay soil. Thick black curls formed a halo around his head. She laughed out loud at the thought. *This man is no angel*! *But he rocks my world.*

"Keith! You're missing the best part!" Maggie leaned over her man and nuzzled his long neck.

"Better than what we just did? I don't want to miss that!" Keith took the joint with one hand and circled the other around Maggie, pulling her closer. One look told her he was ready to go at it again.

"The sky, man! The sky. Check out this sunset! It's psychedelic." She jumped to her bare feet, faced the radiant colors, and raised both arms in salutation. "Go peacefully, Father Sun. Thank you for this day."

Keith sighed, then grabbed his guitar. He picked out the notes with ease. A resonant tone rolled smoothly across the vast plateau. Maggie, still facing the western horizon, swayed in flawless rhythm to the love song. Her naked beauty coalesced perfectly with the blazing day's end. Keith's heart melted for the thousandth time.

It wasn't the pot. He loved her more than anything. *Then why was it always so hard?*

"Maggie. I'm sorry about earlier. It's not so bad here. I just don't know how we'd make it. Who will we hang with? What will we do?"

"Can't we just trust that it'll be okay, Keith? We bought that place in Oregon because we thought the community was perfect. All those hippies, gardens, and babies. It turned out to be a nightmare! Poor old Jonas murdered right down the road from us. Beheaded by those crazy mountain men. It's so peaceful here. Let's give this a chance."

***

Maggie and Kieth had arrived at the property east of Snowflake early in the morning. They parked their van in the shade of a big juniper and walked around the land trying to decide if this place would do for their next home.

The ensuing argument had been so routine it was almost ridiculous. The details were never really the issue, but the core fight repeated incessantly. After five years together, they both knew this. She wanted a baby. He did too. He was scared. She was hopeful. He was angry. She was fearful. She pleaded reason. He demanded sex.

***

They made love quickly this time. The sun dropped into the horizon.

"This place is magical." Maggie held up an agatized petrified rock as if for evidence. A turquoise stripe bisected the relic to confirm her declaration. The air had cooled almost immediately once Sol left the sky.

She stood up and ambled toward the juniper where she had draped her cotton shift. Keith wiggled into his jeans and t-shirt.

"I don't know, Mag. Yeah, the rocks and the sunset are out of this world. But it's lonely here. No other signs of life. Nothing to connect to.

Oregon was a disaster. You're right about that. But what does this land offer…except for the fact my mom will sell it to us cheap?"

Maggie spun to face Keith, eyes flashing, naked body taut. "This land offers us the chance to make a baby, bring our little one into a peaceful world, dammit!" Arms folded across her bare chest, she stared past her lover toward the eastern horizon.

Then Maggie froze in place. She squinted and blinked several times, but the scene didn't change. At first she couldn't get a sound to come out of her mouth. Then words poured out in rapid high-pitched succession.

"Oh, shit! Oh my god. Keith, look! It's a spaceship. It's huge! What'll we do? I can't run; my legs won't move. Help, Keith!"

The intensely bright semi-sphere spread a third of the way across the horizon. It was huge, silent, and ever so slowly rising higher into the dusky sky.

Keith ran to Maggie and wrapped his arms around her from behind. "Wait, Mag," he whispered. "Don't run. They're always faster than the people. Always. Don't act scared. Just look right at the ship and send out good vibes. Throw the best vibes you have right at 'em, Maggie. Love or something. Maybe peace. Peace and love, yes." His voice was shaky, but Keith's stance was strong. He held on to Maggie and gazed at the massive orb with awe surpassing his fear.

Maggie's muscles relaxed a bit. "It's so beautiful. I feel the peace and love, Keith. Do you?"

The young lovers held one another and the sacred space for another minute. They both sent the best vibes they could manage, hoping the aliens would be receptive.

Suddenly Keith burst out laughing. "Oh my god! I can't believe it! Do you see it, Maggie? Do you see it? Oh, my god!"

"Keith, what's the matter with you? Stop laughing. Are you okay? Don't lose it on me now." She turned back toward the UFO. She stared.

Then Maggie laughed too, somewhat hysterically. "Holy shit. Did we really just do that? I think we did. We'll never tell anybody, right? But you have to admit, Keith. That's the biggest full moon ever. It does look like it could be a spaceship."

"They don't make 'em like this in LA, that's for sure!" Keith replied.

They both grinned and sat side by side on the blanket watching as the white globe finally cleared the horizon.

"You know what, Maggie. I want to stay here. I want us to make a baby and build a house and plant a garden right here."

Maggie leaned into Keith. Tears burned her sunburned cheeks as she nodded vigorously.

They held each other that way for a long time, pulling the cover around their shoulders against the chill of night.

###

The Forgotten Log Cabin

by

Myra Larsen

The lonely log cabin stood a few yards east of Silver Creek in Taylor. She had aged through her many years on Tumbleweed Lane. Her front door and window were missing. They were gone and she was forgotten.

Mother Nature sent a wisp of fresh air through the cabin. A visitor stood in the doorway. Those brown, sparkling eyes looked familiar. And the smile. *It must be.* Yes, it was. Gary, the little boy all grown up.

The cabin grinned from open window to door. She wasn't forgotten. A string of a curtain clinging to the top corner of the window waved hello.

She watched as Gary stood for several minutes. She saw him looking at the curtain. He spoke his thoughts, “I remember when Grandma made that curtain from an old sheet.”

The cabin knew Grandma had been frugal and often said, “Use it up. Wear it out. Make it do. Or, do without.” She saw Gary smile. “I wish I had done a better job of following her example.”

Memories came flooding back. That cabin had been home for several generations. Gary was born here with the help of a midwife. Wind hadn't come howling through the windows then. Her door always provided safety from unwelcome critters. The strong walls and roof were protection from snow and rain.

Gary had called it home for several years He and his older siblings and cousins enjoyed great times there in all seasons. The cabin remembered the whoops and hollers as they ran in and out.

Snow wasn't so bad, if they remembered to clean their feet before they hurried in. She was not fond of tracks across her floors. She could almost see them now, through Gary's eyes. They had material for snowball fights and sledding and for wonderful snowmen. Wrapped up in coats, hats, boots, and gloves the children ventured out into the white world.

Snowman needed clothes too, but not for staying warm. Cabin remembered Mother allowed them to wrap an old knitted scarf around his neck. Mr. Snowman looked handsome wearing Grandpa's well-used hat. It didn't matter there were a few holes. No one had a pipe. That was okay. Snowman wasn't a smoker. A whistle stuck in his mouth was just fine for scaring away the birds who wanted to roost on his hat. Whiskers, yes Snowman had needed whiskers. Some dry grass took care of that. Arms were nearly forgotten in the excitement of dressing Snowman. That wasn't hard to arrange. They used a couple of small fallen limbs with twigs for fingers.

Time for pictures. Someone dashed to the door and called for Mother to bring the camera. She responded with, "Close the door." She always said that.

She wrapped herself in her coat and scarf. And grabbed her camera from the shelf. Gloves wouldn't let her operate the buttons. In her rush to make the children happy, she dashed out with no boots.

They posed around Snowman.

Mother snapped the camera and hurried back into the house to thaw her frosty feet. The children followed right behind her to warm their fingers and toes in front of the fireplace. Hot cocoa and gingersnaps warmed their insides.

Happy memories seemed to flash by in seconds compared to the years it took to create them.

The cabin had other visitors over the years especially after the day the door finally fell off its hinges in a windstorm. These visitors had four legs. Some were little critters looking for a nest or something to chew on. Some were big critters looking for hay and shelter. After a meal they stood around or lay down and chewed their cud. She had become a barn! Oh well, she sighed again.

Wind began to whistle through the windows and the doorway where Gary still stood. The cabin remembered the boys who called her Carnegie Hall. Their parents hadn't pressured them to practice their music in the summer. In their own concert hall it was fun. They had an appreciative audience with bales of hay for seats.

One young chap strummed his guitar, Another boy, the one with curly blond hair, played an old harmonica his grandpa gave him for Christmas. The third member of the orchestra played a violin that wasn't always in tune. Sometimes he squeaked, but that was okay.

Tickets were free, but some of the attendees brought milk and cookies. Gary was not one of the musicians. They were his friends and their music gave her happy memories that still brightened her lonely nights.

Those summer day concerts gave him the excuse for saying, *I was born in Carnegie Hall. That's my story and I'm sticking to it.*

Her string of a curtain seemed to chuckle in the breeze as she remembered with him. *Those were the days. The good old days.*

There were plenty of good old days before Gary's time. M. L. Hancock built her for his wife Margaret McCleve Hancock. The old log cabin recalled being filled with happy, noisy children.

One fearful day in 1969 burned into her memory forever.

Gary Solomon, her child born in "Carnegie Hall," tore down the old, barely standing house nearby. Then a crane came and gave her a terrible headache. A crew of men, no friends of hers, arrived and took her roof right off. If that wasn't bad enough, they used unfriendly machinery to lift her from her foundation. She got motion sickness as they moved her all the way into Taylor. The machine plopped her down at the corner of Main Street and Willow Lane.

She was promptly put back together.

Then the cleanup started. She never had such a bath in all her 189 years. Cabin was given a new door and window, and her roof was repaired. They added porches. Then she was filled with family heirlooms. She held her breath when that big wood-burning cook-stove was hauled in. Cabin wanted to hug those two baby dolls before they were carefully placed in the crib. She *saw* the long-ago children as they raced down the stair steps from their sleeping loft on Saturday mornings, ready for breakfast and play. Bits and pieces revived more lovely memories.

The Taylor/Shumway Heritage Foundation became her new family. They gave her a name: Margaret McCleve Hancock Log Cabin. It was a tribute to the first pioneers who had called her home.

With a smile in her log cabin heart, she welcomed her visitors. Cabin wasn't forgotten after all.

She watched as the women admired the handiwork of the patchwork quilt. Men examined the woodwork of the hand made furniture.

Some people were picnicking around the tables on the grassy lawn, below the trees. Children ran and played safely inside her white picket fence. The boys and some of the girls posed for photos in the fort, pretending to be pioneers. A happy tear dropped from her rafters between the hanging dried flowers and herbs. *I won't be lonely anymore.*

###

Four Friends

By

Kaye Phelps

First Friday

They met for breakfast at the Cedar Hills Senior Center every Friday: Harold, a retired chicken farmer; Betsy, working half-time at an insurance office in town; Erica, retired and widowed, raising herbs and spices in a little greenhouse; and Donna, whose passion for baking kept them all in sweets.

As usual, Harold arrived first, setting three cartons of his multi-colored hen fruit by his place at the corner table. He always ordered buttermilk pancakes with real maple syrup and four slices of bacon.

Donna arrived next, set some apple pastry on the table, then went to the window to place her order. She ate something different every week. Betsy and Erica came in together since they lived close and liked to carpool. They always split a Western Scramble.

Harold stood when Betsy and Erica stepped through the door. They were closely followed by a sullen-looking young man and his mother. The kid barged through the door, leaving his mother to catch the rebound.

Harold shook his head. “Did you get home all right last night, son?” he rumbled.

The young man's head snapped around. "You!" he snarled.

Harold was puzzled. The mother looked between them. "Do you know my son?"

"Yes ma'am." He paused. "Last night I saw him slide into that little bend on Concho Ocho Road. He wanted me to drag that big pickup out of the ditch with my little Ranger. I didn't think I had enough power to do that, 'specially with all that mud, so I offered to take him to my place to use the phone but he didn't want to."

The woman glared at her son. "You told me the truck was stolen. And now you've got the sheriff's department involved!"

The kid yelped something that sounded like, "He's lying!" as his mother yanked him out of the Senior Center by his elbow.

The volunteer waiter danced out of the kitchen with Harold's pancakes and the four friends settled in to sip coffee and enjoy their breakfasts.

Second Friday

Harold was late, and when he came in he looked distracted. With no eggs.

He dropped into his chair and wrapped his hands around a mug of coffee that one of his friends had brought for him. "All my chickens are dead," he mumbled into the cup.

All three women paused, forks in the air.

"Why?" Erica demanded. "What happened?"

Harold shook his head. "Somehow the pen got moved. One corner ended up over a little ravine and all my chickens got out. Supper for the local coyote den."

"Oh, Harold, we're so sorry," Donna said. "Are you going to get more chickens?"

The old man's head drooped lower. "I don't know. I've been cleaning up – pieces – all morning. It's all too new right now."

"How could the pen move?" Betsy asked to know.

"I built it sturdy but so I could move it to clean it," Harold told them. "It looks like somebody jerked on one corner and pulled it out of shape. I didn't see any footprints, so I don't know how they did it. Or who got in."

The four friends finished their breakfasts in silence.

On Sunday, the women trailered Erica's and Donna's horses and Betsy's mule up to the Blue Ranch on the hill. They saddled their mounts in the dusty yard among other equines and riders. When the trail boss hollered from the east side of the corral, "Mount up!" pairs started riding in his direction.

Erica glanced into the corral and saw a lean young man practicing roping on a post. The same young man they'd seen on Friday at the Senior Center. She turned to Betsy. "Isn't that the same kid--?"

Betsy stared at the young man, who smirked back. "Sure is."

"Doesn't Harold's chicken pen have a pole sticking up at each corner? So he can drape netting over it to keep the hawks out?"

Betsy nodded. "I'll bet that kid roped the corner post of the chicken pen and dragged it cattywumpus so the chickens could get out. There wouldn't be any footprints."

Donna caught up to them. "That's the kid we saw at breakfast Friday morning. This is his parents' place."

Later, at the after-ride potluck, all three listened but heard no useful information. When the trail boss struck up a conversation with Betsy about her mule, she asked him about their host. Donna and Erica joined them and explained about Harold's chickens being turned loose. The trail boss called the young man's father over and the story was repeated.

The man shook his head. "I'm sure my son wouldn't do anything like that."

Third Friday

The four friends met again for breakfast. The women told Harold their suspicions; he said little as he cut up his pancakes and pushed them through the syrup on his plate. The server and cook came to see if there was something wrong with the meal, but Harold just shook his head and twirled his coffee cup. When he departed he left Donna's banana muffins on the table.

The three women met out Erica's Subaru. "I think we need to do something," Betsy said. "Harold looks awful and I miss those eggs he used to bring us!"

Donna nodded. "I hate baking with store eggs."

Erica frowned. "Let's think about it and we'll ride Black Butte on Sunday and come up with a plan."

Fourth Friday

The three women were cheerful as they ordered their breakfasts. Harold seemed a little less depressed and asked if he could visit one of them who had a computer so he could look at chicks online. Erica said she would be glad to help him. He nodded thoughtfully before he left, this time remembering the date nut bread that Donna gave him.

A few minutes later, their rural mail carrier came in. He handed the cook the day's mail and shook his head. "I just delivered a tub of stuff up at Blue Ranch. Mostly addressed to the son. Catalogs, advertising and what not. Second time this week." He poured coffee into his to-go mug and slapped the lid back on. "The old man said their computer almost blew up with all the emails they got. Must have been ten or twelve from dating sites alone, and a bunch of ads there, too. They can't figure out where it's all coming from."

As the mailman left with his coffee, the three women looked at each other and burst into giggles.

Full Circle

By

Orina Hodgson

Tara liked to say that she and Zoe saved each other's lives.

Six months after Mark was killed by a drunk driver the scraggly long-haired pup appeared at their house.

It started with Banner barking like crazy to warn Tara of an intruder on the property. By the time she pushed the screen door open, the stray had rolled over and tucked a black and white feathered tail across her belly. Banner, a twelve-year-old boxer, sniffed the submissive young bitch thoroughly, then twitched his blonde stub and pranced around. No danger there.

"Come here, girl. I won't hurt you." Tara offered the skinny beast some water and a little bit of kibble. She felt through the tangled mass of hair for a collar and tags, but shot back when the dog yelped. A metal chain was imbedded into the pup's neck. Tara's fingers came away sticky with pus and blood.

"Oh shit! I'm sorry. Who in the hell did this to you?" Tears burned the young woman's hazel eyes. Then she dropped to the ground, put her head to her knees and sobbed. Long brown hair fell forward onto her tightly clasped legs. She had cried so easily since that inebriated asshole crossed the road and stole her husband's life last December. Mark was almost home when it happened-- only one more mile on the Concho Highway before their turn-off.

It isn't fair! Oh Mark, I can't do this anymore. I want to be wherever you are. I'm done here. I'm coming Honey. I'm coming to you.

A low whimper and cold wet nose nudged Tara's dark thoughts. She raised her oval face to meet a tri-colored snout below semi-pricked ears.

"Okay, girl. I need to get you some help before I do anything else, don't I?" Tara sighed deeply. "Come on Banner. In your yard". The old boxer, Mark's dog from before he and Tara had even met, ambled into his large pen and circled around several times before settling into a nap.

Tara coaxed the shaggy stray into her Forerunner and drove eighteen miles to the vet in Snowflake. The pup trembled and whined the entire way. But she never took her intense eyes, one blue and one brown, from Tara's pinched face.

Doc Charles rattled off his assessment as he examined her: "Looks like an Aussie-Husky mix; probably about 9 months old. She's not spayed. Severely undernourished."

"Son-of-a-bitch!" He muttered when he gently parted the pup's hair to expose the noose of a chain and the infection it caused. "Excuse my French, Tara. You, too, Miss." He stroked the shivering animal.

Tara and Doc Charles reached an agreement.

"I'll tend to the pup's medical needs free of charge if you take her until we can find her a home. It wouldn't surprise me if you decide to keep her anyway. Banner is getting old and maybe you could use the company."

No way I'm keeping her! Tara thought. But she needed the doc's help for a while. Money had been tight since Mark died. Tara- an ER nurse in Show Low- had taken a long leave of absence after the accident. She only managed one or two shifts a week now. Besides, she couldn't desert the traumatized stray. The pup leaned hard into Tara while the doc injected a sedative.

"We'll get her cleaned up and get some antibiotics on board. Come back tomorrow about this time to pick her up." The doc's assistant set up the surgical tray as the canine drifted into a deep sleep.

This will work out. I'll find her a family. Someone will take her. The last thing Tara wanted right then was another long-term commitment. She had plans.

Banner loved the new resident. His stub of a tail wagged more than it had in months. He'd been so low since that day Mark didn't come home.

Banner had been the only witness to the furious argument between Mark and Tara the morning his master peeled out in the old Ford pickup.

"All you can think about is getting pregnant! I can't fix this, Tara. Aren't we good enough like we are? We used to make love. Now we have sex on a schedule!" Mark's words meant nothing to the aging boxer.

"You won't even try," she had retaliated. "Why won't you just get tested? Maybe if you quit smoking pot. Maybe if you ate better. Mark, I want us to have a family. I've done everything there is to do on my end. It's your turn to man up!"

Mark stormed out the door and down the icy path to the truck. Banner hobbled after his distressed 'boy'. "Stay Banner! You stay home!" Banner had not heard that voice since puppy training days.

"I'll be back," Mark added. But he never came back.

The killer had been cited three times for driving under the influence. This one would send him to jail. Too late for Tara. Too late for Mark. The old boxer lay by the gate every day, waiting his master's return.

After six months of barely surviving, Tara had made a plan. She knew Mark's parents would take care of Banner. She'd make sure it looked like an accident-- to make her death easier on her parents and brothers. For weeks, she'd been taking solo hikes, photographing petroglyphs, and posting them on Facebook. They were good. It looked to the world as if she was coping. She knew just the place where a "tragic fall" from a high cliff would certainly be fatal.

Then Zoe turned up. That was four years ago.

***

Tara heaved the maul high above her right shoulder. Without pause, she completed an arc, driving the steel wedge into a gnarly round of red juniper. She smiled in response to the loud crack, pungent aroma, and sudden release of pressure.

"Damn, I'm good!" the lithe woman grinned as she kicked the split wood aside and stood another piece on edge, ready to whack it into submission. "You're next," she warned the log.

Zoe interrupted Tara's smug exclamation with a long drawn out howl, nose pointed to the sky as she simultaneously glanced sideways to catch her mistress's eye.

Tara couldn't help but laugh at this familiar comical petition. "Okay, Girl. It's long past time for our run isn't it?" She tossed the fuel into a wheelbarrow, then maneuvered it toward the house with Zoe close on her heels.

Tara tousled the dog's ruff before snapping a leash on the soft leather collar. She spoke aloud to her wagging friend. "Do you remember how long it was before I could even touch your neck without you freaking out? Now look at you. Now look at us."

"Zoe means 'life' you know." Tara stared past the dog toward the high-cliffed mesas in the distance.

Zoe gave two quick barks and turned to face the road. They started out slowly and increased the pace as they warmed up.

"Let's go across the wash today, Girl. I've been hearing some racket at the old Hanson place. Maybe someone finally bought it."

They were a beautiful sight as they loped along the dirt roads. Tara was tall and slender. Her long brown hair, forced from her face by a thick red headband flew wildly behind her. Zoe's once scraggly coat now boasted a shiny mane of black, white, and brown. She held her head high, eyes darting from side to side, not missing a thing.

They approached the previously deserted homestead. Tara eyed crude 'No Trespassing' signs attached to the rusty barbed-wire fence every 100 yards or so. She slowed when she got to the gate, which was chained shut with a heavy padlock securing it.

"Holy cow, Zoe! Looks like our new neighbors aren't too friendly. Maybe we can leave a bag of cookies next time we run this way. With a welcome card or something. It never hurts to try." She squinted toward the scattered buildings set back from the road. Piles of garbage bags and a bunch of plastic bottles obstructed her view. "Phew! This place stinks! The Hansons would be sad, Zoe."

A week passed before they jogged that way again. Tara had the cookies and a card bundled safely in her backpack. She stopped at the gate. The padlock was still secured. She no sooner attached a colorful bag and ribbon to the latch when a piercing blast jolted the silence.

"Shit!" Tara stretched her long neck to look in the direction of the explosion. Smoke rose from a shed standing next to a worn-down trailer. She heard the screams of a child. "Shit!" she repeated and ducked under the rusty wire and onto the property.

When they approached the trailer, Zoe pulled back on the leash with an uncharacteristic whimper. "Zoe, come!" Tara admonished. "They need our help."

"Well, well. Looks like we have company," were the words Tara heard just before a powerful grip yanked her by the wrist into the mobile home. "Can't you read, Lady? 'No trespassing' means stay out!."

Zoe snarled ferociously. Tara dropped the leash just before the trailer door slammed in the dog's face.

"What the hell…." A sharp slap across Tara's face stifled her question.

A toddler screamed in the arms of a skinny pock-faced woman behind the tall scowling man.

"Brandon, stop! B.J. is hurt! She got burned bad out there. We need to get her some help." The woman took a step toward the scruffy man. He shoved her onto the stained couch with the screeching baby in her arms. Acrid smoke drifted through an open window behind them.

Through stinging eyes, Tara spotted Zoe crouched in the rabbit brush in front of the house. *Go home, Girl. Get out of here!* Tara silently implored. Zoe didn't move a muscle.

Tara turned her attention to the agonized cries of the little one. Large blisters oozed across bright red skin on her face, arms and hands. "Please, let me help" Tara beseeched. "I'm a nurse. An ER nurse. It looks like the baby got burned pretty badly."

Brandon's face twisted into an evil grin. Pangs of fear shot through Tara's mind. "Now I know who you are, Bitch! You sent me to jail because your damn husband didn't have the sense to stay home on an icy day. I was locked up for two years after that. Two years of my life wasted!"

Tara's stomach heaved when she recognized the man who killed her husband 4 ½ years ago. She'd sat in the courtroom every day during the trial. Although Brandon's greasy brown hair was longer now, his hollow blue eyes held the same contempt as they did back then.

The baby was screeching and writhing in her mother's arms. "Please let me help her," Tara begged. Intense fear was overruled by the obvious suffering of the burned toddler.

"Oh yes, you'll help the brat all right. You'll help all of us. I can think of a few things you can do for me later," Brandon sneered. "I got a necklace for you, lady." He slipped a choke-collar over Tara's head around her neck. "You're not going anywhere!" He held the end of a leash in his hand.

Tara froze. It took every bit of willpower she had to avoid pulling on the chain.

"She had no business playing by the supplies anyway. The whole god-damned shed is burning up. I ought to whip her butt! Or yours, Cyndi!" He glared at the cowering woman.

"What kind of mother are you anyway? But we'll deal with that later."

He turned to Tara. "Now fix her up. Or else. This screaming is giving me a headache."

"I need to know what caused the burns. It makes a big difference in how we treat them."

Cyndi lurched from the couch with the baby clutched tight in her arms. "It was probably acetone, maybe phosphorus and acid, too. She slipped away from me for just a second. You know how babies are."

No. I don't know how babies are. I never got that chance. And you just threw it away! Tara reached for the screaming toddler who clung tightly to her mama. "It's okay, Sweetie. It will be okay. What's her name?"

Tara learned that the little one's name was Brandy, but they called her B.J. She would turn two in a few months. She asked Cyndi if there were any pain medications in the house.

"Just crank," Cyndi referred to the meth they cooked on the ranch. "And marijuana. A little Tylenol syrup, I think. We're all out of downers. That's why he's so crabby. 'Hasn't slept in days. I keep telling him…."

Tara interrupted, "Let's give her the Tylenol and some marijuana will probably help too." Tara was incredulous that she was considering recommending pot for a toddler. Yet within minutes she directed Cyndi to blow smoke toward the crying child.

Soon, the baby nodded off in her mother's arms. Tara gently cleaned the raw red burns. She applied Bag Balm, the only salve in the house. B.J. whimpered throughout the process, but did not fully wake.

"She needs to get to a hospital. These are serious wounds. B.J. could die if they get infected."

The young mother gently rocked her baby, tears welled up in her eyes.

"She dies, you die!" Brandon yanked on the leash attached to the choke collar.

Tara's hands flew to her neck, grabbing the chain. She lurched toward Brandon to create slack, a terrified scream muffled by the pressure on her throat. Tara wrenched the loosened collar over her head and leapt away.

"What in the hell are you doing, you son of a….." Before she could finish the expletive, Brandon, red-faced and wild-eyed, covered the short distance between them and smacked Tara furiously across the face.

She gasped and stumbled back onto the couch.

B.J. woke and began shrieking again.

"Stop, Brandon!" Cyndi cried out. "We need her to help us with the baby."

Brandon raised his clenched fist to strike Cyndi.

Suddenly, B.J.'s high-pitched wail was overpowered by shrill undulating sirens. Their intensity increased by the second.

"It's The Man! They saw the fire! I told you I'm not going back to jail. Never again!" Brandon reached behind the couch under the open window and yanked out a Glock .45. He spun to face the two women and child. "It's your fault! All of you. Even the god-damned baby started the fire. No one gets out of this alive. I'm not going back to the slammer." He pointed the semi-automatic toward the three huddled females.

Cyndi curled her body around B.J.'s, resulting in more furious screams from the baby.

The wailing of the sirens was louder.

Tara shrieked, "No, Brandon! Don't shoot the baby!"

A flash of brown, black, and white momentarily blocked the light from the window as Zoe leapt through the opening with teeth bared.

"Oh, you too, Mutt? This magazine has plenty for all of us. You first."

***

The sheriff cut through the rusted wire fence next to the padlocked gate. A small red fire tanker entered the property and lurched to a stop outside the trailer and the burned out shed. Just then they heard the gunfire: two shots in quick succession, followed by four more, spaced seconds apart.

Two more deputies arrived before they used the bullhorn. "Drop your weapons! Come out the front door with your hands above your head. No sudden moves."

The door creaked as it opened. Tara held both hands straight up in the air as she maneuvered down the aluminum steps. Tears rolled down her red, bruised cheeks. The first deputy gasped. "Tara Morgan! What the…".

Cyndi came close behind with one arm raised and the other wrapped tightly around B.J. "Please help us. Please! My baby is burned. There's a dead man in there."

Tara blurted out between wracking sobs, "You've got to help my dog! She saved our lives. She's been shot."

The deputies gently separated the women into two cars while they waited for the ambulances to arrive. Their stories corroborated perfectly. Zoe launched through the window when she heard Tara scream. She took a bullet on her way to attack Brandon. Her sharp teeth gripped his wrist and the gun fell to the floor. Cyndi scrambled to the ground, grabbed the gun and fired at Brandon. He went down but was still moving. Cyndi fired twice more, then went and stood over the writhing man. He grabbed her ankle.

Cyndi hissed at him. “No, you don’t. You’re not taking me down with you!” This time the bullet went straight to his head. Brandon stopped moving and the grip on her ankle relaxed.

The officers found the dead man and the motionless dog right where the women told them they would be.

***

“Come away little one. She’s not a pony.” Tara gently pulled B.J. from Zoe’s back. The toddler had crawled on top of the sleeping dog, who only whined and looked up at her mistress. They were both healing well, each day better than the one before. B.J.’s bandages had been removed four days ago and Zoe was starting to run again, at an easy lope.

“We’re going to visit your mama today. Let’s get you all cleaned up and put your birthday dress on.”

“Mama?” B.J. stared solemnly at Tara.

“Yup. We finally got our papers and we’ll be able to go to the… to go visit your Mama almost every week. When she gets out, she’s going to live here for a while. Until the two of you get back on your feet.”

“Feet,” B.J. giggled and pointed to her bare toes. “Feet.”

Tara laughed as she scooped the little girl into her arms. “You are such a smart baby!” Her joy was cut short by a catch in her throat as she remembered that B.J. wouldn’t be her foster-daughter forever.

Zoe nudged Tara’s knee, then pointed her nose to the sky and howled. “Yup, Zoe. It’s you an’ me, Girl. Full circle.”

###

Horses

By

Nico Crowkiller-Scherr

Small town life was wonderful. Living in the high deserts of northeast Arizona meant there were changes in the seasons through the year.

Snowflake was founded in 1878 by pioneers following the Mormon way of life. Like so many small towns it had its traditions.

Sarah Bell was almost thirteen and had lived there all her life. Over the years somethings changed. They had a Super Walmart in the town of Taylor, which meant her Momma didn't have to drive into Show Low to do her shopping. This years school clothes and supplies would come from their Taylor store, but other things stayed the same.

The July 4th firing of the anvil, Trapper's Day, Snowflake Pioneer Days, The Taylor Sweet Corn Festival and Snowflake's Twelve Days of Christmas were all on the family's calendar.

Other things were special to her also. Grandfather Yazzi lived on his forty-nine acre ranch in Hunt, just east of Snowflake where he raised his horses. He was an old cowboy, riding the rodeo circuit for years while Nonna Emily raised their children on the ranch. Sarah Bell's Momma, Bena had grown up on the ranch.

The youngest of six, Bena worked her way through nursing school when she met Cam Lockwood and fell in love.

Cam was in the Army. A Chaplain. They dated for several months when he asked her to marry him. She agreed, but to Mitch Yazzi's disapproval. The Yazzi children were raised traditional Navajo. No daughter of his was going to change that fact. Bena wasn't planning on changing her father. Only living her life.

They married without her father's blessing.

Moving where ever his orders took them, they'd traveled from the US to Germany then Japan and finally when Bena was expecting back to Texas.

That was until Cam's new orders came in. He was to be transferred to Washington D.C. Tired of travel and wanting a stable place to raise a child, Bena chose to return home to Snowflake where they purchased a home in Sundance Springs Community.

So began the rebuilding of bridges between her father and herself. Living in the small town meant she would be able to raise their daughter amongst family, Each morning before Bena drove into Show Low for her shift at Summit Hospital she drove the children out to the ranch.

When Sarah Bell started school she would be dropped off and picked up by Grandfather. He taught her the old ways of tradition. They talked about the family. Sarah Bell found out that her Great Grandfather was a US Marine and Wind Talker during World War II and Grandfather served in the Meikong Delta area in Vietman.

She had questions Grandfather wouldn't answer about her father. Maybe he didn't want to. But what she did know was Grandfather knew his horses.

Sarah Bell stood by the riding ring's fence and watched Grandfather with Sundancer It was mid July, school would be starting in August. This also meant they were in the midst of monsoon season. They already had several storms and now as Grandfather worked with Sundancer, she watched the clouds forming in the incoming darkness and dancing of lightning in the distances. The rumble of thunder rolled in the west. That meant Holbrook was getting it first

"Child," Grandfather called. "Go to the house. I'm calling it a day."

"Yes, Grandfather." She stepped down from the railed fence.

Turning for the home that Great Grandfather built in 1948 when he returned to Navajo Nation. He'd bought the land as a wedding gift for his bride and they'd settled to build the six bedroom home and raise five daughters and two sons on the ranch. Grandfather was to oldest. Born in 1949, he was sent to school at age five then elevated to third grade at age six, graduating high school at sixteen in 1965 he'd joined the Army. By January 28, 1973 he was ready for peace. At age twenty-four he came home to marry his high school sweetheart, Emily Yellow Hair. She had waited for him.

Nonna and Grandfather would be celebrating their forty-fourth wedding anniversary on Valentine's Day. Sarah Bell sighed with a smile. 'How romantic was that?'

She crossed the yard from the corrals, walked onto the porch to open the screen door and entered the living room. She inhaled deeply smelling the lemon oil Nonna used on the furniture and the bees wax she used to polish the wide pine floor boards. In the center of the room sat a circular hearth for the massive fireplace. The furniture was old, but heavy and withstood the horseplay and abuse of the seven original children and many more, including herself, her younger sister, Hannah, who was ten and three year old brother, Camp, who sat with Nonna in the kitchen as she made the evening meal.

Sarah Bell called out, "Nonna, storm coming."

Walking into the kitchen she smelt the fried bread bubbling away in the hot oil and the roast in the oven blended with the scent of drying herbs hanging from the rafters.

"Is Grandfather coming?" Nona asked turning the bread in the pan.

"Putting Sundancer in the barn with the others."

Sarah Bell took plates from the closet to help Hannah set the table.

Moments later there was a crash of thunder and the skies opened loosing a torrent of rain. They heard the screen door open then slam as the wind took it from Mitch's hand.

"Sorry, Em." He ran his hand through his long silver streaked black hair. Rivulets of water streamed onto his shoulders.

"That's okay, Boy. Dinner's ready. Come wash up and eat." Nonna set the fry bread on paper to drain. She took the pan from the oven to remove the roast and carve while Sarah Bell plated vegetables.

Mitch washed his hands and regarded his grandchildren with pride. The girls resembled their mother. Their long black hair hung to their waist matching their dark doe eyes. Camp, he smiled. He called him his Scamp, a little saddle tramp, with the way he rode his pony, Kwam, always having to reset his cowboy hat as it fell over his eyes as they bounced around the coral. His grandson had a dark auburn tint to his brown hair and the most beautiful forest green eyes he'd ever seen on a child. Truly his father's son.

He sat at the head of the table and waited for Emily to plate Camp's meal and cut his meat. The girls fixed their plates as Emily prepared her own. Finally, as always, he plated his own.

"Your mother's going to be late picking you up with this storm. The washes will run. You might miss his call tonight." He never spoke their father's name. Never wanted to. The man drifted in and out of their lives with every transfer order he received. What reason did he have to speak the name of a ghost?

He broke the fry bread to dip into his gravy as Emily and the children began to eat. Looking at Sarah Bell he said. "Tomorrow, you can seat yourself on Sundancer. But not without me. Am I clear?"

"Yes, Grandfather." Her heart burst with pride. He was trusting her with the big Appaloosa.

"We'll work with you and Sundancer for the barrel. But, right now you and he need to find your seat." Grandfather ate. "Emmh... Wonderful as always, Emily.'

Nonna smiled. She took pride in feeding her man. Too many time in the Army, then in the rodeo he went hungry. Not on her watch.

They were in the middle of putting away the leftovers and doing the dishes when Nonna's phone rang. She took it from her pocket, glanced at the incoming number and answered. "Yes, Bena."

"Momma, can you and Dad keep the kids tonight?" Bena blinked away the tears she'd held back since she got the call with the news she was bracing herself for. Her heart pounded as the sweat broke out on her forehead and she hurt with the love for Cam. She knew this was coming. For God's sake she was an RN. Cam was coming home. This was not what they'd talked about. The original news looked promising. Now it was devastating. Six months had passed since the transfer to Texas and the base there. He was now discharged and coming home. Little did the promised surgeries do but make matters worse.

"Yes, we can keep them. What's wrong?" Nonna looked to the children then to her husband. The children hadn't been told about the accident.

"I need to drive to Phoenix. Cam's coming home. It's not good. Momma, don't tell the kids until we get there."

"Is it what they thought?" Emily crossed her arm over her breast. 'Damn it,' she thought, 'the kids have a right to know the truth.'

Bena was already driving Rout 260 into Payson. She watched the wipers force the water from the windshield as she watched for way word elk as the tears ran down her cheeks. She bit her lower lip then took a deep breath to try to to regroup with the meditation she'd learned long ago from Mitch. It didn't work.

"Yes, Momma, Cam's in a wheelchair."

Two

The next day was Thursday. They woke to blue skies. Breakfast was served and Mitch did his usual chores.

While Emily and the younger two children fed the chickens, gathered eggs and milked the goats, Mitch and Sarah Bell fed the twelve horses and the pony that called the ranch home. This was now Sarah Bell's time with Grandfather and Sundancer. Seated in the saddle on the Appaloosa she trotted in the ring around the barrels Grandfather set to regulation standards.

Mitch looked over his shoulder when the Saturn Vue pulled into the lane and up to the house.

"Keep him at a trot, Bell." Grandfather turned for the house as Bena opened the driver's door to step out. He walked to the back of the SUV when she came to the tailgate. "How is he?" He took the wheelchair from the back.

"He's in good spirits and be nice." She leaned in to take the duffel bag.

"I'm always nice," he growled with a smile. Setting open the chair he rolled it around the side of the truck.

Cam offered his hand. "Sir."

"Son, or should I say Chaplain?' He took Cam's hand.

"As long as you don't call me an SOB, we're okay." He moved his right leg with his hands out of the truck then his left as Mitch rolled the chair close. Easing himself down into it he unlocked the breaks to place his hands on the wheels to roll himself back and shut the door. He looked towards the ring to see his oldest on the horse and watched her trot around the barrels. "Can I go watch?"

"You're her father," he acknowledged with a shrug, then started for the ring.

Cam looked to Bena. “Go. I'll bring the others to you. We'll explain in a few minutes.”

He nodded putting his hands on the wheels to roll towards his daughter and the horse.

Mitch rested his arm on the top rail and a booted foot on the bottom. “Bell, put him through his paces.”

Cam saw his girl's eyes go wide. She patted Sundancer's neck then brought him to the start of the barrels for their run at Grandfather's single. He gave it and she was off.

Cam watched with pride as she circled the first barrel and charged the next.

Mitch glanced to Cam. “Son, Bena said you need to speak with me on a matter of the Sweat Lodge. I'm here.”

He took a deep breath. It was now or never and he was not putting his beloved family through his nightmare. He swallowed his pride.

“They have me on morphine. I...” He closed his eyes and lowered his head.

“White man's drugs are never good. You need to be one with the land. At peace with yourself.” He rested his hand on Cam's shoulder as they watched Sarah Bell and Sundancer become one in rider and horse.

The seconds passed, Sarah Bell brought Sundancer back to a trot in the ring.

“Enough for today. Tomorrow you ride again. A little at a time will bring you together. Unsaddle him, brush him down and when you put him in the barn go help Nonna with dinner.” Mitch looked down at his son-in-law as he rested on hand on the fence rail.

Sarah Bell dismounted to bring Sundancer to the rails. “Hello, Daddy.”

He reached out to the horse to pet his flank and looked at his beautiful daughter. “Hello, Sweetheart. He's beautiful, just like you.”

Her cheeks turned a light shade of pink. She smiled turning to start to remove the saddle.

Grandfather spoke, his deep voice a sweet sound to her ears. "Father and I will be in the house. We have things to discuss."

"We do," Cam agreed as he turned his chair for the front of the house.

Long ago the ranch house had been fitted for a ramp to the porch to make it accessible for Mitch's father. Great Grandfather was now ninety-two and lived in a nursing home, but still came home for celebrations.

They went back to the house to settle into the living room to discuss Cam's new assignment.

There was a new non-denomonational chapel on the outskirts of Snowflake to the east of town. Tree of Life Chapel was looking for a Chaplain. Cam had applied shortly after his second failed surgery and been called to lead this flock.

Mitch looked at Cam across the dinner table then to his daughter. "With Bena having a day shift in Show Low, how are you going to get to church?" He picked up his coffee to take a drink and watch the exchange between his children.

"Cam has a van, Dad. It will be delivered tomorrow. In the mean time, I'll take him in and pick him up today. What we do need to ask..." She took a breath.

He cut her off with a raised hand. "Your house... It's no good for a wheelchair. What do you propose?"

She sighed looking to her husband as he began to explain. "We're taking a loan to have repairs done. We're swapping the den for our bedroom and putting in ramps. It will take a month, maybe six weeks to have things done for me." He sat down his spoon to push his pear and berry cobbler aside. This discussion was dwindling his taste for Nonna's good desserts.

Mitch shook his head knowing where his kid's thoughts were going by the way Cam avoided the question put to him. “Not good enough of an answer, Cam. You're not thinking of staying in a motel for the next... Hell, these repairs could take two or three months. So get that out of that thick skull of yours. You stay here. Besides, tomorrow you have your first lesson.”

“Lesson?” Bena looked from her father to Cam.

“The animals come first. Then the Sweat Lodge.” Mitch finished his coffee to rise from the table and walk out of the house.

“Where's he going?” Bena helped the girls and Nonna clear the table.

“To prepare.” Emily smiled, knowing her man of few words.

Three

Saturday morning they woke at sunrise. Breakfast was served, the animals fed. Cam did the scariest thing he had to do. He turned his pills over to Mitch.

“I don't want them. None of them.” He took a shuddering breath to slam his fist into his thighs. Hands on the wheels of his chair his muscles of his arms flexed as he shoved the wheels forward and began to roll out of the office.

Mitch put the pills in the gun safe as he heard the sound of Cam's tenor singing Amazing Grace as he left the house. Spinning the lock, he smiled. 'Boy's got guts.' He had to admire that.

Following Cam he left the house, he watched as his son-in-law rolled to the riding ring.

Several of the horses were out in the field along with Kwam the pony. Mitch came up behind him noting the sad look he gave the two colts that frolicked in the field together.

Cam inhaled the fresh air, raising his face to the warmth of the sun. He looked to the barn as Sarah Bell came out with Sundancer. She led him to the fence rails.

"You'll do this, Daddy. I know you will." She smiled with all the confidence in the world that she felt for her father. They watched her mount, then start into a slow trot.

"Cam. It's time." Mitch said resting his hand on his shoulder."

"Let's do this, Sir." He turned the chair for the open field where the Sweat Lodge waited.

Rolling over tufts of grass, through the land they arrived in front of the skin-covered dome.

"You get in there remove your clothes. Seat yourself on the blanket and wait for me." Mitch directed pulling back the flap from the opening.

Cam took a deep breath and locked his chair. Moving his feet from the rest he slid forward to lean from the chair onto the tarp in front of the lodge. Once down he turned to place his back to the opening and drug his lower body into the shelter using his upper body strength he had from his massive arms.

He seated himself on the blanket near the hot stones and removed his shirt then his sneakers and jeans. Folding his legs under him he waited. Mitch crawled in next to him, stripped naked and ladled water over the rocks. The steam rose as they sat. Moments passed before either spoke.

It was Mitch who broke the silence explaining that this was not a one time fix all. They would be in the Sweat Lodge many times to come. As many as Cam needed and he would be there with him just as he would be there to teach Sarah Bell how to seat and work with Sundancer.

Cam didn't broach the subject of Mitch and Christianity. He learned long ago what the man thought of religion.

Still he asked. "Will you come to church on Sunday? My first sermon."

The man reached for the ladle and bucket of water to lace the hot stones once again and didn't answer.

The hour passed until Mitch rose. “We're done for the day. Cam, visit the horses.”

He dressed and slid his way from the lodge to where Mitch held the chair for him to pull himself up into it and unlock the breaks.

As they went to the circle a flatbed truck pulled into the lane with Cam's Dodge Ram Extension van on the bed. He signed for it to be lowered to the ground. Taking the keys he gave the man a tip. The flatbed pulled out for him to turn back to the ring to watch his daughter and the horse.

Grandfather nodded to her. “Bell, we're here. Proceed.” He gave the single and she was off.

The first rumble of thunder had Mitch looking to the skies then out to his horses and the pony. The clouds thickened bringing in a darkness then the first streak of lightning breached the sky.

“Son, head for the house. Bell, bring him in. Take care of him.”

Cam watched his daughter dismount to lead Sundancer into the barn as Mitch started for the field.

“What's he doing?” Cam asked his daughter as she unsaddled Sundancer then led him to the barn at the second streak of lightning and a roll of thunder.

“Opening the gate so they can come in. Daddy, head to the house. It's-” The rain fell before she could finish and he felt the first chill of many he'd be facing in the long journey ahead of him without morphine.

The tremors began and his body twitched as he placed his hands on the wheels to turn for the house.

His prayers began with a recitation of The Lord’s Prayer.

Four

Cam had fought through the rest of the day and night to withstand the onset of the withdrawal as the storm pounded the land and into Sunday morning.

The skies were bright blue and the air fresh. This morning after breakfast, Mitch had him in the Sweat Lodge. He'd left the care of the horses to Sarah Bell as he cared for her father.

Now it was time to leave for church. They'd gotten the children into the van and Cam behind the wheel. Driving the back roads took extra care because of the mud. They couldn't take Old Hunt because the wash was still flowing so they rode along Ranch Road all the way out to Concho Highway just east of the five mile marker in Apache County. Coming into Snowflake city limits they drove into the parking lot of the Tree of Life Chapel.

The old ramshackle barn had sat abandon by the owners for almost twenty years when they'd decided to donate it and the land it set on to the congregation. It had been restored into the church and fellowship hall.

Cam was now the first Chaplain in residence.

They entered the church to see the old style pews and altar that once had been the area to store oats and feed. The building still held the scent of fresh hay.

"Welcome home," Cam whispered to himself as he rolled up on altar for the first parishioner to enter.

Congregants gathered for the ten thirty worship.

Cam introduced his family and announced his text for his sermon. Today's sermon was of strength and weakness, abilities and addictions. He brought up what he himself was fighting and that no man was perfect, but all were saved by grace.

He looked to the back of the church as the door opened for a latecomer and he stared into the dark brown eyes of Mitch Yazzi, who nodded and slid into the last pew with his beloved Emily who smiled with pride about the two stubborn men she shared a life with,

"In closing. We ask blessings over the snacks that have been provided and blessings over Your people. In Yashua's name, Amen." He closed his sermon and bible to place it in his lap and roll towards the isle as a chill ran through him.

He was joined by the family in fellowship hall where Sarah Bell was talking to a friend, Jenny Kandi, about Sundancer and the upcoming Pioneer Days celebration.

Mitch looked down at Cam as he held his coffee. "How are you feeling?"

"Chills, my hands are shaking. I'm sweating. I'm having allergy symptoms... sneezing. I'm tired. Yawning mostly. I didn't sleep last night with the cramping. I'll make it though." His hands shook as he raised his coffee to his lips.

"Temperature?" Mitch asked watching him closely.

"Hot and cold at the same time." He smiled stretching to relieve the onset of the cramping.

"We'll make it. The Sweat Lodge and horses are waiting for you. They have a calming effect."

Cam looked up at him with a burning question. "Why did you decide to come today?"

Grandfather looked around to his family then focused on Cam. "She's my granddaughter. You're her father. Her life. She loves you. My daughter loves you. Therefore you're mine to worry about. You're mine to care for. The Creator knows that. I listen to Him when He tells me to." He calmly sipped his coffee.

###

A Kidnapping In Arizona

Chapter 1 of Tony Wagner Mystery #9

Scheduled for release in 2018

by

Paula F. Winskye

Tony Wagner surveyed the hotel conference room occupied by almost thirty law enforcement officers, from deputies to FBI agents.

"To summarize, tracking is like any skill. It takes practice. Have someone leave you a trail to follow. Get out on hiking trails and read the signs. Work at it. Are there any other questions?" When no one spoke up, he continued. "Thanks for giving me the privilege of teaching this FBI Academy class. I know that Albuquerque was a long trip for some of you."

His students rose. While some gathered their belongings and departed, others stopped to thank him.

Only a handful of people remained when he heard the familiar ring tone belonging to his FBI mentor, Wyatt Garret. Tony kept Garret in his peripheral vision while talking with one of the students.

Garret's bushy eyebrows formed his infamous "one-brow look." After more than a decade as friends and coworkers, Tony knew that meant trouble. Garret met his gaze and waved him over. Tony excused himself and closed the gap.

"We'll get to the airport ASAP. Don't let anyone disturb the trail." He disconnected and pivoted for the door. "Kidnapping in Arizona. I'll explain on the way."

Tony ran after him to the parking garage. They scrambled into the FBI SUV and Garret stomped on the gas pedal, squealing tires. He flipped on lights and siren before speaking again.

"You know who George Jacobs is?"

"Under-secretary of ... Energy?"

"Right. His daughter was just kidnapped and her bodyguard murdered at Jacobs ranch in the White Mountains of Arizona. They want you there ASAP. A military chopper will meet us at the Albuquerque airport to make it happen."

Tony gritted his teeth as memories of his own kidnapping flashed through his mind. He shook his head. "How old is the girl?"

"Not sure. I saw her in a picture of him awhile back. Ten? Twelve? I'll get more for you once we're in the air."

"Okay."

Garret could drive like a lunatic if the situation required it, making Tony grateful that the FBI had chosen a location near the airport for his class.

When the SUV skidded around a corner in front of a long line of hangars, Tony saw the Black Hawk helicopter spooling up. He reached into the back seat and grabbed the small backpack he took on all his travels. It contained both wilderness survival necessities and crime scene investigation materials.

An airman waved them toward the Black Hawk. "I'll take care of your vehicle, sir."

Tony joined Garret in the back, buckling in as the helicopter lifted off. Both donned headsets.

The co-pilot's voice squawked in their ears. "Agent Garret, I'm connecting you to the head of security on site."

"Roger. Thanks."

In a moment, the head of Jacobs' security detail came over the airwaves. "This is Hunt."

"Garret here. Wagner's keyed in. Give us details."

"When Under-secretary Jacobs and his family are at the ranch, his daughter, Chelsea, goes for a ride with her bodyguard every morning about ten. At 11:15, their horses ran into the yard. There was a ransom note tied to Chelsea's saddle and bloodstains on my man's horse."

Garret checked his watch. "It's only 12:10 now. We usually don't get called so quick."

"Mr. Jacobs' idea. When I insisted that he stay in the ranch house, he said he was calling for Wagner. I heard him say once that if he was ever missing, he wanted Wagner on his trail. We backtracked the horses and found Jamison, dead. And an elaborate trap set up in the wash that Chelsea usually took when she rode."

"How close can we land?"

"Within a quarter-mile."

"Have horses ready for us."

"Horses? All-terrain vehicles are a lot faster."

"Too noisy." Garret glanced at Tony. "We don't want the kidnappers to know we're coming."

"They'll be ready. What supplies do you need?"

"Water. A sat phone. What else, Tony?"

"Something to eat on the trail. We don't know how long this will take."

"You'll have it," Hunt said. "Anything else."

Tony needed to know. "How old is Chelsea?"

"Twelve."

"I'll pray that they left a trail I can follow. Where is this ranch? I want to study maps till we get there."

"A half-hour east of Show Low."

"What's the elevation?"

"About 5500 feet. The weather this time of October is in the low 70s. It drops into the 40s at night. I hope you're as good as your reputation."

"And I hope they didn't load their ATVs on a trailer."

Tony brought up a topographic map program on his tablet. Working with the FBI often took him from his home in Colorado. Once as far as Maine. But never Arizona.

He found the ranch and studied the surrounding landscape. Valleys and canyons separated mountains and mesas.

He turned to Garret. "At least there aren't many roads and even less *paved* roads."

"That's where you can do the most good."

"Amen."

***

Their flight took a little over an hour. The co-pilot spoke again. "After we drop you off, we've been instructed to search from altitude with our IR cameras."

"I'll have a sat phone," Garret said. "Contact me if you spot anything."

Tony studied the wash from the air, noting several people and all-terrain vehicles gathered in a narrow place. Approaching the landing zone, he saw three men holding horses nearby.

He and Garret unbuckled as the Black Hawk settled in and jumped out when it touched down. Tony noted that all three animals seemed calm despite the commotion. *Good to know if things get hairy on the trail.*

One of the men with the horses stepped forward. He did not offer to shake their hands, but yelled above the helicopter's din. "I'm Hunt. I'll be riding with you."

Garret just nodded.

They checked cinches and Tony lengthened his stirrups while the Black Hawk took off. Tony wondered if Hunt's scowl reflected the loss of one of his men or his displeasure at their arrival.

After mounting, Garret spoke. "Lead us into the wash."

Hunt found a steep trail hidden behind shaggy-bark juniper trees and eased his horse down. When they reached the sandy bottom, the trap came into view.

Tony studied what looked like ship's cargo nets strung across the deep wash in two places. *It looks like something they might use to catch big game in Africa.*

After the kidnapping, someone had propped up a place on either side high enough to lead a horse under. Tony dismounted and took his horse through to the far side of the trap. He zeroed in on tracks of several ATVs.

In most places, the wide-wheeled vehicles left little more than depressions in the soft sand. But he kept searching until he found clear tracks. He saw Chelsea's smaller footprints ending at an ATV with a chunk missing from its tread.

He turned to find Garret right behind him. "Has anyone been over here?"

"Only on foot. The tire tracks belong to the kidnappers."

Tony mounted, riding south at a walk. He spoke without looking back, knowing Garret would be there. "We're following four quads. Tell the chopper. I know which one they put Chelsea on. If they split up, I know which one to follow." *Lord, help me find this little girl.*

He urged his horse into a lope, maintaining that speed until an expanse of rock crossed the wash. Pulling up, he dismounted to look for signs. Until then, he had forgotten that Hunt rode behind Garret.

Tony searched the far edge of the rock where it gave way to sand again. "They left the wash. Hunt, do you know the way out?"

"No."

Tony scowled. "Spread out. Look for tracks in any sandy depressions."

It only took moments. "Over here," Garret said.

Tony hurried to the spot and continued toward the west edge of the wash. Between boulders, he found fresh ATV tracks in damp clay. "Here's the one with a chunk missing from its tread. The one they put Chelsea on. They're still together."

The trail took them into a smaller wash. He stayed on foot with his hand on his pistol as the wash became shallower, leading to a wide, flat valley covered with bunch grass, saltbush, and juniper. The mixture of sand and clay on the valley floor made tracking easier. He mounted and followed for a half-mile before the trail eased uphill. Almost a mile later, it crossed a low ridge into another valley.

The sun in the cloudless sky made them sweat under their bulletproof vests. But Tony felt grateful that the elevation kept temperatures bearable.

The ATVs took to a "road"—little more than wheel tracks wide enough for one vehicle. It passed a gated driveway leading to an RV with tumbleweeds piled against its door.

When the tracks reached an intersection, they turned west on a similar road and began climbing a mesa. A cattle guard blocked the way. Tony dismounted and opened a barbed wire gate next to the guard, closing it after the horses passed.

Garret squinted into the distance. "Do you think we're gaining on them?"

"No. They can travel faster." Tony mounted. "I'm praying that they're headed for their hideout or the chopper spots them."

He pushed his horse into a trot until the "road" began to switchback on the steep slope. Pulling up, he studied the side of the mesa.

"This could be dangerous, and it's not good for the land, but we need to gain ground."

He urged his horse off the road, heading straight up. He had to stand in his stirrups, leaning over his mount's neck on the steep slope. Each time they crossed the route, he checked for tracks. Six switchbacks later, the road ended at a shack with its door hanging by one hinge and a corral in disrepair.

Dismounting, he followed the ATV tracks around the shack. He led his horse to rest it and talked over his shoulder to Garret and Hunt. "They had to slow to a crawl here because the junipers are so thick. We'll be able to gain some ground for a little while."

After his horse's breathing returned to normal, Tony mounted. If they trotted in this dense cover, they risked an unexpected encounter with the kidnappers. Tony chose to take that chance. When the cover receded to reveal a view, he scanned ahead for any sign of activity. Despite the circumstances, he could not help but notice the stark beauty of the place.

Though three trails forked off toward the top of the mesa, the tracks stayed on the path below the rim. *It's probably too open on top. They don't want to cross the mesa and risk being spotted from the air.*

Tony checked the sun, creeping lower in the western sky. *We've gone half-way round the mesa now. If we don't find their hideout, the trail should start down soon.* He slowed to a walk, stopping once to listen. Only ravens and the sound of a distant helicopter broke the silence. He moved on. The path forked again and the tracks followed the lower fork.

He heard Garret's satellite phone ring but could not make out the conversation. Garret would tell him anything he needed to know.

Through openings in the trees, Tony studied what lay ahead—a valley, then a conical peak higher than the mesa. He stopped and pointed. "Can you see the dust rising from the shoulder of that mountain?"

"Barely," Garret said. "You think that's them?"

"I'd bet on it."

"Hellfire! The Black Hawk just called that they're going in to refuel. We could sure use them now."

Tony pushed his horse downhill as fast as he dared. Horses could step over fallen trees which the ATVs had needed to skirt. *We're still gaining on them.*

The narrow, rocky valley provided no chance to travel at a lope. They began climbing almost as soon as they reached the bottom. As the elevation increased, a few pines appeared among the junipers. Again, fallen trees had slowed the kidnappers.

The trail moved into shadows on the east shoulder of the mountain. Large boulders dotted the slope, finally outnumbering the trees. Ahead, Tony saw more of the same, with some rocks as big as a bus.

If they made it through there, so can we.

The trail wound between boulders. In places, black marks at tire height indicated where an ATV had rubbed in passing.

I hope they don't know we're here. This would be a great spot for an ambush. When he tracked, he counted on Garret to watch his back. Still, he rested his hand on his pistol just to be safe.

Before them, the trail lay between two boulders almost the size of his house. A smell wafted in the air, making him think of a truck stop. *Diesel fuel?*

He raised his hand, stopping to inhale again. No mistake. He turned to Garret and whispered. "Smell that?"

The one-brow look barely preceded Garret's hiss. "Get back!"

All three horses scraped boulders turning around. Hunt looked confused, but did not question the retreat. When he reached a wide place in the trail, he pulled up. Garret and Tony passed him and he followed until they stopped in a safer location.

"What was that all about?"

"Didn't you smell the diesel fuel?" Garret asked.

"No. Why would there be diesel out here?"

"ANFO."

"An— ."

The blast stopped all conversation. For the next few minutes they had their hands full trying to control horses that wanted nothing more than to flee the noise, shock wave, and debris pelting them.

When the rain of dirt and gravel stopped, the horses settled down to skittering around the small clearing. Tony dismounted and began soothing his mount while he tried to peer through the dust cloud. It drifted away, revealing the trail now plugged with broken rock.

He studied the slope above and below, then almost shouted because he could barely hear himself over the ringing in his ears.

"We can't take the horses, but we can climb across those boulders."

Garret shook his head. "Too dangerous. They know we're here. They could set other traps. We need the chopper."

Tony hung his head. *We were so close.* He sighed, glancing at the cloudless sky. *Thy will be done, Lord.*

Garret dismounted and led his horse north along the trail, the satellite phone to his ear. Hunt followed and Tony took up the rear. Ten minutes later, Garret put the phone away and stopped long enough to explain.

"I saw a clearing back here big enough for the Black Hawk. We should get there about the same time it does. Hunt, you'll take the horses back to the ranch. I doubt if you'll make it before dark. I'll leave you the sat phone."

"How long will you stay out?"

"Till the chopper needs fuel. Mount up."

(To be continued ...)

Kona's Justice

by

Orina Hodgson

September 27th

The Harvest Moon climbed into the dark blue sky and scattered broken light through silhouetted juniper trees. Kona loved nights like this. *I wonder if the kids remember me waking them up to walk when the moon was full.* She smiled at the memories: fresh-fallen snow on cactus and rabbit brush, coyotes howling just over the ridge, and that time they surprised a skunk and backed up slowly before turning away. They never took flashlights or matches. *I'm glad they learned that the world at night is a safe and sacred place.*

The slender woman flipped her long brown braid from front to back and hummed softly as she made her way down the familiar trail.

Out of nowhere, a blinding light struck Kona's face. "Hey! What the heck? Get that out of my eyes!"

The black form behind the beam sprinted toward her. Kona spun and dashed back up the path, her well-developed muscles barely keeping up with the oxygen demand of terror. Her toe caught the sharp edge of a rock. Kona gasped but kept running. The sound of footsteps behind her grew louder. When she felt a hand grab her plait, she pivoted.

"What do you want?" Kona faced her assailant, breathing hard, her voice shrill. A ski mask hid the face of the dark-clad figure in front of her. "Get out of here! Go! Leave me alone!"

The accoster jerked on her braid, snapping Kona's neck sharply to the side. She dropped to the ground, rolled a few feet and sprang up to run. Something cold and sharp slashed across her back, then plunged deep inside her. Kona screamed as she collapsed. The weight of the attacker pinned her down. She thrashed, pushed, rolled and kicked.

Fight, goddammit! Fight! I don't want my children to see me like this. Her eyes faded from clear blue to cloudy gray. She gazed toward the huge moon, now a soft blur in the distance. Kona was silent and still as blood drained from many deep gashes.

Then a form bent over her face, pulled off the mask and stared at her. Kona could no longer speak. She mouthed "*Damn you!*"

***

Shayla stepped into her little courtyard just as the full moon rose above the adobe wall. She sat on her meditation bench and chanted softly. She smiled at the peaceful beauty of the night. Silver should be home soon. Her grin widened.

Shayla had tried to talk Kona into staying until Silver got back from scouting for his elk hunt. She wanted to share a bottle of wine like they used to, maybe smoke a pipe. They could all stay up late talking and laughing. But Kona wanted to get home. She said one of the kids was going to call tonight. *It's never going to be like it used to be,* Shayla mused.

"Chant, you drunken monkey!" Shayla laughed aloud at her wandering thoughts and resumed meditation.

This time her focus was shattered by piercing screams to the north.

"Kona!" She scrambled into some shoes, grabbed a flashlight; and ran down the half-mile trail that joined their houses. "Kona!" She called again and again. Shayla's large breasts flapped against her big belly. Her chest heaved as she fought for breath, but she forced her short legs to keep moving. "Kona!"

The screams stopped a minute or so before Shayla huffed around the *halfway home* juniper. Their children used to meet each other here for picnics and "adventure hikes" years ago. The kids claimed it was exactly 375 steps from each house to the *halfway home* tree.

Moonlight illuminated the still body sprawled across the trail. Kona's unseeing eyes faced the bright globe. Shayla screamed. "Kona! No, Kona! No!"

She ran to her friend and stumbled into dark pools of blood. She tenderly lifted the lifeless woman's head and shoulders into her lap. "Oh god! What happened? Oh my god!"

Shayla heard a crack in the trees behind her. Terror spurred her to squirm free, push to her feet and dash toward her house. Heaving breaths and wracking sobs forced her to slow the pace. She looked back and saw no one.

Silver pulled up in his battered Chevy pickup at the same time Shayla entered the courtyard.

"My god, woman! What the hell happened? Are you okay?"

She reached for his outstretched arms and collapsed

***

October 30th

Kane guffawed loudly. All heads turned toward the burly man whose long grey curls merged with a thick shaggy beard into one mass of unruly hair. Intense hazel eyes, as distinctive as that laugh, stared back at the gathering of men and women at the meeting.

"Look at us!" he demanded. "This is not who we are and you know it. We're going to give hippies a bad name if we don't share a little love here." He hooted again and forty spontaneous laughs echoed. It was always like that with Kane.

"Hug the man or woman on your right. That's more like it. Now turn and hug the person on your left." Kane reached out to grab Silver's bony shoulders, but the tall sinewy man turned away and embraced the woman next to him. His long pony tail, more white than silver, slapped Kane's outstretched arm.

"Thank you, Kane," Shayla held the talking stick now. "You did good to call us into perspective. Hatred will not bring Kona back to us. Blaming will not make her body whole again. I miss her so much! I can't sleep at night with those images. If I lose all of you to hatred, I might as well join her."

Silver sternly held his long slender fingers out for the stick and his wife complied. "You're right Kane. Our community is a mess! We called this council today because none of us is doing very well. We haven't danced or had music or pot luck in over a month. We can't move forward without answers." He glared at Shayla. "Threatening suicide isn't going to fix anything either." Then he locked eyes with Kane. "And we can sit circle and sing *Kumbaya* all night! But what we really want to know, what we need to know, is what happened to Kona. Her kids are coming tomorrow to sort through her stuff. What are we going to tell them? How are we going to face Sunshine and Orion? How?"

Without a word, Blaze grabbed the speaking piece from Silver. He strode to the huge chalkboard they'd used in Council for the past ten years, bright red hair flowing down his back. The board was kind of a joke at first, but they really did need more help remembering things these days. He quickly erased the scrawls that covered the slate. No one uttered a word.

"Okay," Blaze started. "Here's what we know." In his usual precise way, he numbered the entries and wrote in clear sharp letters, reading aloud as he went:

"On the evening of September 27th, 2015, Kona visited with Shayla. They had dinner. Shayla said Kona left to walk home just after moonrise. Around 6:30pm.

"Shayla said she heard screams about five minutes later. It sounded like Kona. She ran down the trail. She said she was yelling Kona's name. She found Kona just past the *halfway tree*."

"Shayla said she knew right away Kona had passed. She took her in her arms and held her. There was lots of blood."—Blaze's voice cracked. He took a deep breath and continued—"Shayla said she heard a noise…"

"What the F!" Silver interrupted the list-making. "What's with *'Shayla said this'* and *'Shayla said that'*. You sound like a god-damned cop!"

Blaze paused for just a moment. "Hold on Silver. I'm getting there. Just hang with me a minute. Please, Brother." He turned back to the board. "Shayla said she heard a noise in the trees behind her. She got scared and ran home. Silver got home from elk-scouting at the same time she did.

"They called the cops. The sheriffs-showed up and in all their glory thoroughly screwed up the crime scene!!!"

"They wouldn't let us be with Kona. They didn't let us sing for her there. We had to stay across the road. We sat circle for her. We sang; we cried; we held one another. They took a thousand pictures of our Kona and of us. Some of us pulled out our cell phones and did some recording of our own. Kane would like to see every one of those shots. Arrange that with him.

"Over the next few weeks, almost everyone in the community has been asked for an interview. Some have been deposed."

Blaze stopped writing. “Silver and Shayla and Kane, I know The Man has run you ragged. No wonder you’re frustrated. But we are not the enemy.”

Silver cringed with the memory of the first interrogation.

***

September 28th

The morning after Kona was murdered, the authorities *requested* that Silver and Shayla drive up to Holbrook to answer a few questions. The deputies put them in separate rooms.

Sheriff Paul Feldman sat across the table from Silver.

“Just tell me exactly what happened Mr. West.;” The clean-cut sheriff turned on the recorder.:

“My name is Silver. Silver James West. It’s been my legal name for 26 years, so quit with the ‘Mr. West’ stuff. I answer to Silver.

“It’s like I told you out there last night. I was scouting for elk north of the rim. It’s the first tag I drew in eight years. I got home around seven. My wife was standing in our courtyard, looking like she was half gone. I didn’t even notice the blood at first. She passed out in my arms. Then I saw the blood. It was still wet on her clothes. I was lifting her blouse, looking for a wound, when she came to.

“Shayla started crying hysterically. I had to shake her hard to get her to calm down enough to tell me what had happened.”

Silver dropped his head into his hands, elbows propped on the table. “I was afraid to go back down there. I actually threw up. Then we…”

Sheriff Feldman broke in.; “Did you say you were afraid to go *back* down there? When were you last on that trail, Mr. West?”

“It’s *Silver*, god damn it!” Bloodshot blue eyes glared at the officer. “I am on the trail between our place and Kona’s a few times a week. We’ve been friends and neighbors for over forty years. But I wasn’t over there at all yesterday. Too busy. Do you want my story or not?”

"Yes, please continue."

"I threw up after Shayla told me what she found. We called the cops. We called 911. Got the dispatch and I think you know the rest. It's recorded. We were told to stay home."

Sheriff Feldman stood and moved closer to the hunched over man. "But you just had to start calling all your friends, right? You had to alert at least forty people before we could even get there!"

Silver pushed against the steel edge of the table and started to stand. "I'm out of here, Feldman You don't understand our community. You don't get it! You never did! Your grandparents lived out there before we ever did. They were good people. I don't know what happened to you. Now I'm leaving." He scowled at Sheriff Feldman.

A firm hand forced Silver back into his chair. "I'm not done, Mr. West. You do realize you and your wife are the prime persons of interest in this case? Who went scouting with you?"

"No one! I told you that last night! I was on Forest Road 95. Went about three miles back. Maybe you can find my tracks. Maybe you can collect some DNA out there....where I took a piss or threw a banana peel. Just maybe you can act like a real detective instead of messing everything up like y'all did last night! None of us trampled the crime scene like your guys did. I was watching you and a couple others scrambling around with flashlights a full fifteen minutes before everybody else showed up with crime tape wearing their moon suits."

Sheriff Feldman clicked off the recorder. He circled back around the table to face Silver. His eyes blinked in rapid succession; "You, you don't know what you are talking about, *Mr. West*! You go around badmouthing my boys and you're going to find yourself digging out of a deeper pile of shit than you're in already! Now just answer my questions."

He turned the recorder back on. “Okay. I’ll send a couple of detectives out FR 95. Maybe they’ll find something to support your alibi. Now, tell me about your and Kona’s relationship.”

“Kona and I have been friends for forty-three years. We both moved *Out East* in ‘72. You know where we live. A half-mile from your Gramp’s old place. The land was cheap. Shayla was pregnant with our first. Kona was expecting too, but she and Mark already had a toddler, Sunshine. We were all kids in our early twenties. We grew up together. We helped each other. We became family. Cancer took Mark about ten years ago. Shayla and I, well, the whole community, got Kona and their kids through that time.”

“Yeah, I heard you helped Kona in a real special way, Silver.” Sheriff Feldman moved closer to Silver. “Tell me about the affair you had with Kona Johnston. When did it start? When did it end? Did it end, Mr. West? Did your wife know about it? Something like that would make a woman pretty angry, wouldn’t it?”

Silver did stand this time, turning away from tthe officer. He strode to the door, fists clenched and arms stiff at his sides. “If you don’t have a warrant for my arrest or deposition, I’m out of here, *Sir*! You’ve got no business asking these questions. And you’d better not be hassling Shayla either!”

“Are you threatening me?” Sheriff Feldman kept one hand on his revolver as he motioned to the officer behind the two-way mirror. The door flew opened and two deputies stepped inside.

Silver stood stock still. The recorder silently documented every word. “No Sir. I am smarter than that. I’m exhausted. Shayla’s exhausted. We’re grieving. Just let us go home.”

“You are free to leave Mr. West.” Sheriff Feldman shut the recorder off. “If you can afford to get yourself a lawyer, you might want to do that soon. We will be getting a warrant. Shayla’s still talking to Deputy Smith. You can wait for her in the lobby or in your truck.”

Silver took three long steps toward the lobby, then turned back. The three officers stood in a line staring at him. "Let me go to Shayla. Let me be with her! I don't trust you guys!"

"I'm sorry Mr. West. That's not possible right now. Shayla is fine. Deputy Smith is a lot less intimidating than I am." The three men in uniform chuckled.

Silver rushed past the front desk and pushed the automatic door. He bolted down the stairs toward his truck. He was almost there when someone touched his sleeve from behind. Silver whirled and swung just as Kane dodged back a step.

"Goddamn, Silver!

"What in the hell are you doing grabbing me like that, Kane? I almost decked you!" He shook his head. "No. I'm sorry. I'm crazy. I can't even think. Those bastards are grilling Shayla, trying to get her to confess or something. I need to get her out of there. What are you doing here anyway?"

"They asked me to come up to answer some questions. I don't know why. I wasn't even home last night. Try not to worry about Shayla, Silver. I've never met a more calm and centered person. She'll have them chanting *ohm* with her before she's done."

Silver spun away and stormed the last few steps to his pickup, opened the door and slid behind the wheel. He rested his head against the back of the seat and tears rolled into his white stubble.

Shoulders slumped, Kane trudged into the county building, taking deep breaths as he went.

***

Deputy Sheriff Cassie Smith led Shayla to a molded plastic chair behind an oval table. She sat on the opposite side. Both women were short, but the likeness stopped there. Deputy Smith was trim and muscular with a youthful face and short curly hair. Shayla noticed that she hadn't changed much from the days they car-pooled their kids to high school events.

"It's been awhile, Shayla. Almost twenty years, I reckon. I'm real sorry about Kona. This is all so terrible. I do have to ask you some questions about last night. I'm glad I wasn't on call and didn't have to see that. I looked at the pictures this morning though. Awful!"

Shayla cringed. "Can we just do this, Cassie. I need to try to get some sleep or something."

Deputy Smith turned the recorder on. "Let's just start by having you tell your full name and what happened last night. Your words, from the beginning."

"My name is Shayla Renae West. Kona and I canned applesauce together yesterday and I asked her to stay for supper. Silver was scouting elk and didn't expect to be home until later." In a monotone voice, Shayla recounted the events of the night before. When she got to the part about finding Kona, she dropped her head into her hands and sobbed.

"Do you need a minute to collect yourself?"

"No, Cassie, I think I need a lot longer than that! Have you gotten so jaded being a cop? I found Kona dead and covered in blood on our trail. How much time would you need?"

The deputy turned the recorder off. "Look, Shayla. I feel sick thinking about Kona. And sick for you, too. But this is my job now. Feldman wanted me to interview you because he said you might open up more easily to a woman. I don't really have a choice about this. I am sorry, but let's just get it done." She turned the recorder back on.

Shayla described finding Kona, holding her, hearing the noise, and running home. "I'm so fat now, I thought I was going to die from a heart attack or something. I couldn't catch my breath and my chest hurt. When I got to the yard, I saw Silver's headlights pulling in at the same time. That's when I really lost it." She told the rest of her story.

"Why did you and Silver start calling other folks out there as soon as you got off with the dispatcher? Feldman is concerned all those people might have compromised the crime scene."

Shayla sat up straight and stared hard into Deputy Smith's eyes. "If anybody messed up the investigation, it was Feldman! He and his men trampled all over the place before the medical examiner even got there. We gathered across the way at the Hanson's place. The cops were taking pictures of us like we were suspects. We sang for Kona. We held each other. It's what we do, Cassie. You never did understand what the community was all about. And that's okay. It's not for everybody. But you were my friend. And Kona's too. Our kids hung out together! Try not to forget that, Deputy!" Shayla was crying again.

Deputy Smith stood up, turned around, then sat to face Shayla again. "I'm sorry for your loss, Shayla. I need to ask you about a few more things. Sheriff Feldman told me that Silver had an affair with Kona. Tell me about that."

Now Shayla's green eyes flashed across the table. "I don't know where the good sheriff gets his gossip, but let me set the story straight! Silver and me met Kona and Mark when we all moved out east of Snowflake in 1972. We built our houses together. We had our babies together. We grew up together. We were best friends. Yes, we were, we are, Hippies, Cassie. And you have no idea what that really means. You never wanted to know. It isn't nonstop drugs and orgies. It's about community and love and sharing life. Anyway, after the kids were all grown up and gone, Mark found out he had cancer. For three years we helped him and Kona. The whole community took turns with whatever needed doing. Silver and I were there the night he died. Then we helped Kona and the kids plan the ceremony. After that we hung out with her a lot, just keeping an eye on things. She was in a bad state. Crying, staying in bed.

"One night, Silver was over at her place holding her while she wept. They said later that it just sort of happened. You know how beautiful Kona is. Silver got carried away with it all and they made love a few more times over the next couple of weeks. That was it. I don't even know why I'm telling you this! That was almost ten years ago! Do you think I murdered Kona because of that? Do you?" Shayla's chair screeched on the floor as she pushed it back. She stood, wobbled a little, then eased back down again.

"We aren't accusing anyone at this point. We're just trying to gather as much information as possible. We need to know who had issues with Kona, who would do this to her. Who else was Kona intimate with after her husband died? Do you know of anyone who was upset with her?"

"Everyone loved Kona! She was beautiful, smart, funny, generous, and yes, she was attractive. I'll bet you have it written down that she and Kane were together for about seven years. His wife had divorced him and moved away from the community. They were both lonely. Kona and Kane were a sweet couple. He even moved in with her. She didn't want to remarry, though, and broke off with him last winter. Said she needed to figure out who she was without a man.

That wasn't too long after Kona's oldest girl, Sunshine, had moved back home for a bit. She was tangled up with meth and got arrested for stealing from the Corner Store. You probably have that in your notes too. Kane helped get her into rehab and she worked out a plea with the county. I think Feldman had something to do with that." Shayla's gaze burned toward Deputy Smith. "If you're thinking Kane did this, you're crazy! That man wouldn't hurt a fly. He was sad when she split with him, but not hostile."

"What about Sunshine? Did she ever steal from you or her mother? Is she still on drugs?"

"Sunshine is doing great! She's been back with her husband and kids for months. What makes y'all so sure a complete stranger, a maniac, didn't murder Kona? Why are you looking at the people who loved her?"

"As sad as it is Shayla, well over half of violent crimes and homicides are committed by someone who knows the victim, often someone who is loved and trusted."

"Well, that's all I have to tell you. I want to go to Silver now. I want to go home."

***

Kane faced Sheriff Feldman and a deputy across the table. He pulled on his shaggy grey beard and spoke first. "I don't know why you wanted to talk to me this morning. I wasn't even home last night. I got a call at my son's house in Albuquerque and drove back right away."

"Hold on Mr. Jordon. I'm going to turn the recorder on. Start by stating your full name and tell us where you were last night."

"My name is Michael Kane Jordon. But everybody calls me Kane. Like I said, I was in Albuquerque visiting my son since last week. Silver called me at about one in the morning and I drove straight back. I can't even think. I can't believe Kona's dead."

"Write down your son's name and phone number and we'll give him a call to confirm your alibi. We want to…"

Kane shot up, his formidable bulk resulting in both officers standing in unison, with hands on their service weapons.

"Who the hell do you think you are! We just lost a beloved member of our community. She was murdered horribly in cold blood! And here you are dragging in the people who cared about her the most. Do you even know what my relationship with Kona was? I loved that woman more than anything in the world." Kane paced back and forth in the small interview room.

"Kane, please sit down." Sheriff Feldman used his preferred name and spoke in a softer tone than he had with Silver. "We do know that you and Kona were together, were partners for several years. That's why we need to talk with you. We're not accusing anyone. We just need to gather information to help us with the investigation."

The interview dragged on for more than an hour.

***

November 4th

Silver walked around from behind the shed and saw Shayla sitting on her meditation bench. Her eyes were closed and her hands rested in her lap. She was chanting softly in the warm fall sun. He sat beside her.

Shayla opened her eyes and smiled. "Hi Honey. Are you ready for some lunch?" She leaned into him, longing for a response from the strong body she knew so well. He'd been so distant since Kona died.

"Shayla, I need to talk to you. I need to tell you something. I've been a mess since our community council last week. I can't keep this to myself anymore."

His wife froze. *Oh god, no. Don't tell me Silver. I don't want to know!*

The white-haired man put his arms around Shayla and held her close. "I'm so sorry," he started. "I never meant to do it. I'm afraid that Feldman knows anyway, and I don't want you to find out like that. I love you so much. I'm so sorry."

Shayla's breaths were short and fast as she listened to Silver's confession. He told her everything. When he finished talking, she got up without a word. She stumbled to her bed and stayed there for a week, moving only to use the toilet or get a drink.

***

November 11th

Kane slipped into the room, his soft steps seeming a contradiction to his burly physique. Silver walked in behind him. Shayla turned to face the wall when her husband entered.

"Shayla, we need to talk. The three of us." Kane spoke in a clear and gentle voice. "Silver told me everything. I know this is really hard for you. Well, it's hard for me, too. I know how much Silver loves you. I think you know that too. And I love the bastard for some crazy reason. I can't just turn away from him after forty-one years of being brothers." Kane smiled toward Silver, who slumped into a chair. "We can't let him hang for this, Shayla. He's already suffered enough. And I told him about that other thing that happened with Kona ... when Sunshine was here last year."

Silver broke in, his voice unsteady. "Why did you keep that from me, Shayla? It might have changed everything if you'd told me back then! Didn't you trust me?" He hung his head, knowing how that question must sound to his wife.

Kane broke in. "You know what hasn't changed since we held council last week? What hasn't changed is that throwing blame around isn't going to do anything to bring Kona back to us. We can't change what happened up to this point. But no more secrets, okay?"

Shayla stirred.

He pulled an envelope from his shirt. "Sunshine found this letter a couple days ago. Kona wrote it. And someone brought these cell phone pics to me yesterday. Take a look. We need to do something before Feldman makes a move on you, Silver. We're all in this together."

***

November 15th

"There's fresh car tracks out here, Kane. Just like Silver said there'd be," Shayla whispered as she squeezed between the barbed wires Kane forced apart for her.

"We have about forty minutes at least," Kane told her. "Silver has his cell phone and he's watching the church parking lot. He'll call us as soon as they walk out the door."

"This feels like such a long shot," Shayla muttered. "I hope we're not too late."

They walked to a run-down wooden shed next to the corral. They found it locked, but a window in the rear was easy to pry open. Kane helped Shayla scramble over the sill into the dark room. She put gloves on while her eyes adjusted. She turned slowly to face one wall, then another. There were two large metal drums on the far side, next to the door. Her heart raced as she carefully lifted the lid of one. Nothing. She opened the next drum and was disappointed to see that it, too, looked empty. Then she saw a black bundle in the bottom of the barrel.

At that instant Kane's hoarse whisper came through the window. "Shit! Silver just texted. They left church early! We've got to get out of here! Now Shayla!"

"Wait! I found something!" She snapped a picture of it sitting in the drum and then another of that whole side of the shed. She pulled a small black river bag from the barrel. It was rolled tight and secured with straps. "Got your gloves on?"

She shoved it out to Kane, closed the barrel, and clambered through the window, remembering to shut it behind her. She turned and took a picture of the shed from the outside. They left the property the way they had come, from the back side. Just as they dropped into a ravine, they heard a car coming up the road.

Shayla and Kane took a few minutes to catch their breaths, before silently working their way to her car. Their dust covered faces were streaked with rivulets of sweat. Kane drove.

Shayla tried to slow her racing heart and announced, "I'm too old and fat to be doing this stuff!" They both laughed, bordering on hysteria, as they turned from one dirt road onto another, then onto Highway 77. They drove north toward Holbrook, but took a right on to Woodruff Road, shortly before reaching town. That's where they were meeting Silver.

Shayla's freshly-gloved hands shook as she fought the clasps on the sack. She carefully unrolled the bundle letting the bottom rest on a clean plastic bag on the floor of the car. The first thing they saw was a blood-stained hunting knife. It was sitting on a black ski mask. Shayla recognized the charcoal grey sweatshirt under that. It belonged to her husband.

A wave of nausea overtook Shayla. Her face prickled. "Oh, Silver," she cried. "Oh my dear Silver."

***

December 9th

Paul Feldman sat behind the polished brown table and scowled across the courtroom toward Silver West. When the judge entered the room, Feldman looked toward him with a smirk on his face.

The judge called the court to order and said "Will the defendant please stand." Reading from the paper on his desk, he spoke in a clear stern voice:

"The Grand Jurors of Navajo County, Arizona, accuse Paul T. Feldman, hereafter referred to as the defendant, on this day of December 9, 2015, charging that in Navajo County, Arizona:

1. On or about September 27, 2015, the defendant committed felony murder in the first degree according to ASR Section 13 1105; to wit: with willful premeditation and intent to cause severe bodily harm, the defendant lay in waiting for Kona C. Johnston, the victim, and proceeded to inflict multiple knife wounds upon said victim, causing injury which resulted in her death ..."

The evidence was extensive and had been preserved meticulously when they presented it to Deputy Cassie Smith. There were six charges in all, including the intention to frame Silver. As the judge read through them, one by one, Silver, Shayla, Kane and many other community members clasped hands with whoever sat next to them and held back tears. There was no cheering in the courtroom or in the parking lot after.

***

December 22nd

The circle was bigger than it had been on Winter Solstice for the past ten years or so. Almost everyone from the community had gathered for the annual ceremony. Many of their kids returned home and brought grandchildren with them.

They sang in voices strong and timid, baritone and soprano, on key and hopelessly lost. But they sang in unison as each turned his or her unlit candle into the flame of the taper held by the person standing alongside. In a few moments, the community center was aglow with eighty-four candles.

After the ceremony, Silver, Shayla, and Kane held court for any interested adults, promising to go over details as best they could in a half hour.

“We want to get on with the night.” Kane said. “There’s music to be made, food to be shared, and kids to play with”.

They told their stories, interrupting each other at times, but pretty much on the same page. They warned those who stayed to listen. “It gets pretty ugly.”

It was painful to hear details about how Sheriff Feldman had met with Kona at his grandparents old place the previous year after Sunshine was arrested. He claimed he wanted to go over the plea agreement the prosecutor was trying to work out. It would be good for Sunshine. No jail time. Minimal parole.

Then he raped Kona. He threatened that if she told anyone, Sunshine would face maximum charges and end up put away for a long time.

"Kona did what many of us would do for our kids." Shayla put her arm around her oldest daughter. "She told me about it a few months later, but made me swear not to tell anyone."

Kane interjected. "Kona broke up with me a couple weeks after this happened. I didn't know. But now it all makes sense."

Silver almost whispered. "I was an idiot. I really messed up. I went to Kona's house the week before she died to help her get some firewood in. We were sitting together on the couch. We'd had a little wine. She leaned into me. We made out like stupid teenagers. But that's as far as it went. That's all we did. Good old Blaze popped in out of nowhere and surprised us both. He was embarrassed. So were we. He told me that Feldman pulled that story out of him when he had his interview. I was scared that Feldman would use it against me somehow, that he would tell Shayla. So I did."

They told about how Sunshine and her brother had been going through Kona's things and found a copy of a letter she wrote to Sheriff Feldman. She told him she couldn't live with what he did to her, that she was depressed and feeling crazy. She wrote that she didn't know what she was going to do next, but something had to give. The letter was dated September 23, four days before she was killed.

They passed around the photographs from the video someone had found on their cell phone after the community council. It was from the night of Kona's murder. They clearly showed Feldman taking a black bag out from under his jacket and sticking it in his patrol car.

"The rest is history." Shayla smiled. "It's all history, really. And herstory. Now let's go celebrate solstice! Let's celebrate Kona's life and Kona's justice."

###

Market Day

By

Kaye Phelps

I was up before dawn, the girls harnessed and pulling my cobbled-together wagon out of my box canyon hidden in the hills.

The first of every month, many of my neighbors met at the old Country Store grounds to swap or sell our products. We had even developed our own currency, the cluck – approximately the value of one chicken. Ten peeps (chicks or eggs) equaled one cluck. Goats usually went for about a hundred clucks and beef five hundred to a thousand.

Of course we didn't actually print money but it gave us a basis for barter.

I arrived at the grounds on old Concho Road a little over two hours later. I parked my wagon and led the big black Morgans to the long lean-to west of the old store. I'd brought several crocks of honey, some necklaces of dried apples and peaches from my small orchard, several dozen eggs and agreed-upon payment for work I had contracted.

I hoped to score containers for my honey and something to preserve my garden vegetables in. Since the end of the war, most of the cheap plastic had worn out or fallen apart, and glass jars and pottery crocks went for a lot of clucks.

Maria Tsosie approached my wagon. She must have been on the road several days from the reservation. But her medicinal herbs were always pure and she favored my orchard honey. We were able to make a good trade.

Doc Whitman limped over and brought me several empty crocks to trade for one of honey. He asked how I was doing; he was one of the few people who knew that I live alone.

My canyon was hidden in the breaks of the Little Colorado River. My partner Jenny and I found it ten years ago, a beat-up old stone homestead and tarred, wood-frame windmill. We repaired what we could, put a metal roof on the house and installed passive solar for hot water. Our canyon, fortunately, had a high water table.

Five years ago, when the enemy took out large portions of both coasts and bombed the big dams here in the Southwest, there wasn't much left of what we used to call "the Valley," meaning Phoenix, Tucson and points south. Flagstaff was pretty ragged, too. By then Jenny and I had our canyon planted and cross-fenced. I developed a reputation for good horses, well-trained.

Jenny was a Type I diabetic. When we couldn't get insulin any more, she passed quickly. I laid her to rest in a cave about halfway up the canyon wall. I still miss her enthusiasm, her bright ideas and her kindness.

These past five years have changed all of us. Once the electrical system failed, we never learned much of what happened to the rest of the world, or the rest of the country for that matter. Train tracks still ran through Holbrook to the north but that was a two-day trip, one way, by horse and wagon. Gasoline and diesel were scarce and very expensive, used mainly by the railroad and some folks who were better off than most of us. I suspect that what we used to call the Middle East had been bombed into oblivion since what few petroleum products we saw were crude and probably local.

The man I only knew as PJ brought me the scythe blades he had fashioned from old leaf springs. I handed him a big crock of pickles with a wooden lid, a bag of goat jerky and some dried fruit and vegetables. He agreed to return my crock after he ate the pickles. The blades would be used to cut hay.

Someone I didn't know traded a couple of loaves of bread for two bracelets of dried apples. I asked where she got her flour; she said she sent for it from someplace back East and had picked it up in Holbrook.

We congregated in the middle of the circle for a bite at mid-day. I had corn tortillas from home, wrapped around egg and goat cheese I'd bartered for last month. But I didn't see my neighbor who made the cheese.

A woman I didn't know asked if I had children. She was establishing a school in her home.

I checked my mares and hauled a couple of buckets of water to them from the store's tank.

A small group walked up to our sales area after lunch and offered scavenged goods to trade. Most of it was useless; dried-out leather bridles with rusty bits, one fairly decent saddle that was far too small for me to use, a bunch of beat-up plastic water bottles and some dented, far-outdated canned goods.

Sales slumped for some time after lunch and some of us stood together in the middle of the grounds, trading gossip instead of goods.

Doc told us that Ellen Bybee, the goat lady, had passed. Her husband Elmore had followed a few days later. Poor Doc – fancy education based on drugs and nothing much he could do for his patients now.

Someone mentioned that the LDS church was developing a pony express mail system to serve local areas that would feed into the rail line in Holbrook. I wondered how much it would cost. Would the Mormons accept barter? Clucks?

John Cramer, who used to be an attorney, said the county was trying to reorganize itself and commissioners were discussing how to hold elections, raise taxes and deal with legal issues. After a short pause, my neighbors chuckled. Navajo County covered a lot of territory and peace officers would probably have to patrol on horseback. How would they communicate? For a while folks with solar chargers had cell phone service, but batteries failed and few were left working.

Out of the corner of my eye, I saw a man leading my horses from the lean-to. "Stop!" I yelled, sprinting after him. "Those are my mares!"

He gave me a strange look. "But I just bought them."

I didn't know him; he was a skinny, dirty, hairy man who could have been anywhere from thirty to fifty.

"That would be difficult, since they're mine and I have no intention of selling them."

"My family's hungry."

This imbecile wanted to *eat* my beautiful young mares, both of which were due in late summer for foals that I already had buyers for? That sort of thing hadn't happened since about a year after the war ended. I still had ammunition for my shotgun then, and many nights I slept by the gate to protect my livestock.

He yanked on the lead ropes. "Look, lady, I just traded for these horses and I'm taking them now!"

John Cramer and the rest of my neighbors caught up to me at the edge of the road. "I know this woman, and I know these mares belong to her," he said, trying to calm the man.

"Prove it!" the man challenged angrily.

"Got a bill of sale?" Doc asked.

"No paper," the man spat.

"Who sold them to you?" Cramer asked.

The man looked around. "Guy in a tan shirt."

We discussed it; none of us had seen a man in a tan shirt all day.

"Can I go now?" he whined. "My kids are hungry."

"Not with my mares," I said.

"Can you prove they're yours?"

"They'll come to me when I whistle," I told him.

"Hah!" he answered back. "That don't prove ownership."

"It does in my book," John told him. He gestured to one of the teenagers in the group. "You, take the mares up the road a ways. Hold them loose."

The kid nodded but had to yank the lead ropes from the man. The young man walked the horses west along the crumbled highway and waited.

The thief snorted and kicked dirt. "What are you going to do, hang me?"

I whistled. Judy and Trudy whirled and trotted to me, trailing their lead lines.

"Can you do that?" Cramer asked him.

"Not fair!" the fellow whined. "I bought those horses! Traded my gun for them."

Doc pulled up his shirt tail. "This gun?" he asked.

The thief whipped out the revolver. "I've had enough of this!"

"Do you even have ammo for that relic?" Cramer asked.

One of my other neighbors took the piece from him. "Empty," he reported. Most ammunition had been used up during the first year and no one knew if more was being manufactured. Some reload was available but was notoriously unreliable.

John told me to take the mares back to my wagon and declared Market Day over. As I looked over my mares for injuries, my neighbors took the thief to the east side of the building and pummeled him.

We sent him off with an old, threadbare towel wrapped around a loaf of bread, some jerky, some dried fruits and vegetables and an admonition to ask, not take. "I wanted meat!" he protested through a split lip.

"We don't always get what we want," John Cramer told him. Steaks and roasts were scarce since there wasn't an easy way to keep meat cold, but most of us had figured out how to grow and preserve what we needed. I lost a lot of weight – many of us did -- but we survived.

Maria Tsosie stepped over from her cart. "You have law here."

"Of a sort," I replied as I placed Trudy's collar over her head.

"More than on the rez. I am afraid for my granddaughters."

I gave her my full attention.

"My son is a good trainer of horses."

I waited for her to continue.

"It is said that you live alone in a good place. You could use some help."

My box canyon is isolated but defensible. And I had repelled some folks bent on taking it away from me during that first year.

"I ask that you allow us to come to your place. We will work."

Maria was right, I could use the help. And there was relative safety in numbers, after all. My old farmhouse had three small bedrooms and a loft; there is plenty of water and graze for the livestock I had. Maria told me her sheep and goats could live outside the canyon if we could get water to them. She asked for a small plot of ground for her herbs, to which I readily agreed. She told me she, her son and granddaughters would arrive in a weeks' time. I didn't ask her how she knew where I lived.

On my way home, I wondered where the horse thief came from. He gave the name Jim Smith, which none of us believed. "Smith" had headed north on old Hay Hollow Road while I went south a few roads to the east, but I kept looking behind my rig. Not everyone had adjusted well to the new norm. I still found human remains out in the desert now and then of folks who failed to survive in some way. I felt fortunate that I had my canyon and friends and neighbors.

###

A Matter of Trust

By

Conni de Wolfe

It was a lovely June afternoon in the "Valley of the Sun." Not as hot as usual because a monsoon shower had passed through an hour ago. Kelly was in the kitchen preparing dinner when she heard her husband, Joe, pull into the driveway. He was early.

As he came in the door he barked, "Honey, get ready to throw out all our junk, we're moving," and threw his briefcase down on the kitchen table in front of Kelly.

"Moving? Moving where?" Kelly asked calmly as she continued to peel the potatoes for dinner. She was used to these occasional aberrations of her husband.

"Just what I said," Joe said in explanation. "I told old man Bartholomew to take his job and put it where it will do the most good."

"You did *what!"* Kelly stared wide-eyed at her husband, the potato and knife forgotten in her hand.

"That's right. I told him where to get off. Ah, honey. It'll be all right. I know just where we're going to go, too."

Kelly carefully laid down the potato and knife. She knew that if she wasn't careful she would throw them both at him. Slowly she raised her eyes from the cutting board and studied the man she'd been married to for ten years.

He was still slim, had most of his curly brown hair and at that moment his still boyish face wore a lopsided grin that, at another time, would have melted her heart. Even now the look in his longlashed green eyes made her pulse quicken.

Kelly took a deep breath as a shot of fear shook her to the core. "You...you're kidding me. This is a joke, right? Joseph William Garrett, you can't be serious!"

Joe sat down at the table and paused before answering. He took a good look at his still beautiful wife. At thirty-four, and after bearing three children, she still had a trim figure that would put some models to shame. She wore her long, ash blonde hair in soft waves, just like she had when had married her fresh out of college. Kelly Louise Garret, he thought. He was so proud of her, but when she flashed her sapphire blue eyes and used his full name like that he knew he was in trouble and had better explain fast.

"No joke, Kelly," he said seriously. "I've been thinking about this for a long time now, and today at the office it was just the last straw."

Joe held up his hands as he could see Kelly was about to explode. "Now take it easy, honey, I swear everything will work out fine."

"But...but, don't honey me!" Kelly spluttered. "What about the house, the bills, the children's school? Oh, Joe," she put her hands to her face and shuddered... Then in a desolate voice said, "You can't be serious. Where on earth do you plan to go and what can we do now? Besides, I like it right here in Chandler, Arizona."

They heard the front screen door slam. Both were grateful for the interruption. Kelly gave Joe her, *I'll talk to you later when the kids are in bed,* look and turned towards the kitchen door as a youthful voice hollered, "Mom! I'm home!" It was Joey, back from the park. He followed closely by his older sister Vickey, who in turn, was trailed by four-year-old Nathan. They both knew it was time to finish preparing dinner and completing the evening chores. Anything to put off the confrontation they both knew was coming.

***

Kelly sat down wearily on the end of the couch in her nineteenth–century living room. One they had both worked so hard to make just right. She propped her feet on the coffee table in childish rebellion. Something she never allowed Joe or the children to do. She didn't know how she had managed to finish cooking dinner and clean up the kitchen. Too much had been running through her mind. *With Joe out of a job, how will we survive?*

There was the house payment, the van payment, Joey's orthodontic bill. The worst scenario she could visualize was the five of them living out of the van, homeless, wondering where their next meal was coming from. What Kelly really recognized was her returning fear of lost security, and that bothered her the most.

She thought she had gotten over that long ago, when her father had left her mother for another woman when she was five. She'd been tossed from one grandparent to another. Her mother had gone back to school in order to get a job that could support the two of them, and had done it in style too. But after going to fourteen different schools, in twelve years, living with two stepfathers, never staying in one house for longer than two years; Kelly never got over her feelings of being unwanted and insecure, until she met Joe. Now the feeling of insecurity had returned with a force she could barely control.

Chief, their German Shepherd dog, came tearing into the room to greet her and Joe followed. As she ruffled Chief's furry neck and scratched his ears, Kelly told Joe, "Kids all tucked away. Now tell me, why did you quit, and why so suddenly that you didn't even warn me?

Where do you plan for us to move? Do you have another job: and what--?"

"Whoa, slow down Kelly. I'll answer all you questions. It'll be all right, you'll see." Joe reached down and plucked up their cat, Whiskers, who had been playing with his shoelaces, and started petting him as he gathered his thoughts.

"I quit because of office politics. Do you remember Charlie Taft? The gung-ho college preppy? Well, they just promoted him over me. All because he's a graduate of the same college as Bartholmew's son. He hasn't been with the company half as long as I have, nor come up through the ranks, but they booted him up anyway. For me that was the last straw. I haven't been that happy lately anyway. You know that."

"I understand, but to give no notice and just walk out? I can't believe you did that, Joe."

Bartholomew jumped on me about my *supposed* attitude toward some of the office personnel," Joe said. "Unfortunately for me, and him, I'd just had a rough two hours soothing a client's feathers for something Charlie hadn't done. I'm afraid I gave him a taste of the bad attitude he accused me of having and let him have it with both barrels. I'm sorry honey, but I just couldn't help myself."

"I believe you, and I've felt like doing the same thing about some of the principals I've worked for. But Joe, don't you realize what your being out of work means to us. My occasional substitute jobs won't keep a roof over our heads or even make the van payment. I just can't see how we're going to manage and not lose everything."

"Ah, that's where my real news comes in. Kelly, you're going to have to trust me. Really trust and have a little faith in me to make it work out right. Do you thnk you can?" Joe watched her apprehensively.

Kelly knew she should answer him right away, but her anxieties gnawed at her stomach. It was just like the time when she was fourteen and her mother left her with her maternal grandparents while her first stepfather, Howard, took her mother to Baltimore and she had to change schools in the middle of the year. That's when her nightmares started. Kelly looked at Joe and tried to hide her fear, but her eyes couldn't quite conceal the anxiety that was beginning to overwhelm her again.

"Joe, I believe in you. You know that. I always have. Give me some time, I'll come around." She gave him a hesitant smile. "Now tell me, what's your brilliant idea."

"Do you remember that little town where our old truck broke down on our vacation five year ago? Remember how friendly everyone was?"

"I remember." Kelly nodded. "It was such a beautiful, quiet place. I thought at the time how great it would be to raise the kids there. It was in northern Arizona wasn't it? It was something like St. John or that funny name, Snowflake?"

"It was Snowflake, Kelly. I've been talking to the Chamber of Commerce people there. They've got some new commerce starting up and their law firm needs more legal help to get it started. If we can get settled in, I know I can get a job with them and help advise when they start up in August, probably even before. I've talked to them already."

Joe continued, "Well put the house up for sale and sell off some of the stuff we don't need. We may have to get rid of the van but we'll manage. You've got to trust me on this, Kelly. It's just a feeling, I know, but I've got to try. Do you still believe in me?" Joe asked anxiously as he slid across the couch and sat beside Kelly, putting his arm around her.

"You know I do, honey," Kelly answered and gave Joe a kiss. "Like I said before, just give me some time, I'll come around. Why don't you go on to bed? I really need some time alone for a while. I'll be up a little later. Ok?"

Joe didn't say anything, just leaned over and gave her a long lingering kiss. A kiss that said, *I'm still me. Please trust in me.*

After Joe had gone upstairs, Kelly lay back on the couch and listened as silence permeated the house. This had always been a favorite time for her. The children in bed, safe. The security of her love for Joe wrapped around her like a warm blanket. Tonight, however, that feeling was missing and she didn't quite know how to handle it.

***

Kelly sat up and looked around at the house they lived in for five years. They had saved and worked hard for every piece of furniture in this room alone. The couch she was sitting on had taken a year to save for and buy. The original Duncan Fyfe table in the dining room wasn't easy to find either. It had taken another year of haunting all the antique shops to get the two end tables and the beautiful coffee table to match.

It wasn't just the furniture, but all the labor they had put in; painting, replacing the floors, and then staining them, and all of the woodwork in the house. It was all the memories they had gathered. Nathan had been carried and born here. Could she turn her back on all this? Give it to a stranger who might not care about such things. The house was her security blanket. Was she strong enough to turn loose and face a new life? A new beginning?

Kelly got up from the couch and went into the kitchen. As she poured herself a glass of iced tea, she caught her image in the mirror next to the breakfast bar. She stepped close to the mirror and stared deeply into the eyes reflected back at her. "Well Kelly girl, are you a woman or a mouse, forever hiding form the cat?" she asked herself. "You have a loving husband, whom you know you love, three wonderful children, and you're still young enough to do anything you want."

For the first time since Joe had come home with his news, Kelly felt the fear and insecurity that accompanied his announcement, ease, if not completely disappear. She was strong, she had everything in the world she could possibly want in her family. All else was just window dressing. She nodded, winked at her image in the mirror and said "I'll tell Joe yes tomorrow, first thing."

***

The weeks that followed became dreamlike to Kelly She would surface occasionally to catch her breath, then plunge ever deeper into the maelstrom of clearing her house of the unessential paraphernalia that had been collected over the five years of living in one place.

Though not one to collect things for the sake of saving them for later, she was amazed at the amount of junk they had acquired and stored. A broken tricycle, her old iron, and at least three different Christmas tree stands, were just samples of what was stored faithfully away in the garage. Her biggest problems were with her children. Most of all with Vickey, who was a packrat and refused to turn loose of anything.

Eventually however, it was done. The last load to the dump had been run. The garage sale was successful. The house was sold to a couple their own age with one child and another on the way.

The mover's truck would be in tomorrow to pack and take their belongings to storage until they could find a new house in Snowflake. They had traded the van back in for an older SUV along with some cash borrowed from Joe's dad. That debt was no longer hanging over them. A new life and a new adventure, was awaiting them.

***

It was late July when they finally drove into Snowflake, Arizona. The deep summer sun smoothed a golden touch over the small, sleepy town. A light breeze whispered through the leaves of the old towering cottonwood trees that lined some of the residential streets. As they pulled up to a motel in town, Kelly smelled the faint fragrance of late summer sage, mixed with the tang of slow-moving water from Silver Creek. A feeling of peace seemed to invade her soul and ease the anxiety she had felt since leaving their old home in Chandler.

The same questions came again to plague her. Would Joe get a job in this slow-moving town? Would they find a new home? Would she like it here and find new friends? Were they crazy to cut loose with no prospects on the horizon and take this kind of chance? Kelly sighed and mentally shook herself; she must trust in Joe. If she didn't, what else did she have to keep going with.

It all happened fast. Within days Joe had a job with the new law firm business that was being organized. Kelly had talked to the school board and had credentials cleared to be a substitute teacher in Smowflake and other areas. She found a house that was her dream come true and it was empty, ready to move into.

This couldn't be happening like this, Kelly thought. She just knew she was going to wake up and find it a dream. The children had already found new friends and were looking forward to school staring in a few weeks. She had even found someone to take care of Nathan when she was working. Now Kelly was afraid the bubble would burst. It just seemed to fast, too easy to be true.

***

Kelly sat down at the kitchen table in her new kitchen and sipped a cup of coffee. Her furniture had been delivered two days before and she was just now getting everything in order. She looked out the kitchen window at the quiet street where late summer flowers were showing their latest colors. A bird sang in the tall cottonwood tree in her front yard. It was so peaceful.

She sighed and a faint smile touched her lips. She finally realized that by believing in, and trusting Joe, she had come to find this peace.

Joe walked into the kitchen, poured himself a cut of coffee and sat down across from Kelly. "Well, honey, was it right to ask us to make this move? Are you glad you trusted me?" he asked.

Kelly got up and moved behind his chair. She reached over, put her arms around his neck and hugged him "Yes, Joe, you were right. I should never have doubted you. But a life change this big would scare most anyone. There's one thing I've learned from all this, though."

Joe turned, pulled her onto his lap, and looked into her sapphire blue eyes. “What’s that honey?” he asked, as he gently kissed her cheek.

Kelly reached up and ruffled Joe’s hair. “A house and belongings are just things. It’s the people in the house that make a house full of warmth and love.”

The front screen door slammed and a youthful voice shouted, “Mom, I’m home.”

###

Monsoon

By

Paula F. Winskye

Greg studied the sky as he drove east on Concho Highway. Thunderheads had been building throughout the early August afternoon.

"Maybe today," he said to his empty pickup.

Other parts of eastern Arizona had received nice rains this monsoon season. His property had only managed one shower significant enough to wet the ground. The rest of the "monsoons" had been mostly thunder, lightning, and blowing dust.

A gust of wind made the pickup swerve left. Sprinkles dotted his windshield, attracting dirt.

He passed the Country Store, planning the rest of his day. His wife Carla had already left for work. She had placed supper in the slow cooker to give him time to change oil in the pickup before feeding the horses.

With the kids growing up, they could help with many chores. But the hundred pound bales were too much for even 12-year-old Annie. She milked the goats. Nine-year-old Kevin fed the chickens and gathered eggs. Gary, at six, still could not do much. He fed the cats. All three kept the garden weeded and helped their mom gather and preserve the harvest.

Greg felt grateful that the family had made it through the pre-school years. He and Carla no longer had to struggle to pay their bills.

When Gary had started kindergarten, eliminating the school-year daycare bill, they were able to pay off Carla's SUV. This summer, they had entrusted Annie with the boys during the couple hours both parents were gone. By the end of the year, they would have the pickup paid off.

This would be the brightest Christmas in many years.

The sight of Hay Hollow Wash jerked him from his thoughts. A muddy torrent, not yet the width of the wash, rushed under Concho Highway.

They got monsoons further south.

He turned north on a dirt road while the sprinkles continued. On high ground the wash came into view, with brown water now extending across its width. Greg paused at a location he knew well to estimate the depth of the water.

"About three feet deep." He accelerated again and flipped his wipers up a notch. "Hey, I think this qualifies as a drizzle. Might actually get some mud out of this one."

He slowed at his driveway on the left. The pickup rumbled over the cattle guard and he eased through potholes all along the quarter-mile stretch. If they got substantial rain it would be a rutted, slimy mess. *Maybe when we get the pickup paid off we can have some cinders hauled in.*

Greg pulled into the carport and immediately noticed the missing quad. He climbed down and listened for the ATV's motor, a futile gesture with raindrops hitting the tin roof.

He stepped into the rain. "Annie!"

No reply. The horses and goats regarded him over and through the corral fences.

He hurried into the house. Annie had to follow rules to keep her quad privileges, including leaving a note with her destination.

When Greg saw the words on the whiteboard in the kitchen, his chest constricted. “We went to the fort.”

He bolted from the house. The kids’ fort was *in the wash.*

The goats stampeded away from the lunatic sprinting toward the barn. The horses raised their heads and tails. One of them snorted.

Greg grabbed a halter with lead and a lariat from the barn. He forced himself to slow when he reached the gate.

“Harley, come on boy.”

The black-and-white pinto approached, always interested in the man who fed him.

Greg slipped the halter over Harley’s big head and knotted it, threw the rope around his neck and tied it to make reins. He led the stout gelding from the corral, then swung up.

A squeeze of his knees sent Harley off at a fast walk. When Greg pressed his heels into the white sides, his mount moved into a lope.

They followed the familiar, winding, half-mile trail through shaggy-barked junipers as the drizzle increased to wind-driven rain. The junipers provided little shelter.

Greg tried to reassure himself that the fort’s location at a bend in the wash made it safer. Cottonwood trees had taken root there a hundred years ago, catching soil, creating a spot about five feet higher than the floor of the wash. But on the other side.

If they had headed back before the wash filled, I would have met them by now. How will I get them across? Please, God, keep them safe.

His mind considered possible rescues. A grown man *might* be able to climb the almost vertical clay wall behind the fort on a dry day. Today it would be impossible. Somehow, he would have to help them from this side.

The rain had begun to make the footing treacherous, forcing him to slow Harley. Above the rain, he heard water roaring through the wash.

“Please, Lord, protect my kids,” he kept repeating.

He pointed Harley down the trail leading into the wash. The gelding braced himself, sliding in the mud, nearly sitting, until it leveled off.

Annie stood in the scant shelter provided by the driftwood fort, her arms around her brothers. When she saw him, her lips moved. The boys waved.

Greg forced himself to smile. "Hang on! I'll get you!" *How will I get them?*

He dismounted, fighting panic, and tied Harley to a juniper. *Stay calm, Greg. You can't help your kids if you lose your head. And acting like you're in charge will keep them calm.*

Determined to save his children, he assessed the situation. Standing on the highest point of their little island, they were in no immediate danger. If he had been dealing with adults, he would have told them to just tie themselves to one of the cottonwoods. *You can't ask kids to do that.*

Because the wash narrowed here, only about twenty feet of water separated him from his children. But forcing the muddy runoff through a smaller opening made the current faster and more dangerous.

The lariat hanging over his arm was not long enough to do him any good. He studied his children again. Just having him there seemed to reassure them.

Then he spotted the quad.

"Annie! Pull out the cable."

She stared for a moment, then he read her lips. "What?"

"Pull out the cable." He waved toward the quad. "The winch. Pull out the cable."

Annie still looked puzzled. He pointed to her right. She turned her head, then darted to the quad and began fumbling with the winch. Greg prayed that she would remember how to play out the cable.

After what seemed like hours, she began unwinding it. The lariat and cable, when hooked together, would reach across the flood.

But how will I get them hooked together? He smiled and gave Annie a thumbs up. "Start the quad." He made a motion as if turning the key.

Annie handed the cable to Kevin and climbed on the quad. When the headlight came on, Greg gestured for her to drive closer to the water. Kevin walked beside her with the cable.

Greg clenched his fist. Annie stopped and took the quad out of gear. He made a slashing motion across his neck and she turned it off.

He gave her another thumbs up before uncoiling the lariat. After tying one end to another juniper, he slipped the loop around his waist, prayed again, and waded into the shallows.

He backtracked and removed his cowboy boots. By ankle depth he felt the soil being washed from under his feet. Before the water reached his knees, the current pulled at him. He kept the rope tight and pointed at Kevin.

"Annie, get the cable."

She nodded, grasped the hook at the end, and lay the cable in front of the quad without kinks. She pointed toward the fort and her brothers retreated there.

Annie stood closer to the deadly deluge than Greg would have liked, but they needed all the advantage they could get.

He took another step, fighting the current, aiming for a place where foam sprayed into the air. A submerged boulder would give him something to brace against.

The flood knocked him down. Because of the tight rope, he managed to keep his head above water until he could pull himself into the shallows.

Greg smiled at his children and started over. This time, as he neared the boulder, the water swirled and threatened to topple him again.

His shin bumped against it. He braced his hand against the smooth surface, but the speed of the current even made that difficult. When he had both legs maneuvered against the rock, the water pressure helped hold them in place.

He gestured to Annie. “Throw it.” He extended his arm.

She took a side-arm wind-up and launched the cable. It fell about five feet short.

Greg nodded. “Try again.”

She retrieved the cable and threw the hook again. This time it came close to Greg’s outstretched fingers.

He smiled. “Almost.”

On the third attempt, the hook hit his shoulder. He tried to grasp it, but failed.

“One more.”

The cable landed in his hand. His fingers closed around it, but in the process he lost his balance. The merciless flood knocked him down. This time he could not keep his head above water.

The steel cable slid through his hand and the loop tightened around his waist, but he refused to let go. He got both hands on the cable and surfaced, coughing and choking. Hand over hand, he worked his way up the cable until the hook could reach the lariat.

But hooking them together meant holding the cable with only one hand. He gritted his teeth, wrapped the steel around his left hand, and slid his right to the hook. The line bit into him, but he managed to secure the hook to the lariat. He unwrapped the cable, then worked hand over hand again.

Everything to this point had been easy compared to the next maneuver. He had to get the loop off his waist to reach his children. With the flood waters beating on his body.

Slipping his right arm under the still-tight noose, he passed it over his shoulder, then his head. The current carried him downstream until the slack left his line.

Please, Lord, let it hold.

The line held.

He began working his way toward his kids. When he staggered into the shallows, they surrounded him.

"Annie ..." He coughed. "Start the quad."

She rushed to it and he followed on his hands and knees. He grasped the front rack and pulled himself to a sitting position, then reeled in the cable until it hung taut above the water.

"Shut it off." He rested his head on the rack.

"Daddy," Gary sobbed. "Your hands are bleeding."

He just nodded.

"Dad," Annie said in a strained voice. "Are you okay?"

"Just tired." He raised his head. "I'll rest a little, then get you out of here."

Gary's eyes became saucers. "Across that?"

"It will be easy now that we have a line," Greg lied.

Annie wiped her eyes. "What do you want us to do?"

"What's in the tool box on the quad?"

She checked. "A fencing tool, staples, fasteners, tarp straps, and a pair of leather gloves."

"Got any rope in your fort?"

"Some we made from twine."

"Get it!"

Annie retrieved a coil of braided rope made from the black plastic twine which bound their hay bales. "Is this enough?"

"That will work." He pulled himself to his feet, then sat on the quad to hide his shaking knees.

Annie handed him the rope. He uncoiled it. *About ten feet.* Enough to fashion a harness to secure a child to him. As he worked on it, he explained.

"I'll have to take you one-at-a-time. And, boys, I need to take Annie first, so she's on the other side to help me. So you'll have to be brave. Can you do that?"

They both nodded, their tear-streaked faces solemn.

"Good boys. Stay in the fort. I love you all very much. Okay, Annie, I'm going to kind of tie you to my back. You need to hang on to me, but don't wrap your arms around my neck."

"Okay."

"Get me those gloves."

When he pulled the glove on his left hand, he had to grit his teeth. He used his teeth to get the glove on his right hand. "Let's go. Walk as long as you can. The current will catch you, but don't worry. I won't let you go."

"O-okay."

The trip began as he expected. Within a few feet the current stretched him out from the line. Pain shot up his left arm every time his hand took another hold. The rope securing Annie to him bit into his shoulder.

Finally, his feet touched bottom. He held the rope to keep himself upright until Annie had her feet on the ground too.

"Get out ... of the rope."

When she had freed herself, he sank to his knees.

"Dad, are you okay?"

He nodded. "I need you ... to take Harley ... home. Call the Wilsons. I may need some help to get out of here." He forced a smile. "This is a lot of work."

"What if they aren't home?"

"They milk goats about this time of day. There'll be somebody home. But if you can't get through, call 9-1-1."

Her brow furrowed. "But that's just for emergencies."

"This is close enough. They won't mind."

"Okay."

He struggled to his feet, untied Harley, then lifted her to his back. "Let him pick his speed. It's slippery and he'll keep you safe."

"You can count on me. I love you, Dad."

"I love you, Annie."

She wheeled Harley and the pinto picked his way up the trail. Greg turned toward the water again. It had risen another foot since he reached the wash.

Can I make four more trips across? Please, Lord, for the boys' sake, give me the strength to do this. He waded into the water.

When he reached the island this time, he stayed on his hands and knees for much longer. He only responded with nods to the boys' questions. He sat back on his haunches.

"Kevin, I need to take Gary next."

"Yes, sir."

"You wait in the fort, and you stay there no matter what. Understand?"

"Yes, sir."

"Good boy. Gary, come here." He knotted the rope around Gary, below his arms, forming a figure-eight. He slipped the larger loop over his head and across his chest. When he stood, Gary hung from his back.

"Ow, Daddy."

"I know. Hang on to the rope. It won't hurt so much when we get in the water."

He waded in as fast as he could, forcing himself to keep going, ignoring the pain and exhaustion. Somehow, they reached safety.

Gary slapped his shoulder. "Daddy. Daddy!"

"Let me rest a minute." He worked the rope off, freeing Gary, then rolled over in the mud.

The little boy wiped a muddy hand across Greg's forehead. "Daddy, you're so tired."

"Oh, this is nothing." He lied again. "You should have seen how hard they worked us in the Army. You head back to the house now. We'll catch up to you."

Gary looked across at his brother. "But ..."

"Don't worry about us. I want you to get home and into dry clothes as soon as you can. I'll be too tired to carry you." Greg sat up. "Okay."

"Okay."

"Get going. It will be hard work. But you can do it."

Greg forced himself to his feet and hooked his left arm over the rope for support. He watched his son crawl up the slope and fought tears. He could not allow his baby to see what might happen next.

With his arm still hooked over the rope, he waded in. But when the current caught him, he needed both hands to make progress. Near the middle of the wash, everything went black.

***

"Daddy." Kevin's voice sounded like he was in a barrel. "Daddy!" Now the voice sounded shrill. "Daddy, wake up!"

Greg groaned.

"Daddy?"

"I'm okay."

It took all his strength to roll over with a splash. Only then did he feel the water around his legs. He squinted, noticing tear tracks on Kevin's muddy face. He wanted to reach up and reassure his son, but could only manage to pat his leg.

"I thought you died."

"I'm fine. We need to get out of the water."

"I'll help you."

"Grab my arm. Help me roll over."

Every fiber in Greg's body protested, but he made it to his hand and knees. He could not put weight on his left hand. Kevin walked beside him as he hobbled to the fort. He flopped down with his back propped against the wall.

"I'm sorry, Buddy. We'll have to wait here till somebody comes. I can't make it across again without help."

"But the water's still getting higher."

"Don't worry. These trees have been here a hundred years. If we have to, we'll just tie ourselves to one of them. You keep an eye on the water for me."

He passed out again.

***

Greg woke to small hands shaking him. "Daddy, Mr. Wilson's here. How'd he know?"

He opened his eyes. The rain had stopped and he saw patches of blue among the clouds. "Annie called them."

The water still roared. But when he forced himself to a seated position, it had receded at least a foot. Don Wilson and his young adult sons stood across the wash next to their quads. Greg made a half-hearted wave. The Wilsons huddled, then Don tied a rope around his waist and began crossing on Greg's line.

When his feet hit the island, Don grinned. "Hi, neighbor. What's new?"

"Are Annie and Gary okay?"

"Met Gary on the way here with Annie. They should be back to the house by now."

"Thank God." Greg began sobbing.

"Daddy, what's wrong?"

"Don't worry, little fellow," Don said. "Your daddy's just very, very tired. Let's get him home to bed."

***

The next morning, Greg woke himself by smacking his nose with the cast on his arm. X-rays had showed three broken bones in his left hand.

Every muscle ached when he forced himself to sit up. He swung his legs over the side of the bed and shuffled to the kitchen.

His children leaped from their chairs and hugged him. Even that hurt.

"Finish your breakfast," Carla ordered. "Let your daddy sit down."

They obeyed, but Carla wrapped her arms around his neck. He winced.

"Should I ask how you feel this morning?" She smiled.

"Pretty dumb," he whispered.

She frowned. "Why?"

"Because I could have just stayed there with them."

"You didn't know that. We've seen that fort torn apart by a monsoon. You couldn't take that chance."

"Guess so."

Carla kissed him. "I've prayed a lot in the past twelve hours. Our financial struggles don't seem very important anymore. I've never felt quite so grateful."

Greg nodded, fighting tears again. "Amen."

###

A Motion Away

By

Jonathan S. Pembroke

PRESENT

He wasn't the first man I'd killed but he was the easiest.

He never moved, not even I worked the bolt handle--a horrible clanking sound in the still of the night. But he showed zero reaction.

Had the radiation damaged his hearing? I knew plenty of people that had lost some hearing. I'd never know but I did wonder at the stupidity of posting a deaf guard at your back entrance.

I took a deep breath, exhaled half of it and squeezed the trigger.

The round punched through his padded coat and into his chest. The man pitched forward without a peep.

I cycled the bolt, ejecting a spent casing and slamming the next one home. I didn't celebrate my kill. Alive or dead, he didn't matter.

Only one thing did.

Casey.

I waited for a cry of alarm from the building but it never came. Perhaps random shots were common enough in town that unless the raiders felt the snap of a bullet whizzing past their head, they ignored it.

Better for me.

Bent low, I scurried to the back door.

TWO DAYS AGO

"Hey, Julie. Want to give me a hand down here?"

I wiped the sweat from my brow and straightened. The tin sheeting of roof wobbled. Royce stood below, wearing that ever-present shit-eating grin of his. He clutched a bulky hay bale.

I snorted. "Yeah, I'm not busy up here or anything."

"You could take a break, walk with me a little, help me carry this."

"You've carried plenty on your own. You can handle it."

Royce's eyes lit up. "I could come up and help you."

"I'm good."

The man's shoulders slumped. "All right." He hefted his bale and walked deeper into Cedar Point, looking like a kicked puppy.

I watched him go. I hadn't meant to hurt his feelings but I did wish he'd take the hint. Casey always said I was too abrupt for my own good.

As if my thoughts had summoned her, a thin teenage girl emerged from the shack on which I stood. She stretched and tilted her head back. "You ran him off again."

"I don't want any misunderstandings, Casey."

She grinned in that infuriating way teenagers do. "You could cut the guy some slack, hang out with him a little."

"No, that would only lead him on."

"He has no one, Mom. He's completely alone. Most everyone else who was alone have already paired off, like Will and Madeline. They were married before, but...." Casey shrugged.

"That's their business. Besides, Will and Madeline are just screwing. It's not like they're in love."

"It's not even that, Mom," Casey said, her face sad. "They just don't want to be alone, like Royce."

"That's pretty cynical."

"So is life, Mom. At least, it is now."

My poor Cassandra, I thought. *I wish I could have spared you such a grim existence.*

"Well, Casey, I appreciate your interest in the community spirit of Cedar Point--" Casey snorted at that. "--but I'm not afraid of being alone."

I hammered the last nail in place and gave the tin sheet a tentative pull. It held tight. The roof would see us through another season. I shimmied down, ignoring the grind in my joints. My knees were going to hurt tonight.

Only forty and already feeling ancient, Julie.

I guess after all that happened, I was lucky to feel anything.

Casey waited for me. Her face was pensive. "Mom, you know Dad isn't coming back, right?"

She wasn't wrong but the thought renewed the old hurts--the ones I'd fought to bury. I bit my lip. "I know that."

She slipped her arms around me and embraced me in a gentle hug. "I don't want to see you alone either."

"I won't be. I'll have you."

Casey pulled her head back to stare me in the eye. "What if something happens to me, Mom? Or what if I meet someone?"

"Casey—"

She disengaged herself. "I won't wait. If I meet someone, I am not going to hang back and wait to get with him. We're all living on borrowed time. I have a chance at happiness--even for a while--I'm taking it."

Moisture filled my eyes but I didn't say anything. I guess Casey saw the look on my face. Her countenance softened and she took my hands. "Mom, I do love you. Just promise me you won't be alone just because of Dad, okay?"

"I promise," I lied.

Casey narrowed her eyes but before she could say anything further, a gravelly voice sliced the air. "Julie, you still on for a run today?"

A heavyset woman leading two horses tramped up the lane. She wore a fleabitten duster and scuffed riding boots. A battered cowboy hat perched atop her cropped gray hair.

I jerked my head at our shack. "Yeah, let me grab my stuff."

Casey followed me in. "Where are you and Tammy off to today?"

"Just over to Concho Valley to drop off crops. They're supposed to have boxes of screws and nails for us and maybe some more potassium iodide pills, which we're very short on."

"Radiation pills?"

"Yeah." I strapped on my gunbelt.

"Cool."

I raised an eyebrow. "Really?"

"Nah." She grinned. "Sounds lame."

"Come here."

I embraced her, again fighting tears. Her wit and carefree attitude...it reminded me of Dan so much it hurt. I said, "You be careful. We'll be back before sunset, okay?"

"Sure thing, Mom."

PRESENT

I was terrified the back door would be locked but it squeaked open on rusty hinges. Each squeal made me wince and I expected more men to burst from the darkness to grab me. But there was nothing.

I crept into the darkened room. My heartbeat hammered in my ears like a bass drum. I concentrated, straining my ears. All I heard was the soft moan of the breeze dritfing through a shattered window.

Is this the wrong place?

It couldn't be. Nowhere else in town would work for them. Unless they weren't in Snowflake at all.

My mind shied away from the implications of that possibility.

I slung the Remington across my back. Indoors, the rifle was unwieldy.

I pulled one my revolvers from its holster. A Smith and Wesson 627. Eight rounds of .357 pain. I loved my old nine millimeter but it was so hard to keep functional now. Dan's voice drifted through my memory: *you can put a revolver in a drawer for years, pick it up, and it will still fire. With semi-autos, in this Arizona dust...not so much.*

I smiled sadly. *You taught me so much, Honey. We sure could use you now.*

I tapped the second revolver in my belt and crept further into the building.

YESTERDAY

The cresting dawn did nothing to wipe the scowl from my face. As soon as the sky lightened, I nudged Tammy with my toe. "C'mon, let's go."

She groaned, half-asleep. "A few more minutes."

"You can sleep when we get back to Cedar Point. Get up."

She struggled into a sitting position. "What's the rush?"

"You know damn well what the rush is."

"She's sixteen, Julie. You can't shield her forever."

"I'll do it as long as I can." I fidgeted with the cuff of my sleeve. "Tammy, I'm leaving in five minutes, with or without you."

"All right, all right. God, you're a nervous bitch."

I didn't argue with her.

The trade with Concho Valley had gone smooth enough. One of them had stumbled on an abadoned big rig off Route 180A, loaded with hardware. They were happy to barter with us.

Sure, there was always one jerk who wanted to lowball the deal but we worked it out. The crops in our saddlebags were gone, replaced with boxes of screws and nails, a few cans of machine oil, tools, and other items.

Best of all, I had a whole box of the iodide pills. We still had showers of fallout now and again so they were more valuable than gold.

But just as we were set to leave, a fire broke out.

We could have left. There was enough daylight for us to reach Cedar Point. But the way Tammy looked at me....

I caved and reluctantly agreed to help. My gut told me I was making a mistake. We lugged heavy buckets of water from the water tank, back and forth, back and forth, until the fire was out. Exhausted, I headed for the horse when a hand clamped over my bicep.

Tammy pointed with her free hand at the darkening horizon. "Julie, the sunlight's almost gone."

"So?"

"You know we can't travel at night."

I glared at her. The worst part is that she was right.

It was too far to navigate without visible landmarks. We could follow the highway but raiders and killers tended to set up ambushes on the road and the last thing I wanted to do was stumble into one of those in the darkness. Or get lost, which might be worse.

I wrenched my arm from Tammy's grip.

I barely slept. I tossed and turned, cognizant of Tammy's heavy snores. The moment night began to fade from the eastern sky, I sprang up, ready to go.

Despite her protestations, Tammy was ready within moments of waking. We set out and pushed the horses as hard as we could. After a short gallop, Tammy shouted, "Julie, we need to slow down for a bit."

"No!'

"You kill that horse and you'll be walking."

I yanked the reins. The horse nickered and slowed. Impatience chewed at my mind. Tammy pulled alongside me. "Julie, they were just stories."

"Doesn't matter."

She rolled her eyes. "Just 'cause some scavenger nosing around Snowflake said the warband moved in doesn't make it so. He probably spotted a single guy on a donkey and by the time he got back to Concho Valley, it had grown in his mind to a Mongol Horde."

"Tammy, I know what you're trying to do but I won't feel better until I have Casey in my sight."

"She'll be all right."

I didn't answer. I kept my eyes fixed on the horizon.

Only thirty minutes later I saw the smoke.

This time, I was oblivious to Tammy's cries. I spurred my horse at full speed, driving the poor animal up and down the ridges. The inevitable happened; the animal stumbled and fell. I sensed it coming and rolled clear. My elbow jarred against a rock but I scarcely felt it. I was on my feet in a flash, sprinting towards Cedar Point. Behind me, the dying horse thrashed impotently on the ground.

I crested the last ridge and my heart quailed. Cedar Point lay in ruins. Some of the shacks were down, others aflame.

"Casey."

I took off in a sprint yet again.

As I reached the outskirts of the village, a form emerged from a pile of rubble. I skidded to a stop, my hand on my revolver. Then I all but slumped in relief. "Royce!"

"Julie?" The man's eyes were glazed and unfocused and blood trickled from his hairline.

"Royce." She lunged forward and grabbed him by the shoulders. "Casey! Where is she?"

"Casey? I...I don't...."

The man's knees buckled and he would have fallen had I not held him up. I grabbed the canteen on my belt and brought it to his lips. "Drink."

Royce took a sip, paused, then another. I guided him to the shade of the nearest building, where he slumped against the tin sheet siding. "Royce, listen to me. What happened?"

"They came out of the night."

"Who?"

His eyes focused, suddenly afraid. "Them. The ones from Snowflake."

"How did you know they were from Snowflake?"

"I heard them talk about going back. And when they left, they rode off to the west, along the highway."

"How many?"

"Twenty, maybe more. They...they took people with them."

A chill seized my heart. "Casey?"

"I don't know."

"Rest, Royce." I handed him the canteen.

I ran straight to our shack. The door hung askew from the hinges and the interior was ransacked. No Casey.

The next fifteen minutes were a waking nightmare. Blood pooled everywhere but there were no bodies. Save Royce, everyone was gone.

I returned to him. His eyes were more coherent but carried a haunted look I knew so well: survivor guilt.

"Julie." I spun at the new voice but it was only Tammy. Her wide-eyed stare roamed across the devastation. "What--"

"Not now. Tammy, listen to me. Take Royce and get out of here. Head back to Concho Valley. You have to warn them."

"But Cedar Point is our home."

I pressed my lips into a line. "Not any more."

"What about you?"

"I'm going to Snowflake."

"Why?"

"That's where they took her."

"But—"

"No more 'buts,' Tammy." I kept my voice firm. "Just do it, all right?"

"All right."

She helped Royce onto her horse. He was still weak and swayed in the sadlle. "Julie, don't go."

"If there is any chance, Royce--*any* chance that Casey is still alive--I have to go."

"Julie, they'll get you too."

"Goodbye, Royce. Tammy...thanks for everything."

I marched out of Cedar Point for the last time. Tammy said nothing. Royce however, called after me like a lost little boy.

"Julie! Don't go. Please come with us. Julie!"

I kept walking.

PRESENT

Some of the rooms were filled with debris or were crammed with empty cots. Many were empty. One contained stacks of clothes, boots, and shoes. With each passing moment, my despair grew.

I rounded a corner and stopped. A shut door blocked further progress. A thin, flickering light emanated from beneath the door and even as I watched, a shadow passed beneath the door.

"This one's not bad." I flinched at the sound of the gravelly tone. It was the voice of a dead man.

"Get out of that," chided a woman's voice. "We have to have it ready for breakfast."

"Sure you don't want a taste?"

"Is that a rib?"

The man chuckled. "Yeah these are my favorites."

"Okay," the woman said, "but just a bite."

I eased the hammer back on my revolver, and stretched from my crouch into a low stance. My hand craned towards the doorknob.

Just as my fingertips touched the knob, the door yanked open. The dim yellow light revealed a huge, bearded man in jeans and a flannel shirt. He saw me and his eyes went wide.

"What the--"

I pulled the trigger.

The discharge was deafening in the enclosed space. The slug ripped through the man's stomach. He screamed and toppled to the floor.

I fired again. The man flopped and quivered. But there had been two voices in the room. I hopped across him.

The inside of the room was a slaughterhouse. Literally.

Two rows of hooks filled the left side of the room, hanging from the ceiling. Some bore parts of animals and some held what I could only believe were parts of people. My brain refused to analyze the bloody chunks too closely.

There were several bloodstained butcher blocks on the right. By one stood an ashen-faced young woman. She clutched at her belt but froze when I leveled the revolver at her head.

"Where is she?"

"Who?"

"Teenage girl with long brown hair. You took her from Cedar Point."

The woman's face changed to a smirk. I realized she was only a few years older than Casey.

"Wouldn't you like to know?" she said in a sing-song voice.

"Do not play with me, bitch. I will kill you right now."

The girl pointed at a door opposite the one I'd come in. "Through there."

"Anyone in there with her?"

She shrugged.

"Last warning."

Her eyes had all the warmth of a shark's. I'd seen the look before; she'd witnessed or endured too much. The trauma had pushed her humanity into a sealed box, just so she could survive, until only the animal remained.

Then what does that make you, Julie?

The girl spat at my feet. "You're going to kill me anyway."

"Maybe. But you can make it easy or hard."

The girl closed her eyes and rotated her body until she faced the wall. "You'll have to shoot me in the back.

"Don't think I won't."

She said nothing and it hit me like a thunderbolt. She was stalling, which could only mean there were more of them nearby. The realization made me madder than anything up to that point.

I fired.

A FEW HOURS PAST

It was just after sunset when I reached the outskirts of Snowflake. Crumbling buildings and burnt-out shells lined Hwy 77. I worked my way south, pausing every few minutes to listen for any telltale signs of danger.

Before I had gone far, I heard the thunder of hoofbeats. I concealed myself in the space between two dumpsters, where I could still see the street. Not a moment later, a dozen riders pounded past. I waited until they were out of sight and sound before moving on.

I found the factory easy enough. Some subsidary of Toyota noticed the derelict rail spur into town, low taxes, and generally depressed economy (meaning cheap workers) and thought it would be a good place to set up a production plant for brake parts. Desperate for incoming industry, the city fathers had pretty much given them the keys to the kingdom.

I shook my head. Those were problems for better times. Before the bombs fell.

Several large groups of riders milled around the parking lot. One man strode between the groups with a flashlight and what looked like a map. The man gestured at the map and pointed before moving to the next group. Some of the groups rode out as soon as the man moved to the next cluster. Some hung around and then suddenly took off at some unseen signal.

I worked my way around the factory, towards the rear. I knew there was an entrance there, as the rear parking lot butted up against the personal property of one of the town elders. The issue had turned into one of the big points of contention for the factory coming into town. Dan thought it was amusing. *That's what it always comes down to*, he said. *Screw the people but once it affects someone rich, it's a major deal.*

Dan. I still missed him so much.

I never should have let him go.

Correction, Julie: it should have been you.

A lousy quirk of fate, was all. I had a crate of stained glass in Phoenix, at the distributor. I could have had them ship it up the mountain, at a prohibitive cost. But Dan, God bless him, volunteered to take the truck to Phoenix and pick it up for me. He knew how much I wanted it. He grumped about the drive but I knew he did because he loved me. I told him I would go with him but stayed up too late the night before. He let me sleep in. He drove to Phoenix. He was there when the balloon went up. Forty-five minutes later, the whole city, along with most of the country, was a radioactive wasteland.

We never saw him again.

All because I wanted some pretty glass.

I clung to Casey. For the last year, we'd pulled together with our neighbors. We'd rebuilt somewhat, survived. I never let anyone hurt Casey or come between us. I'd killed to protect her.

Until yesterday. I'd put someone else ahead of her and I wasn't there to protect her. And now, I might have lost her too.

The last group of riders galloped away from the front of the building. I thumbed the light on my wristwatch. Just after midnight.

A new day.

I hoped it would be a good one.

PRESENT

The girl howled and fell to the floor. Blood fountained from the wound in her shoulder. Her voice rose to a shriek. "You mother--"

I pulled the trigger again. She fell still.

"Damn right. I *am* a mother."

Footfalls echoed from the hallway. I holstered the revolver, drew my backup, and knelt with the gun trained on the doorway. Five seconds later, two bruisers shouldered their way inside. I fired and fired until the hammer fell on two empty chambers in a row. Both the newcomers lay dead in a tumbled heap in the doorway, sprawled across the man from the room.

I reloaded both guns as quick as I could. My gaze settled on something and the blood drained from my veins.

Will and Madeline lay on the floor. At least, their heads did. Both were bug-eyed and fixed in shock, as if they could not believe what was happening right up until their last fleeting seconds of life.

Did these fiends butcher them alive?

There was the other door. No one had come bursting through it. Was it empty or was someone lying in wait for me to come through.

More than that, was Casey even there?

As I reached to open it, a deep horror ripped through my mind.

What if she's already dead?

What if she's already...the same as Will and Madeline?

The mere thought made my hand shake. A wracking sob escaped my lips. I stood paralyzed, hand halfway to the doorknob.

She was a motion away, a mere flick of the wrist. I prayed she was there--and then that she wasn't. I couldn't bring myself to do it. The possibility was too terrifying.

If she was gone, I was truly alone. My husband, my community, and now my daughter. Opening that door was crossing a line I could never uncross.

And in every case, it was completely my fault.

I might have stood there forever if a voice from two days earlier hadn't drifted back into my thoughts.

Just promise me you won't be alone, Mom.

"But Casey," I cried out, "I can't go one without you."

I'll always be in your heart, Mom.

I bit my lip. There were only two things I could do. I could turn and walk. Or I could open the door.

Either path offered heartache and devastation.

Only one offered relief.

I steeled myself, grabbed the knob and flung open the door.

"Mom!"

I slumped to my knees as she flung herself into my arms. Casey collapsed against me, her cries wracking her body. She was naked and filthy. Had those monsters--

Don't think about it right now.

"Mom, oh Mom. You came for me."

"I always will, sweetie. Always." I gave her a long squeeze. "Now come on, we have to go."

"Julie?"

My eyes flicked to the sound. A handful of people stood around the room. Some of them I knew, some I didn't. The speaker was a heavyset bald man from Cedar Point, named Brian. Like Casey, he was nude and covered in sweat and dust.

Brian pointed at the open door. "You alone?"

"Yes. We have to go. Right now."

I helped Casey to her feet. I led them back to the clothing-filled room and stood guard while they dressed, my anxiety increasing with every second.

We had no more than crossed the parking lot and entered the trees surrounding Silver Creek when I felt a faint rumble. My voice was a hiss. "Down, everyone down."

A group of horsemen galloped up main street and into the Toyota factory parking lot. As one, they swung down and trotted to the doors.

I nudged Casey and kept my voice low. "Okay, everyone up. Follow me. Single file."

We worked our way through the trees and into the fields beyond, leaving the ruined city and its murderous inhabitants behind.

THREE WEEKS LATER

I pulled the charging handle and nodded at the satisfactory *click* as it snapped a round into place. I handed the weapon back to the man. "Works fine, Kenneth. You're ready."

"Thanks, Julie."

Kenneth placed the weapon's safety on, slung it over his shoulder, and ambled away.

Casey looked up from her disassembled pistol. "It's funny."

"What is?"

"Watching these macho guys ask a girl how to load and fire a weapon."

I chuckled. "I guess when it comes to survival, pride takes a back seat."

"Yeah."

I sat next to her. She leaned against my shoulder and I put my arm around her. "You sure you want to do this, sweetie?"

"I have to, Mom. I...I can't just sit here the rest of my life." She gestured. "This is our home now. We have to defend it."

"I know, baby. Trust me, I wish you wouldn't but I...."

"What, Mom?"

"No matter what, I can't protect you from everything. I know that now."

I stood and jerked my head at her fractured weapon. With a speed that impressed me, she reassembled the gun, ops-checked it, and shoved a fresh clip in. She thumbed the slide forward and jammed it in her holster.

My eyes lingered on her gun belt. I wanted her to use the revolver--for simplicity--but she said she was more comfortable with the semi-auto.

Let it go, Julie. She's growing up and you have to let her.

Around us, the citizens of Concho Valley scurried about, grabbing up supplies and ammunition. Some stared off into space, some prayed.

It had taken a week to convince the citizens that they would have to fight back. It took another two weeks of reconnaissance to get down the search pattern of the Snowflake Butchers, as we now called them.

They'd gotten sloppy and predictable, sending their bands out in a recognizable pattern, which left them open to ambush.

I nodded. Tonight, we were going to make them pay.

Me. Casey. All of us.

Was it the first step to taking back our land? Reclaiming Snowflake for the civilized people?

I didn't know. I hoped so.

I chambered a round in my rifle.

Until that happened, I'd settle for vengeance.

###

Navajo-Apache Wedding

an excerpt from *Robert Yellowhair, Navajo Artist*,

upcoming authorized biography by

Myra Larsen

This little story is a great example of how many things can go wrong and all turns out right anyway.

It was all set for Carol Yellowhair and her groom, Fernando Lupe, an Apache, to have a perfect wedding and a perfect start to their lives together, her parents, Robert and Louise thought. It was a combination of a Navajo, Apache and White event.

Carol had been planning the wedding for months. She was excited as she discussed the details with her mother. They went shopping for the reception. Her mother, Louise, helped her select the satin and lace for her dress and the pattern, as they giggled like two school girls. They planned the refreshments; cake and punch and cookies. Carol wanted simple decorations because they would just be torn down later.

While Carol worked on her dress, Fernando tried to sneak a peek, but they shooed him out of the house. There was a huge cake made by a couple who owned the Jack Rabbit store.

Fernando had a suit purchased for the wedding. It would later be his church suit.

Instead of the marriage being performed in a hogan, it would be held in a gym with plenty of indoor space for the guests on that warm evening in 1980.

The location was Whiteriver, on the Fort Apache Reservation in Navajo County with plenty of camping, fishing, and hiking opportunities. There weren't many weddings among a population of less than 4000. Formal invitations had been sent out and a crowd of people would come to celebrate.

Finally the happy evening arrived. As any bride would be, Carol was nervous. Her fingers seemed all thumbs as she tried to arrange her hair just so. Her mother was there to assist, but she was just as nervous as Carol. She was having as much trouble with her own hair, but it was not as important. She got dressed and returned to help Carol with her dress and veil. Carol had given up on her hair and decided it would be hidden anyway. When her dad, Robert, called them for the tenth time, she said, “Okay. I'm as ready as I can be. Lets go.”

While that was going on at the bride's parent's home, a similar, but less spectacular, event was being played out at the groom's parent's home. Work had delayed the groom and his father. So, even the groom was concerned about his hair. It kept wanting to stick up in that irritating “rooster's tail”. His mother was the one there rushing everyone out the door.

It was planned to be a 6:00 PM wedding with a reception to follow. The Yellowhair family needed lots of help for their first wedding.. They counted on friends to assist them with the preparations.

Larry and Shirley Nelson, were asked to bring their silver punch bowl and ladle. They agreed and promised Robert to be there about 5:45 and have it ready to fill, “Oh no, that would be much to early.” Robert told them. Larry was also asked to share a few words of advise to the couple.

“We'll be there. We don't want to be late.”

At 5:45, the Nelsons were right on time, but the gym was empty. The door was open so they went inside. There were a few decorations around the perimeter of the room. There were no tables set up, so they took care of that and put the bowl and ladle on one.

They found chairs and sat down to wait. And wait, and wait some more. They were sure it was the right date. Could it have been canceled or postponed?

Sometime after 7:00 PM the pianist finally arrived. She didn't seem concerned about arriving so late, but where was the piano? A search of the building revealed none. The Nelsons invited her to take a chair and wait with them. Larry suggested, "Someone will probably bring a piano soon."

"I hope so." she calmly answered.

The bride and groom were still missing and there was a discussion about the possibility of cancellation or elopement. The pianist reassured the Nelsons there would be a wedding.

Some friends of the groom appeared and Larry told them there was no piano and asked if any of them had one that could be brought. One couple had one and offered its use if the men would help them bring it in the back of their pickup.

The pianist was relieved even though pianos should be tuned with every move. It would do. She sat down and arranged her music. She would be ready when it was time.

Another 30 minutes passed and the groom arrived with his family. His family found chairs among the guests and sat down. Fernando paced the floor. He stopped suddenly when the piano began playing "Here Comes the Bride."

The bride had arrived with her family. It was not as she had planned. All they could do was find seats and sit down as the music ended.

The program began.

Larry gave his advise to the distracted couple in a brief ten minute presentation with intermittent cheers from the guests.

The Apache tribal chairman, a family member, was also on the program. He shared a few words about the couple he had grown to love and wished them a successful and happy life.

But there was a problem – no minister to perform the ceremony; the Nelsons wondered why no one was concerned. They looked around the room. There was quiet visiting. Some of the restless children had began squirming until their parents let them go to the back of the room to play.

Larry asked Robert what would happen now and was asked to help find someone.

It seemed that Larry was now in charge of solving that problem. After a discussion with the guests someone remembered a possible minister. A couple of guys rushed out to find him.

Larry observed,"The minister was falling-down drunk. In filthy, ragged clothes, twigs in his dirty, stringy hair he looked like a homeless desert man. Boy, did he smell." But, Larry was reassured by the man's escorts he was a real minister; he wore the white collar. He was accepted by everyone else, so Larry did also.

Larry had set up a podium and microphone for the ceremony, but the minister propped himself on the podium and kept moving away from the mike. Robert asked Larry to help, but every time Larry adjusted the mike the man moved again. His whole ceremony was whispered, so only the bride and groom could hear his words.

Finally, rings were exchanged, the "I dos" were said and a "kiss the bride" was mumbled. They were now Mr. and Mrs. They had a certificate, a squiggly signature and witnesses.

No one saw the minister leave. He had done his job.

The vows were completed but, the challenges were not over.

Everyone moved to the refreshment area. There was no punch to go with the cake. There were no cups to go with the bowl and ladle. The assigned people had failed in their tasks. That didn't stop the children from sneaking between the line of adults and grabbing cookies or a brownie.

A guest quickly went to a store and returned with bottles of punch and sodas. No cups. That problem was accepted by filling the ladle and handing it to one guest at a time. Larry and Shirley declined.

Music was provided by The Apache Spirit Band, playing a variety of selections.

The Money Dance began with the newlyweds alone on the floor. They were claimed by different partners who gifted them with paper money pinned to their clothing. Other dancers joined them on the floor. Gifts were opened by a family member who held each one up for all to see and recognize the giver.

Everyone cheered each gift.

A sister-in-law collected all the gifts to deliver them to the couple's home.

Instead of the bowl of cornmeal for the Native American ceremony, there was a bowl of rice to toss on the couple as they left the event. They went straight home because Fernando had to go to work the next morning. The evening began late. The reception would continue longer while the guests celebrated the happy event with the parents of the newlyweds.

***

While driving home, Larry told his wife, "That is one wedding I will never forget. At least, we were on time."

"Now, I understand what Robert had meant when he once said, *Indian time,"* Shirley laughed. "I'm glad we remembered to take our punch bowl and ladle."

"All is well that ends well." he replied.

###

The Old Mountain Home

by

Myra Larsen

For me, one look at the home on First Street West in Snowflake conjures up a myriad of memories and I smile. Horses in the corral. A little boy with a flashlight. Thanksgiving dinners with the house, porch and lawn filled with family from toddlers to old folks.

By the late1800s, the home was owned by Evan Larson and his wife Zella. It passed to their son Ivan in the mid-1900s. He remodeled it at the desire of his wife, Erna, even though he thought it had been just fine. At least, the exterior remained the same.

The house is in the family to this day.

Grandpa Ivan enjoyed sitting with the children and grandchildren on the front porch. Back and forth the porch swing moved beneath the weight of three or four noisy grandchildren, or their parents when they could sneak a turn. Usually, the adults found lawn chairs or, places on the porch wall.

Zella, the oldest grandchild remembers the day that swing appeared. “It was an exciting day that created the foundation of my childhood. My dad and uncle installed that swing. The porch with its swing and beautiful flowers was the coveted spot.

Grandpa always wore long sleeves, even in the summer. He also wore a cowboy hat whenever he went outdoors. He enjoyed being with a horse or two in the corral when they were brought up from the field. He had a hayfield separated from the big field.

"And, oh yes, homemade ice cream. Grandma mixed up a batch and Grandpa sat in his chair in the garage door and tended the salt and ice till it was just right. The freezer was the old-fashioned hand-crank style."

It was a great gathering place, not just for family, but also for friends and neighbors out for a stroll. If Grandpa was sitting there alone a neighbor walking by was invited to *sit a spell.*

Grandpa's favorite place though was the garage connected to the enclosed back porch. With the door open, he enjoyed relaxing in his best-loved chair, totally ragged from many years of use. His grandchildren never tired of gathering around him to hear his stories about when he was a kid just like them.

One of their favorites was about the skunk family. They could almost tell it themselves.

At about age seven, he was walking and skipping home one evening when he saw a family of skunks crossing a bridge over Silver Creek. They were not the family's favorite critter.

"I'll take care of those beasties and mom will be so happy. I'll kick them into the creek."

He ran toward them and managed to get them into the water, but ... not before they got him. Spray, spray. Whew!

Not discouraged, but excited about his news, he raced home. He ran into the kitchen where the family was having dinner with friends. The welcome he received was a disappointment.

His dad, wasting no time, assisted Ivan, with confusion written all over his face, back outside and straight to the barn. He stripped off Ivan's clothes and threw them in the burn pile. With a bucket of cold water and a bar of Lava soap, tearful, shivering, Ivan scrubbed and scrubbed and couldn't rid himself of the stinky skunk perfume. Dressed again, he entered the garage and waited fearfully until the visitors left. “Do I still smell bad? Will Mother be mad about my clothes?”

I remember Grandpa telling them about the lost wallet. It involved Zella's dad and uncles, when they were younger.

The family had come for Thanksgiving. Grandpa's horses were in the barnyard and his sons wanted to go for a ride. Wayne and Monte, fathers of some of the grandchildren, saddled the horses and rode to the family field outside of town, returning a few hours later. As they washed up for dinner, Wayne realized his wallet was missing. Dinner could wait.

They returned to the field to search for it, with no success. Wayne’s younger twin brothers volunteered to lend a hand. Even with a 120 acre field to search, they found the wallet. This story really excited the children of Ivan. They cheered and waved their hands, “Yeah. Yeah. Now we can eat.”

One of Grandpa's holiday pleasures was dessert. There was always plenty of dessert, dessert, and more dessert. The children, and sometimes bigger folks, were caught sneaking a cookie or brownie. “Grandma, I'm hungry.”

Grandma made several kinds of candy and her famous steamed carrot pudding with a scrumptious sauce of butter, cream and sugar. It took what seemed like hours to make and the long wait was torture. And oh so rich. A wise person would eat only a little. The recipe was passed along to her children who continue the tradition in their own homes.

“Being at Grandma and Grandpa's house was a lot of fun. It was a break from regular life with homework and chores. In Grandma's kitchen, only she, my mom and the aunts took care of meal preparations and clean up. Many times we kids just hung out with cousins or swung on the porch swing.” Zella said.

The grand-kids liked to hear Grandpa tell about his son and the flashlight. When Wayne was just a little tyke, he was crazy about his grandparents, who lived next door. Grandpa Ivan told them Wayne always wanted to take a flashlight and walk across the lawns to tell his Grandma Zella goodnight. Perhaps that had something to do with the chocolate chip cookies in her cookie jar.

Grandpa Ivan's stories were sometimes about work. He wanted his children to do chores, including milking the cow, which he assigned to Wayne. Even if Wayne went to a community dance before milking, she was waiting for him when he got home. He knew Grandpa would not do the job for him.

The barn was a cool place to play for generations of children. It had hay for climbing and mice to find in the corn bin. There was even a window on the second level to jump out of. It was also the location of Grandpa's tools and he expected to find them where he left them.

Snowflake corn has a reputation for being extra special. Corn growers in Taylor will still argue that point. They think theirs is best.

Grandpa planted nearly half the garden to corn.

Zella remembers the strawberry patch surrounded by a little metal frame. She remembers the grape arbor. She talks about, "the sweet peas smelled so good, but you can't eat them, the snap dragons, that don't bite, and the horses across the fence in the barnyard were a backdrop for the huge garden."

He prepared the soil and did most of the irrigation. At harvest time, children and grandchildren traveled miles from their homes to help Grandpa and Grandma.

Grandpa said, "Everyone eats corn so everyone shares the work."

The older boys helped Grandpa collect the corn into tubs. They brought it to the driveway and the shucking began. Silks clung to clothes and hands and made a sticky mess on the driveway.

Everyone big enough to use a sharp knife trimmed the ends and the bug-eaten portions.

Grandma and her daughters and daughters-in-law gathered in the small kitchen and continued the work. They cooked the corn in big steaming pots and cooled it before they cut off the kernels and froze them. Every family took some home.

Of course, there was plenty of eating to be done as the corn cooled. There seemed to be a race to see who could eat the most with butter dripping off hands. Someone usually brought up memories of a cousin who ate more at reunions than anyone else.

Some people grabbed an ear and ate from one end to the other and back again. Some ate the delicious corn around and around from one end to the other. Some liked the mature ears and some liked the baby stage. Grandma, with her false teeth, couldn't get every last bit so she used a knife to scrape the cob to get the rest. Either way, it was messy and no one cared; it was finger licking good.

Friends near and far benefited from Grandpa's kindness. I remember a few stories which included assisting a few of the Navajo men. If they needed cash, they brought a watch or, some other item, for collateral. He accepted the item and kept it until the man returned with cash. He never asked why they needed a loan. Of course, he didn't tell those stories. He left them for others to share.

Zella said, "Sunday was very important to him. He honored the Sabbath more than anyone I knew. He took great care dressing for meetings and being prompt was top priority. After church, he spent hours in his recliner reading church books and magazines. He had a collection in the bookcase and was always willing to share. I remember reading Charlie's Monument."

His desire to be prompt with everything extended to visitors leaving early enough to arrive home before late at night. Zella may remember, as I do, he tried to rush our family out the door when he thought we needed to leave.

If local visitors were in his home close to his bedtime he might say, “Turn off the lights before you leave,” as he rose from his chair and headed to the bedroom. It was an unmistakable hint.

Zella remembers bubble gum! “When Grandpa was older and Grandma had already passed away, I took my family of seven to his home for a visit. He had bags and bags of bubble gum. He loved sharing it with my children, daring them to stuff as many pieces as possible into their mouths. His ornery side of previous years seemed to have softened and we had a pleasant visit.

His ornery side was almost a joke, just part of his personality. Some people realized it was a cover-up for the emotion he wanted to hide. He loved his family dearly and visits often brought a few tears.

In the lonely months after Grandma's death, he loved company. I often sat on the porch with him for a visit. When it came time for me to leave, he gave me a hard hug, looked teary and said, “You've made my day. Come back again.”

If my visits to his house did not come often enough he came to visit me. I was usually at work in our gift shop downtown. He got on his scooter and crossed Main Street, making traffic give him the right-of-way. It was never a problem because he did it so often that local drivers were accustomed to it.

When he got to my door, he couldn't easily get off the scooter and open the door. He reached out his cane and tapped on the glass. I never wondered who was there. He greeted me with a hug and a big smile. We visited a while about this and that. When he was finished talking, he headed toward the door and told me, “Come see me.” I helped him out and watched until he was safely across the street.

Even though Grandpa and Grandma are no longer here, the younger generations enjoy retelling their favorite memories about life and visits to the Old Mountain Home.

###

One Helluva Commute

by

DEUM

My teeth chattered. Goose bumps threatened to morph me into a creature from Star Wars. It must have been sub-zero that predawn morning. I tripped on a piece of petrified wood, stumbled in the loose red dirt, and cursed the dark.

I glanced up and, awestruck at the crisp clarity of the Milk Way, forgot my sore toe and frozen breath. The galaxy stretched across a sky full of brilliant planets and stars. My little piece of Arizona's Colorado Plateau was illuminated with a cosmic glow. The celestial light-show pointed me to my frosty pickup.

I pried my icy fingers from the bite of the frozen door handle. My sphincter puckered as I placed my butt on frigid upholstery. The blessed truck battery turned the engine over first try. Another forty-five mile commute ahead. Clock in at 7 A.M. Another day, another dollar.

Nothing in my Bostonian youth had prepared me for this. This was no subway commute! I was practiced by now. It still didn't make the deep winter trek any easier. At least the mud would be frozen solid for the first ten miles. I shifted and crept up the driveway hoping yesterday's bright, distant Arizona sun had melted enough ice off the pavement to make the last thirtyfive miles somewhat less treacherous.

I turned the heat on high gritting my clattering teeth as the first blasts hit me like a winter gale on the Charles River Bridge. By the time I reached the swing gate, it blew tepid. I imagined my blue lips beginning to thaw.

I shivered my way through opening the gate, pulling through and closing it behind me. The cab began to feel more like a refrigerator than a deep freeze. The possibilities of the road stretched before me.

Experience told me I wouldn't be bored. Suicidal rabbits and potholes to dodge, rutted roads to navigate, cows with hides blacker than the night around any given corner, the occasional odd crazy driver. These would require all my attention and skill if I wanted to make it to work on time and unscathed. These and so much more.

I'd left the concrete corridors and tarmac covered terrain. I'd felt my hands and feet in the dirt. I'd seen the magic of uncluttered skies. My senses had expanded. I'd found a Sisterhood of sensitives and learned the power of Spirit and Ritual. My connection with All-That-Is deepened and became conscious. This had changed the commute more than anything.

I shook my long, thick hair; shrugged my shoulders, and prepared to go the distance physically and metaphysically from the rugged, housebuilding, energy healing, tribal drumming hippy woman I was to the highly educated, experienced, skilled, lifesaving RN I also was. I was and am a two-world walker. The one hour commute was sufficient for the transformation.

The cab's ever-cozier temperature allowed me to begin my traveling ritual. My morning chant rose in my throat in gratitude for the power and beauty of the precious predawn silence. Then three breaths of protection for my body and my aura (the energy field that organizes all beings into the bodies that we have and connects us to Earth and to the All-That-Is). Breaths to shield me from the dangers of the road and the psychic and physical toxins of the ER where I worked. I chuckled at the paradox of connecting my auric root, to the rutted, hard packed Earth even as it flowed beneath me at thirty-five mph. Prayers formed on my lips for my beloveds, for the land, the country, the world, the universe. Through it all mindfulness, present moment awareness, kept me alert for the next placid cow sleeping in the middle of the road.

Five miles out I hit billows of hoarfrost. *Could be dicey getting through the wash to "Nincompoop Ranch" (*as my husband and I called it). Irresponsible farming had left the fields a dust bowl in the wind. The icy fog would make it hard to avoid the dogs and livestock the fools always let roam the road between their fences.

I greeted the Spirit Lingerer on the east rim of Hay Hollow wash. I remembered first sensing him years ago. Initially I felt fear and uncertainty about my safety. But he was willing to deepen the connection quickly, and it became clear he had been a part of the land for a long time. He was a Protector long ago. He greeted me solemnly and benignly on every trip. Today his aspect was much darker than usual.

I slowed for the dip into the wash and reached a practiced hand into my food box for my carefully packed breakfast. The apple slice smelled sweet as I brought it to my mouth and downshifted up, out of the wash.

Damn! There ahead. A large, still, dark shape barely visible through the icy mist. I slowed further. Dread filled my heart.

Fear! Turmoil! Confusion! These slammed my psyche as I inched toward the figure ahead. Its hide, not yet cool, steamed in the frosty air. I closed in. I barely made out 4 legs, each one trapped nearly to the belly in the metal grated cattle guard. My gaze traveled to the hanging head. No air escaped the nostrils. Not a twitch rustled the mane. The horse's eyes showed only white. They never blinked.

I hit the breaks as a ragged breath turned into a mournful whistle on my lips. This horse was dead. No doubt about it. It just hadn't figured that out yet.

I sat stunned and battling for center amid the wordless ethereal assault. The mare was caught in a maelstrom of terror and disorientation. I was caught behind its massive carcass an hour from my professional obligation.

Breathe! Again! I had no time to mourn the creature's sorry, soul-trapped Bardo state. *Gaia, Earth Mother, help me!* I was in over my head.

The next breath brought fury. Nincompoops had done this! What kind of rancher lets horses wander in the dark boxed between two fences and two cattle guards? All this suffering from their neglect or ignorance. Either way, I raged and cursed their folly.

Breathe! Again! I forced myself to reach out to the All-That-Is. All my rage and curses would not help this poor animal or the night nurse waiting for my relief. I needed to find my center, handle this. Now!

Logic told me I could probably squeeze by the rump if I drove on the furthest edge of the road. Anger told me I could then drive to the ranch house and confront the assholes who let this gentle creature come to such a tortured end. Compassion told me I should immediately make the psychic connection needed to help this increasingly panicked spirit.

Every fiber of my soul fought that necessity. I didn't have the balls to reach into such agony, to touch the mare and help her leave her corpse behind.

Horse. My totem and my heritage. Pictures from ancient family stories flooded my mind. The very meaning of my Polish name-Ulan:

Horse Soldier. Her death was too much for me! I wanted to flee her pain and never look back.

Breathe! Again!

Gaia glued my gaze to the miasma of chaotic formlessness around the horse's remains. Gently she asked, "Did you run from the trauma patients, those with broken bones, amputations or hemorrhaging? Could you forgive yourself if you ran from this?"

The next breath brought calm resolve. I shifted to first and eased forward with the truck and my mind.

Relief! Help! The mare's flood of gratitude as she recognized my intention to assist tore at my heart and hardened my resolution. *You are not alone!* I surrounded her with silent white light and deep caring. She began to settle. Her fear diminished and confusion dominated her energy field. Thankfully, she was past physical pain. With a mental stroke to her aura to comfort her, I promised to explain in a moment. Then I turned up Nincompoop drive. Time to vent the wrath inside of me.

Breathe! Again! I struggled to quash the ire and practiced a cold, clear message of the facts. Rage was winning.

I felt my eyes flashing, my face flushed despite the frigid temperatures. I rapped hard on the first door with a light behind it. No response. The door rattled with my second blows. I was ready to pounce.

The knob turned, the door squeaked open, but no one stood before me to receive my tirade. Then I looked down at tangled blonde locks and sleepy blue eyes. She was probably four.

"Get your parents." My words were stern and brief. She only looked perplexed. A little louder but not unkindly, "Get your parents!"

She turned and toddled off. My anger dissipated in the bounce of her curls. I got a grip on myself and remembered my dual purpose. Help the mare, get to work. *Focus! Don't waste time on these idiots.*

My foot tapped the seconds until an even sleepier woman with hair mirroring her daughter's mop waddled to the door.

A breath, and then "I think you have a dead horse in the east cattle guard." Cold and clear. I thanked the All-That-Is for that small blessing of self-control.

She looked as confused as the child, saying "Wha…?"

"A dead horse! Yours! In the cattle guard. You'll want to take care of it. There's more traffic coming." As understanding and dismay broke upon her face, I turned away and trotted to my idling truck.

The shield of my anger gone I crumpled into the seat, found the gearshift and drove. My duties would have only a few extra minutes to wait.

It took fifteen miles to help the dead mare understand she was done with her body, another five to guide her to see the path free of this plane. At that point I lost contact. I could only hope she ascended and couldn't help wondering what I'd find on my return home.

At the hospital, the night nurse I relieved was glad to see me in her sweet forgiving way. My ministrations turned to the physical as my shift began.

Thirteen hours later, the cattle guard was empty of corpses and souls. Driving up the east side of the wash, I felt the Protector. He nodded a terse acknowledgment of my obligation met.

One helluva commute.

###

Pearls
By
Kendra Rogers

Vina shoved a clip into her blonde hair so she could apply her eyelash extensions. She picked up tweezers to remove the new set from the package.

Her husband Dave appeared in the bedroom door of their Concho mobile home. "You have a windfall of easy money?"

"Yep." She laughed. "Bill Rawley's old lady is out of town. I'm going to clean his house this morning."

"Like you eviscerated that old guy's house in Albuquerque six weeks ago?"

She snorted. "The word 'eviscerate' sounds like gutting a fresh caught fish."

"Isn't that what you did?"

"Pretty much." She tried to keep a straight face as she applied glue to her upper lids.

"You did good." Dave slapped her on the seat.

"Stop that." Her curls rolled as her head shook. "You made me get glue on my face."

"We got over four thousand off that job."

"Almost as good as that old biddy's place in Pinetop. I still wish you hadn't sold that pink diamond ring we got off her. I wanted that for myself."

"You'll get another. You can't go around the White Mountains wearing something people could recognize. And I got six thou for it."

"I could have kept it hidden till we move on to Idaho. Nobody there would know it was hot."

Dave changed the subject. "I forgot to tell you, last Tuesday in Gallup, I found a box of cash in the fridge."

"And we got paid twelve bucks an hour for cleaning the guy's house." She giggled. "By the time he woke up, we were out of New Mexico and had a different vehicle."

Vina made special brownies for her cleaning clients. After a couple of them, Dave could even bring in a furniture dolly to haul out their victim's possessions. If the client started to wake up, she flirted with him and fed him another brownie.

Dave studied her four feet, eleven inch, size two figure. Lonely men could not resist her charm.

"I have more fantastic news," Vina said. "Two weeks ago when I was at church in Show Low, I saw the Rawley bitch wearing real good lookin' pearls. A double strand."

"Was that the morning you got baptized? How many times you been dunked now?"

"I lost track."

When they moved to a new town, Vina checked out the local churches, attended the camp meetings and retreats. She knew how to talk the "god talk," even carried a worn Bible they had stolen off one of their victims.

Once she joined a church, the other members would try to convert Dave. They received many invitations to Sunday dinner, allowing them to look for prospective victims.

At just the right time, Vina would give them her business card. Depending on the circumstances, she had one that said "Home Janitorial Specialist" and another proclaiming her a "Certified Nursing Assistant."

Vina finished putting on her face, then walked to the closet. "You would've been proud of me at the Saldas' place yesterday. There was a twenty dollar bill on the coffee table. Thought about picking it up, then decided to leave it so they'd know they can trust me."

"Good girl."

She began pulling on her blue satin shorts.

"You don't look like a cleaning lady in that hot outfit. You're only supposed to wear those pants when we're alone." His fingers trailed across her shoulder, then down the front of her shirt. "Just seeing you slide them on lights a bonfire. Come on, now, you can take five minutes before you head over to Rawley's place."

She waved her husband off with the back of her hand. "I promise I'll be back with that double strand of pearls. I'll bet Jack will give us a pile of cash for them. We can have quite a party with that kind of money."

"I wish you'd put out my fire right now." Dave lit a cigarette. "But it's a good idea to wear your shiny shorts for the job. It will make him fall in love with you."

"Exactly. His wife went to Nevada to take care of her sister. Old Man Rawley will be lonely and easy."

***

Vina held the cell phone close to her ear. "Get over here right now. There's a locked gun cabinet. Bring a dolly. It's heavy. You can pick the lock later."

"How about Rawley?" Dave asked. "Is he out of it yet?"

"By the time you get here, he'll be unresponsive. I sat on his lap. Gave him a French kiss. He's in love. He was more than happy to eat my brownies."

Dave laughed. "I'm on my way."

Vina sighed. She had seen Rawley's bank statements. *We should leave all this stuff and try to get guardianship of this guy. We'd be rolling in dough. I don't think we could get away with killing his old lady, but we could run her off.*

She and Dave could get a quick divorce, then she could marry Rawley. *If I kept him drugged up and claim he's not competent, then I could bring Dave in to help take care of him.*

But Dave would never go for it. He liked to get in and out fast, then move on.

While Vina waited for Dave to arrive, she scooted things off the kitchen counters into boxes. Anything she thought she could sell or use, even the dish towels and canned goods. She sat the containers near the door for her husband to cart out.

In the bedroom, she found a nice-looking dresser. *I could sell that easy.* She pulled open the drawers, finding the jewelry box and the pearl necklace she'd seen on the old biddy. She crumpled the double strand into her pocket, then jerked out a ruby choker.

Dammit. The red necklace broke and pieces scattered on the floor. *I can sweep it up later. Let's see what else is here.*

When Dave arrived, he had their friend Clayton with him. Clayton had helped on a couple other big jobs. Vina fumed but said nothing. *Now we have to split it three ways.*

But after she saw Clayton steady the dresser on the dolly as they took it down the steps, Vina was happy to have the extra help.

A little later Dave found a bucket full of .22 shells. He laughed. *Rawley asked us to clean the house. Here we go.*

Clayton trotted into the room holding a key ring. "I found this on a hook beside the kitchen door. It says 'back shed'."

"Let's go have a look."

The storage building was a prize. They found a generator, tools, and a collection of Louis L'Amour novels. Clayton helped Dave wrestle the generator into the pickup while Vina packed the books into boxes.

After they finished cleaning out the shed, they locked it and returned the key to its place. Clayton strapped the load down and Vina began working on the bathroom.

"Hey, Vina," Dave said. "Is there a basement?"

"No." She stooped to pick up a couple of pill bottles that had fallen on the floor. *Percoset and Vicodin, now that's a good find.*

"The old turd is waking up."

"All right. I'll take care of him."

"Sit on his lap and see if you can get his wallet."

"No. If we leave the cash in his wallet, he'll think we're his friends. We're just cleaning the mess out of his house." She grabbed another brownie from the kitchen.

Clayton came inside. "What's with his dogs? They're sprawled out in the yard. They're still breathing, but their eyes look dead and their tongues are hanging out."

Vina and Dave laughed.

"I gave them some of these." Vina raised the brownie. "They're big Labs. They'll be okay." She chuckled. "When we hit that place in Oklahoma City, the smaller mutt died."

Clayton said nothing, but began to worry about his future. *Old man Rawley's nothing but skin and bones. If her recipe can kill a dog, it could happen to him. If he kicks off, I'll be an accomplice to murder.*

***

The tires on Dave's truck threw gravel when he turned into his driveway. His face throbbed and his left eye had begun to swell shut. *Wait till I get my hands on her.*

He leaped from the pickup and threw open the back door of the mobile home, screaming, “Let me tell you about them genuine, high dollar pearls.”

Vina ran. She had seen her husband in this mood before and it was going to be bad for her.

“Get over here, you little bitch.”

She cowered into the closet, pressing her ninety-four pound frame against the wall.

Spit dribbled from the corner of Dave’s mouth. His face was purple with rage and the veins stood out like cords under his skin.

Vina slid to the floor and curled up in the fetal position with her arms over her head to protect herself.

“Jack said those pearls were worth *two dollars!* He gave me a beating and now you’re getting the same.”

###

A Piece of Earth
By
TDL

I sit in silence against the back wall of my bedroom observing life through a large window. I hear quacking sounds which filter through the glass. Dawn is rising and with it, a new adventure awaits.

These characters are fowl, different shades of brown highlighted by the sun. Their feathers flutter wildly, forced back against their bodies by a gust of wind.

I had named all four ducks: BG (which stands for Bitch Gimp), who chases Bob (a large drake, bought on a whim in Globe AZ), Blue (a Swedish drake), and Sitting duck, (a large bright white female). They waddle around in a large pen made from two trampolines stacked on top of each other. Picture this; top rail bolted together legs on ground and legs in the air. The ground cover is cut grass and straw which offers an easy floor to walk on. They start swimming in the large kiddy pools filled with water, which are in different locations, so there will be no fighting among the males over the females.

***

My childhood was all country life. My siblings and I played outside from morning to night. I didn't know about cities or crowds of people all living together. I only knew the woods and rivers, moon and stars.

Dad died when I was in my teens. Mom left the Earth when I was in my twenties, I became disconnected from my family members as they married and moved elsewhere. I found myself with strong feelings to see and smell other landscapes, So I left everything I knew and loved. I bought a new van, then hit the road! My dog and I traveled for ten years, enjoying the pleasure of sharing with so many people east to west across the USA.

My age grew higher and the money became lower, which made me decide to settle down. "*Where I wondered?*" I felt at peace in the high desert. I had always lived on other peoples' land and was very content. Now I felt a need for security/stability, I thought, "*a piece of land of my own.*"

***

Adobe whose land I lived on, came home from town and jumped out of her truck hollering "Hey wimmin! I heard about cheap land up north. Let's go check it out." Three days later four women in a Chevy truck, drove five hours to see a parcel of property. An old cowboy realtor named Merrill took us far out into wild country with no houses in view. He pulled up next to a newly hung "for sale" sign. We hopped out of the truck and shamelessly started filling our pockets with rocks. There were so many different shapes, colors, and sizes.

Magic Dance held up a glittering fist size stone. "I need to take this home, it is so incredible!"

Janet turned to Merrill. "Is this petrified wood I just found? I love all the mix of colors."

Before Merrill could answer Adobe screeched. "I just found some pottery. This place is magic."

We ran here and there picking rocks up. Merrill just sat and watched, scratching his head. I wandered along the ridge where the sandstone rocks cascaded to the valley floor. Then and there I fell in love, plain and simple. This land had a vista that seemed to never end. Big boulders and tall snags dotted this piece of Earth. I wanted to live here forever! Merrill asked us if we wanted to stay the night at his house.

"Yes!" we chorused. The next day we drove back to Tucson. On the way, we talked and three of the women thought paying for land over twenty years was too long a commitment and bowed out. I felt disappointed and could not do this on my own. I let it go.

Months later, I was sitting in a friend's house and a woman named Judith walked in. She overheard me talking about the inexpensive land up north. She asked more questions and spoke of others who might be looking to "invest".

Three weeks later, five of us met Merrill again; I was thrilled to walk on these forty acres once more. We stood on the ridge together and committed to buy.

It was a thirty-minute drive to sign the Deed. On the way, my thoughts ran, *Wow! Whoa! what am I doing? Committing with four wimmin whom I know zero about!* This was going to be my life and I wanted more info about them. I collected phone numbers and worked on learning more. It was not to be. Decades passed and I still do not know much about the other four women who helped me find a place to live. I am forever grateful for them.

***

How to start my life on barren land? I thought living for a time on each perimeter would give me a sense of the best place to put a house.

Starting on the north side of the property, there was a road leading into the valley on the easement, set back in the trees, I built a small enclosure of reed fencing. Six by eight feet with a dirt floor; I wanted to be able to leave no trace as I moved around the land. When the first rain occurred, I learned about red clay! I walked across the clearing and became taller as the clay stuck on my shoes. Nope! Not this border.

I moved everything to the direction of the East. This side had more trees and less mud, warmer too.

My new dog Jack, (my old dog died before living here) who loved the freedom of no fences or other people around, ran with delight. My nearest neighbor was two miles away. Time stood still as I lived simple and free, naked under the sun and moon. I woke each sunrise not knowing the exact date of the month.

I lived in the east for two weeks. The land was sandy loam with tall Juniper trees and very little cactus. I set up another hut back from the edge of the big rocks tumbling into the valley. When the sun came up behind the ridge across the valley, Jack and I walked to greet the dawn. Camp fire coffee, dog food and crackers with peanut butter to nourish us. For me this was my way of life. It was so quiet, just the coyotes, birds, and wind. When rain came, I threw plastic over my hut and stayed dry. Then I moved south and found I really liked this side of the forty and decided to build a sturdier home. The money crunch arrived, just as I was feeling established. Now to find a job and save for a house.

I realized that I could make more money back east, so I left home. I moved to New England for two years and saved enough to build a house. I decided to not include the others in my choice where to build and started making a home. With just a saw, hammer, and ladder, I created a twelve by twelve structure which was not square and had a dirt floor. I put in a wood stove and three windows (not level either) and lived happily for two years. Sometime I would wonder about the other women who owned this wonderful place with me, yet knew they bought it as an "*investment*". The only contact with my land partners was tax time, a phone call and a check in the mail.

The money was all used up again, so I went to find work. I made enough in eighteen months to stay for a year, I drove back home and had a well dug which allowed me to grow food. I had never garden before so,

I just winged it. I found that truck bed liners work great! That year I ate well.

Living on one area of the land offered insight into animal lives. One night while keeping warm by the fire, a "HUGE" horned Owl landed on a large snag with the full moon behind her. I was awestruck and blessed. She stayed awhile then silently swooped down over my head. Mule deer and Antelope cross the valley and climb the mesa.

One day Jack and I were on a walk and his hair stood out all over his body, "Jack what's up?" He sniffed and turned toward a fence. I crouched down and saw a perfect foot print made after the rain and thought, "What in hell?" The print showed a heel of a person and four claws. I had never seen this foot track before. I followed it to the fence and found a piece of black rough hair and knew it was a bear, which I did not know lived in this area. I have seen a Bobcat, a baby road-runner swimming in a puddle with its mother, and so many other beings. This was better than television. Life was full.

***

Living east of town, I listen to stories from the town folks about the bad people who rob and do drugs out here, I even heard of cannibals and laugh out loud at that rumor. Over the years many people have moved near me and in the valley, Gun fire, dogs barking, vehicles driving by, my peace has changed. I made new friends and shied away from the neighbors who were not friendly. When I tell my friends back in New England I live outside the town of Snowflake which is named from two last names, (Mr. Snow and Mr. Flake), they laugh and ask, does it really snow there? People have always been friendly towards me here and I feel welcome even though I am not a Mormon.

***

My most fearful time occurred years apart and started with a man who squatted across the road/border in an abandon silver RV. He drove a jeep and hauled fifty-five gallon barrels of water from somewhere. I would hear him at all hours and wondered what he was about. I was hiking around my forty one day when he showed up. I asked him to stay on his side of the road, he laughed and said, "Well, we're the only ones up here." I felt sick seeing the smirk and glint in his eye. Another time he said "Hey! I had a dream about you." Then he winked at me!

My mind went to how could I protect myself. I thought, *Cross bow and burn it*? He always carried a very large cup, had stinky body odor, yet had barrels of water to wash in. He just kept walking over to my property, offering me no respect. So, I went south for months, hoping his intention would come back to him sevenfold, so says the Bible, and I left it at that.

Four months later while driving back home, I saw yellow caution banners flapping in the wind. White things were blowing everywhere. His Jeep was gone so I drove closer. There where Styrofoam takeout boxes littering the grass, a large pile of other trash outside of the trailer; bed, chairs, kitchen stuff, garbage all over. Beside the trailer were gallon rum jars and quarts of cola faded in the sun! Now I know why the huge cup. I called the Police. Apache county sheriffs had caught him. He had a warrant and was stealing water from the local rancher for his marijuana plants. YEA! My peace returned; he would never be here again.

Another scare was with a neighbor who shot dogs. While reading in my room, I heard shots and walked outside to check my dog. I stood still in my driveway looking for the shooter when a bullet flew past my head. I hit the ground and saw legs by a tree. I started screaming; "Hey the bullets are coming this way." Zing! Another shot. I shouted, "It's against the law shooting so close!"

He hollered back, "So call a cop!"

Well, at this point in my life I didn't own a cell phone, so the next day I drove to the station. An Officer heard both of our stories, and

I quote "Well it's your story against his. Did you see where the bullets went?"

I retorted, "When they were flying by my head I didn't turn to look." This guy was here for the duration and no amount of talking changed anything. I built a fence around the house to protect my animals. He still shoots rabbits for his cat to eat.

As time moved on my world grew larger—more animals and new friends. Thirty-five years have passed and now I have comfort and ease that I enjoy. One day recently I called Amy in California and encouraged her to come see this wonderful place. For over thirty years now her answer has been the same, "someday!"

Life is wonderful and finally my age caught up with the money. Retired and at peace. Funny, my friends in New England still ask if it snows here! Living simply on this piece of the planet, I am never bored and always thankful. Six ducks, three cats, three dogs all stretch their bodies then turn to wait for the sun to rise on a new adventure.

###

OUT EAST

by

Conni de Wolfe

They call it *Out East,*
this land where we live.
where people are friendly,
with their hearts they do give.
The hills can be rugged,
the dirt is bright red,
with the trees mostly Cedar,
the land is not dead.
A coyote, a lynx, an eagle or two,
where wildlife does flourish,
under skies that are blue.
You'll see grazing cattle
and often a deer,
but after a rain,
the land is sparkling with cheer.
So I'm glad I am living upon this bright land,
enjoying warm feelings with my family and friends.

Hearts That Care

By

Conni de Wolfe

See the earth in boughs of green,
shining waters, sparkling , gleam,
watch the birds in winging flight,
hear the children's laughter bright.

Joys of summer, joys of love,
rays of sunshine from above,
memories of our loved ones shared,
captured in the hearts that care.

Wagon Wheels

By

Connie de Wolfe

Wagon wheels bring memories about the long ago,
of straining, pushing, rolling, fast and slow.
Across the plains and rivers, they did roll and strive,
carrying dreams and hopes of those not now alive.
So look and listen friend, before you start to go,
you'll hear a little whisper as the wheel says, "Westward Ho!"

Seasons

By

Nico Crowkiller-Scherr

The wind whips, raking its cold fingers through the high desert and mountains.

Along with it comes snow.

In some areas just a dusting to lay atop the cacti.

In others, it's measured in feet on the tops of plateaus and mesas.

Rains come to the desert. Light in drizzle, the spring breeze warms the cold land as new life begins.

The long prong antelope give birth as do the rabbits and coyote.

The trees that have been planted on surrounding ranches start to blossom, bringing a sense of change.

The summer heat elevates to the low one hundred mark.

Dark clouds form as the humidity climbs for the monsoon to come to parched lands.

Washes flow freely with speed and the intent of bringing dead-falls, rock and sand to dislodge what lay in its pathway.

The coyotes call at the full moon and bring song to the desert.

The temperature cools. A light breeze brings forth the new found chill to the air.

Leaves in the town's trees change into beautiful gold, yellow, and red.

They twist and fall, swirling in the winds.

The seasons have turned once again in the high desert and mountains of northern Arizona.

I am blessed to live here. Thank You Lord for this time in my life.

###

Sometimes Love Whispers

By

Trish Zaabel

The mid-morning July sun beat down with intensity. The air was humid and thick promising another round of afternoon rains. The weatherman predicted yesterday's storm system would clear out of northeastern Arizona but as usual, Mother Nature had other plans.

Jasmine McBride had started at five-thirty. Early morning was the best time to get yard work done. She was proud of her small garden and orchard. Watering, weeding, and checking for bugs had taken the good hours of the day. Thick, red hair was tucked under a floppy wide brimmed hat to protect her light skin from the sun.

I need to cut the grass she thought opening her tool shed. She let her eyes adjust to the dim sunlight streaming through the wall boards. The building was actually an old barn built sometime before the house, which had 1906 carved on a cornerstone of the foundation.

Jasmine loved the place. Partly because it still stood strong and partly because she owned it. There was no other place in the world she would rather be.

Jasmine checked the gas in the push mower and pulled it to the front yard. Glancing at her wristwatch. Nine-thirty.

I should be done by ten. Plenty of time to get ready before one.

A half hour later, Jasmine was glad she had decided to only

landscape a small part of her two acres. She wiped her brow with her long sleeved shirt as she let the mower engine die. The rumble of her brother's diesel engine told her she had company.

"Let me help you with that," Tom offered as he walked up to her.

"Your timing is perfect. I'm finished but you could put the mower away for me. I'm wilting."

"You sure are." He wrinkled his nose playfully. "You're a mess and you stink like sweat too."

Jasmine was in the process of pulling her work gloves off. Even her hands were wet from the heat of the morning.

"Ladies perspire, they do NOT sweat." She sniffed then swatted him with her gloves.

"Sorry, darling, you stink" Tom drawled in a southern gentleman's accent as he pushed the mower away.

It was an old joke between the siblings. Their mother's family could trace lineage back to colonial Virginia. She had been raised in a privileged household with the children of many of Washington D.C.'s elites as her friends. Elizabeth Clarke had admired Jackie Kennedy Onassis. After meeting the sophisticated woman at a garden party she tried to emulate that same cultured and poised look as a teenager. Mother had very strict rules about correct behavior. Formal etiquette was deeply ingrained. Jasmine and Tom spent much of their childhood mocking it.

Mother's one rebellious act had been their father, Flynn McBride. Elizabeth met the tall, devilish man at a dude ranch in Scottsdale. She was on vacation with her parents. He was a horse wrangler working his way through college. It had been a breath-taking, whirlwind romance according to Elizabeth that left her pregnant at twenty years old. Of course, Flynn had not been acceptable husband material in the eyes of the older Clarkes. Their father would not be denied his opportunity for happiness and a family so convinced Elizabeth to return home with him.

Their mother never felt comfortable with the desert, the mountains, or at the ranch. The man was the only thing that held Elizabeth in Arizona. When he died, she left the same day as the funeral, taking fourteen year old Tom with her.

Eighteen-year-old Jasmine was left with her grief, a horse ranch, and drunken great-uncle Shay. The old man had raised the orphaned Flynn when his parents were killed in a plane crash. Jasmine felt obligated to take care of her elderly relative. Somehow, she pulled herself together to sell most of the horses to pay the debt on the property. Sobering Uncle Shay up enough to care for the remaining livestock had been more challenging. The only easy task was earning her degree as an Elementary School teacher.

Shaking off thoughts of her mother, Jasmine entered the kitchen and opened the refrigerator.

"Do you want some strawberry lemonade? I made it this morning."

"Yes, ma'am," Tom pulled off his sunglasses. Accepting the glass, he said "You should hire some kid to cut the grass for you or get a landscaping company. You're getting too old for this. I could find someone for you, if you like me to?"

Jasmine pulled off her hat and her blue eyes flashed. "I AM not that old."

Tom just lifted an eyebrow.

"Thirty six is not old." Jasmine shifted her eyes down defensively.

"It is not young either."

"I would appreciate a change of subject." She wagged a finger at him.

"Okay, can you watch the twins tonight? I want to take Alicia to Show Low for dinner and a movie."

"I can't. I have plans."

"What plans?" Tom asked casually as he sipped the lemonade.

"Bet I can talk you out of it."

"I have a date." She felt smug. *He thought she would always be available to babysit.*

Her brother had returned to Arizona from the east bringing his young wife with him. They both were ready for a simpler, quiet lifestyle after the hectic pace of the New York Stock Exchange where they worked. When her nephews were born eight months ago, Jasmine had been willing to watch them whenever needed. She figured it would be her only opportunity to experience these stages of a child's life. *That doesn't mean that I can't have a social life also.*

"With who?" Tom's voice deepened with the question.

"With whom?"

"What?" He looked confused.

"Sorry, teacher's habit."

Tom shifted to his full height of 6'5. Jasmine refused to be intimidated by his size. She knew she had her brother on defense now.

"Okay, with whom?" he grumbled.

"His name is Harry. I met him online. He's driving up from Fountain Hills right now. He is going to be here soon so I need to get moving." Jasmine rushed through the answer and started to leave the room. "Sorry I can't watch the twins for you." Jasmine didn't feel sorry at all.

"Hold it! Just wait. Let me get this straight. You are going out with a man you met online? A man that lives four hours from here?" Tom's tone rose with each question. "How do you know he's not a serial-killer? Or a sexual predator? Maybe he's already married and just wants a mistress?" He stood in front of the door, not allowing her to leave the room.

"You watch too much TV." Jasmine shook her head as she smiled at him.

"I could still be right."

She tried to ease his worry. “It was a Christian dating site.”

“So? He could have lied. Harry what?”

“He did not lie. His name is Harry Jones. He has two sons that are 7 and 9. They go to a private Christian school. He is a real estate agent in the Phoenix area. He owns his home and is on the financial board for his church. Harry is a nice, polite man.” Jasmine ended her monologue and tried to leave the room again.

“How do you know for sure?”

“Because I spent the evening with him when I was in the valley last week shopping for school supplies.”

Tom’s voice thundered as his face tightened. “You are not implying what I think you could be implying, are you?”

“You’re the one who said I was an old maid.”

“I did not and don’t change the subject on me.”

“I am a big girl and definitely old enough to make my own decisions.” Jasmine rose up to look Tom in the eye.

“I’m not going to win.” Tom sank back against the kitchen counter in defeat.

“No, you are not.”

“Okay, please be careful and call when you get home.” Her brother didn’t look happy. He was used to getting his way and could usually persuade her into agreeing with him. The fact that she was defying him gave some spunk to her step as she headed up the stairs.

***

Jasmine checked her appearance in the full length mirror one last time. She sighed. It was really rather disappointing. Sharp angles existed where she should have gentle curves. Harry wanted to do some four wheeling with his new Jeep. Jeans, cowboy boots, and a long-sleeved cotton shirt seemed like the best attire. *But what about my hair?* She most often wore it in a ponytail or a braided bun. She rarely let it frame her face and never in public. She could still hear mother say that with her hair undone, Jasmine looked like a wild child. Leaving it down made her feel a little reckless. *A semi-blind date called for recklessness.*

Jasmine didn't consider their first meeting a real date. Harry invited her to dinner at a sushi restaurant in Scottsdale. He failed to tell her it was a business meeting to celebrate the closing of a multimillion dollar land deal with corporate buyers. She felt woefully underdressed and ill prepared to socially interact with executives. Most of them had haircuts that cost more than the clothes she wore. She left early in the evening.

Jasmine was surprised when Harry called the next afternoon to plan this trip. They had very little time the previous evening to chat privately. Although, when they were alone, he had been very attentive and actually seemed interested in her. The problem was she didn't feel she fit into his world. Jasmine was a realist. She was a small town teacher who didn't appreciate big city life. Fancy and expensive were not her style.

Plain and simple. The two words fit her like a leather work glove molded to one's hand. Jasmine believed she would never be called pretty. That was a useless fantasy on her part. Like believing the romantic fairy tale her parents shared would ever happen to her.

Far better to conserve her dreams to small pleasures. A rose blooming. A child reading their first sentence. A beautiful sunset. Those were the things that Jasmine could see and know were true.

The crunch of gravel signaled Harry's arrival. Jasmine hurried from the room and down the stairs. She smoothed her hands on the front of jeans to calm her nerves. Then she opened the front door before Harry had a chance to knock.

"Oh-ah. Hello." Harry stood with his hand in midair.

Jasmine realized she appeared too eager, which flustered her more.

"Hello." She felt the unbecoming glow of red fill her face.

An awkward silence filled the space with neither knowing how to proceed. Jasmine looked over her date. He was dressed in shorts, polo shirt, flip-flops, and a sun-visor. It was a big change from the high powered broker of last week.

Harry broke the quiet. "Are you ready to go?"

"Yes, of course."

Harry took Jasmine's arm and escorted her to the lime green vehicle parked in her driveway and helped her into the seat. Jasmine was grateful for the time of day. Her elderly neighbors, the Vasquez, took naps right after lunch. She was sure they would be laughing at the ridiculous sight that the bright Jeep made. It was so out of place in this small town.

"You won't get lost in a parking lot, will you?" Jasmine asked dryly.

"I always liked this color and when I found I could get my Jeep in it, I bought one."

"Obviously."

He put his sun glasses on. Matching color.

"Oh, dear," slipped out of Jasmine's mouth.

"Everything alright?'

"Perfect." Jasmine tried to remain bubbly.

"Great, just give me directions to the best place to try this baby out."

***

Harry and Jasmine stood beside a very stuck Jeep.

"Do what I tell you and everything will be just fine." Harry's tone showed he was trying to sound in control.

If Jasmine had known this was Harry's first time driving off road she would have taken him to a different place. She warned him the Jeep could not make it up the high embankment. Now, the vehicle was high centered with one rear tire in the clay mud.

"I only have flip flops so you'll have to push. Your boots can gain traction."

"I don't think this is going to work. " Jasmine said as she eyeballed the situation.

Harry huffed out an explosion of air. "Of course it's going to work. Just push a little harder the next time I step on the gas. We can rock it out of here. I'm sure"

Jasmine wiped her brow with a dirty glove and moved in behind the right tire. Her boots made a sucking noise every time she stepped.

This is disgusting. She thought as she prepared to push on the Jeep frame. *Why didn't I listen to Tom's warnings?*

Harry yelled back. "Are you ready?"

"Yes!"

He gunned it. Tires spun and the Jeep slid sideways, throwing mud into Jasmine's face as she pushed with all her strength. The vehicle struggled to climb out of the hole. Jasmine pushed harder, slipping as it moved forward.

"Just a little more baby. We can do this." Harry said in encouragement.

"There's no 'we' in this," Jasmine yelled back.

With a final push, the Jeep broke free. Harry drove it to a high spot then looked back at Jasmine.

"Are you alright?" His face was beaming with success.

Jasmine brushed a clump of mud from her hair and straightened her six-one frame.

"What do you think?" Her voice dripped with sarcasm.

Harry's face fell. "Think of it as an adventure," he offered with a half-smile.

"Could you just take me home before that storm hits?" Jasmine pointed towards the dark clouds gathering ominously.

"Uh, sure," Harry said flatly.

Jasmine scraped most of the mud off her boots off and climbed into the Jeep. Harry stared straight ahead.

She waited for him to move. "Is there a problem?"

"I'm lost."

She sucked in a deep breath. Then another. After the third, she felt ready to talk. "We just have to find a road, any road will lead us back to the highway, eventually."

It started to rain. Big, heavy drops hit the windshield as the Jeep bounced over uneven ground.

"Is that a road?" There was hope in Harry's voice.

"No, it's a trail but trails start off a road somewhere." She was trying really hard to keep her irritation under control.

"Ok, left or right?"

Jasmine accessed the landscape. She was unfamiliar with this area but the terrain suggested that going left was the wiser choice.

"Left."

Harry eased the Jeep along the trail. Heavy rain had turned the tracks into mud already. The Jeep's big wheels flung clumps of clay everywhere.

"There's the road." This time it was Jasmine who sounded hopeful.

A red cinder rock surface told them where the road began. It gave more traction and cut down the mudslinging. But Harry could not pick up much speed.

"You call this a road?" Harry sounded skeptical. "I might get stuck in the loose rocks on this *road*."

"I can drive if you're afraid to?" Jasmine offered. Maybe she would get home quicker.

"No, it's alright." Harry eased his way down the road while daylight faded. They drove into the storm as they approached the paved highway.

Windshield wipers on full blast, Harry peered at the dark road. "Which way?"

"Right should lead us to town." She was grateful they were at least heading in the correct direction.

After a few miles, with no letup in the rain, Jasmine saw blurry emergency lights ahead.

"The wash must be out. We can't get through this way," Jasmine said. "We are either have to wait it out or drive seventy miles to get around to the next road that leads to town."

Harry gripped the steering wheel like he was ready to pull it from the dashboard. "This is too much. What have I done to deserve all these mishaps? I just wanted to explore a little with my new Jeep." He sucked in his breath, held it, and finally breathed out. "Okay, I've got a plan. I'll just drive real fast through the wash so we can get you home ASAP."

"What?" Jasmine stared at him. "You can't do that. We will be sucked under by the water current or stuck in the mud. Ever hear of the 'Stupid Motorist Law' in Arizona? I don't want to make the ten o'clock news tonight because you're an idiot!"

Harry hit the brakes hard. The vehicle jerked to a halt.

"Did you just call me an idiot?" he asked in disbelief. Harry's eyes glittered with anger as his jaw tightened. He pounded his left fist on the dash as he turned towards her.

Jasmine chose not to answer him but bolted from the Jeep instead. She felt nothing but relief as it did a U turn and sped away.

"Hey, are you okay?" A flashlight bobbed toward her.

Jasmine shivered. She was getting soaked but answered automatically. "I'm fine."

The tall, dark figure in a rain slicker, a deputy, got close enough to shine light in her face.

"Jasmine? Jasmine McBride?"

She vaguely recognized the deep voice. "Yes."

"It's Jake Gibbs. Sophie's dad. I used to be friends with your brother Tom before he left."

Jasmine tried to peer through the light.

Jake must have realized he was blinding her and lowered it. "Sorry."

"It's okay." Jasmine started shaking from the cold.

"C'mon back to the truck."

Jasmine fell in step with him. Fortunately, he was taller so he could lift his arm over her head to give some shelter. Jake led the way to the passenger side of his police truck.

"In you go."

Jasmine was grateful for the dry if not warm cab.

"Let me get the heat on." Jake said as he tried to unfold his large body out of the rain slicker in the driver's seat. "Here's my jacket," he said as he shoved the wet slicker in the back seat and grabbed the dry garment.

"Thank you." Jasmine accepted the jacket and put it on. Immediately she noticed the faint scent of his cologne. It was a clean and pleasant. Simple not overpowering like Harry's obviously expensive smell. Perhaps it was the uniform but Jasmine felt safe for the first time in hours.

He reached for his dispatch radio.

"Please don't't"

"I have to. It's policy."

Heat flooded Jasmine's face. Everyone would know by morning that she had been ditched by her date.

"Dispatch, this is Apache forty-seven. I have a stranded motorist in the car with me."

"Do you have an identity on the motorist, Apache forty-seven?"

Tanya Blair's chipper voice clearly came through the radio. Jasmine's heart sank. Tanya was the biggest gossip in the county.

"It's Jasmine McBride," Jake said with a half-smile.

"Good Lord, what's she doing out in a storm like this?" Tanya began digging for more information. "Hope she's alright?"

Through the soft light of Jake's laptop, Jasmine shot him a pleading look. *Please don't tell.*

"She'll be fine. When the wash is safe to cross, I'll drive her home."

Jasmine let out a soft sigh only to suck in another sharp breath when Tanya asked "Do you need a tow truck?"

Their eyes met and held for a moment before Jake smiled. "No, I have it covered. Apache forty-seven out."

They sat in silence for long minutes listening to strong wind and raindrops batter the truck. The windshield wipers were on full speed but could not handle the force of the storm. Visibility was limited to the small cab because of the dark sky and heavy precipitation.

"Are you going to tell me what happened?"

Jasmine opened her mouth, then closed it, not sure where to begin. "I have just been on the strangest date of my life. I believe he doesn't like me."

Jake started to laugh. Jasmine felt like an angry cat that had been thrown into a water tank. She folded her arms across her damp chest and glared.

"Easy, Jazzy Girl, easy. I am laughing with you, not at you. Probably better off without the jerk anyway."

Jasmine's face lit up. "It's been a long time since anyone called me that."

Jake stopped laughing and shifted in his seat. "Sorry, I didn't mean to be too casual. I guess I never stopped thinking of you as Jazzy Girl. I always thought your dad nailed it with the name."

"Mom hated that name. She said it encouraged me to be bold and wild. Just like my untamed hair."

Jasmine found it easy to talk with Jake. He felt familiar and safe. *There it was again. Safe. She felt protected. Like nothing would hurt her while she was with him. She had thought she would never experience that security after her dad had died.* In some small way, Jake reminded her of Flynn McBride.

As a teacher, she had been immediately drawn to his daughter, Sophie. The little girl acted much older than her other first grade students. Jasmine believed Sophie was so independent because she was raised by a single father.

"I seem to remember hearing your mother say 'Jasmine! Braid your hair'. It seemed such a shame because when you put hair up, the laughter would go away."

Jasmine studied him. "What do you mean?"

"You got quiet. It was like when you put your hair up, you couldn't be yourself."

"Ladies are to be admired not heard."

Jake snorted. "THAT sounds like something your mother would say."

"Gentlemen prefer demure, soft-spoken female companions."

Jake rolled his eyes. "I would like to think that I am a gentleman, at least more of a man than the jerk who abandoned you. I prefer a woman who speaks her mind."

"Oh." Suddenly, Jasmine felt shy and nervous. Maybe Jake wasn't so safe after all.

The rain had stopped. The barren landscape seemed strangely still after the passing of a violent thunderstorm. Dark clouds covered the sliver of light from a half moon night. Eerily calm.

"I'll be right back." Jake exited the truck. Twenty minutes later, he returned to radio in that the wash was clear. "Barricades are down and the highway is open."

"Apache forty-seven, Tom McBride called because he couldn't reach his sister on her cell phone. Seems she was out with a strange man. I told him not to worry, she's with you."

"Now, Tanya, are you saying I'm strange?" Jake playfully asked Tanya. He glanced over at Jasmine to share a smile. She squirmed in her seat. She realized she jumped out of the Jeep so fast she lost her cell phone.

Tanya chuckled. "Well, if the shoe fits…"

Like a true gentleman, Jake came to her rescue. "I said I will be driving her home. Apache forty-seven out."

Jake shut the flashing lights off and shifted into drive. They drove in silence, while Jasmine searched for something to say.

"At least your job is not as dangerous as being a cop in a big city."

"Sometimes it's more dangerous if you want the truth of this county."

"I don't understand, it's such a rural area. You've got ranchers, farmers, and summer cabins. I wouldn't think that population creates a lot of trouble."

"When the call comes, you're it and it might take a while for backup. There's only so many of us to cover a large region. Apache County is almost the same square mileage as Maryland. " Jake turned in his seat to look at her "Even though we have the most land designated as Indian Reservation of any county in the U.S. there's still no time for hesitation, no second guessing. That's life or death."

That ended their conversation until Jake stopped in front of her house. Jasmine took his jacket off and left it on the seat. She started to get out but Jake met her at the side of the truck. For a big man, he sure moved silent and quick.

"I will walk you to the door." He smiled as he shut the truck door behind her. "In case of strangers lurking in the bushes."

"Of course, you never know." She chuckled slightly nervous by his close proximity.

At the door, Jake surprised her by taking her hand. He gave it a gentle squeeze before letting it go. "Would you like to join us on the Fourth?"

"Um, sure. I guess that would be fun." Heat flooded her face. *What a stupid thing to say to a man when he just asked you out!*

"Great, I'll call you tomorrow."

"Okay." Jasmine entered the house. Shutting the door, she leaned against the solid wood surface. Her stomach fluttered. She could still smell him. It was as if he was wrapping his arms around her.

"Oh my."

She had just agreed to a date with Jake Gibbs. Somehow that sounded far more reckless than going out with plain old Harry Jones.

###

An Unusual Friendship

By

Connie de Wolfe

Here he was again, in a place he swore he'd never return to. Lieutenant Curtiss L. Tappon, USPN, United Space Navy, stood under the only tree left on the barren countryside where he had grown up. It had been a valley ranch not too far from Concho, Arizona.

The tree had grown taller since than the last time he was here as a young space-cadet in 2058. It stood as though guarding the valley where nothing had grown in ten years but red dust. The wind played with it swirling and wreaking havoc with the crimson powder.

The feelings that ran through him hurt even more now than the last time, but he could visualize the way it had been before. The memory he carried in his heart moved like a kaleidoscope across his mind.

He saw the three generations old, two story ranch house with its long rambling porch. He saw his mother sitting on the swing shelling peas for dinner. His small sister, Cathy, was petting the kitten in her lap.

Here came Uncle Ben with Curt's little brother, Willie, tagging behind, their arms full of wood for the evening fire. Dad was down by the barn tossing hay to the horses he was so proud of.

Anger and pain overwhelmed him at that moment, so strongly he didn't feel the tears stream down his face and it almost dropped him to his knees.

The damned Destroyers had wiped out his entire family from the oldest to the youngest baby. They waste to the entire valley where now not even a weed would grow, just rivers of red dust.

Only his oldest brother, Charles, better known as Hawk, now a commander on the space ship USPF, United Space Frigate, Patton, was still alive, and Curt had just learned that the ship was missing somewhere near Saturn.

That was why he was out here in the wilderness alone. He needed to try and pull himself back together.

Curt gathered his inner forces, and thought to himself, I *guess I'd better find a place to camp for the night.* He turned, not looking back at the barren valley, and walked away for the last time.

Curt thought of a spot he camped at long ago. If he remembered correctly it had a snow runoff stream close by it.

***

Curt jerked awake from the same old dream of his family. Not moving, he listened but all he heard was the chill September wind gusting down from the mountains of the high Arizona desert and the quiet babbling of the nearby stream. He lay stiffly in his bedroll; the abrupt awakening had set him on his guard. Curt put his hand on the knife he always kept close at hand. He then remembered his dream and flinched as the word Destroyers crossed his mind.

They had appeared ten years ago and wreaked death and devastation, apparently at random, upon an unwary population.

They had never been seen in all these years, and when their ships were almost captured, they would self-destruct. Earth had become a world besieged by the unknown.

Curt pushed the pain back into the mental box where he kept it hidden. His features resumed the granite look he usually wore, as he began to wonder what had really awakened him.

Not hearing anything out of the ordinary, he brushed his sandy, sun streaked hair away from his eyes, turned his head, and came face to face with a very large wildcat sitting quietly two feet away.

Not daring to move and barely breathing, Curt spoke softly, "Well my friend, what brings you into my camp so early? Are you lost or hungry? I'll bet you scattered my horses to hell and back."

"No," an answer came, *"your horses are still there."*

Startled, Curt's eyes darted around the camp, and not seeing anything, the hair rose on the back of his neck, "Who said that?"

"I did."

Steel grey eyes met golden yellow ones as the cat switched its tail. A warmth unlike anything he'd felt before, filled the inside of Curt's head.

"No," the voice came again, *"you not crassy. It is I who speaks."* The cat moved a step closer and the warmth again moved softly through Curt's mind.

"What's all this?" Curt asked himself aloud and sat up very aware he didn't want to startle the cat.

"I wish your help, Man," came the reply to his question.

Curt studied the cat he now recognized as a mountain lion, closely. He could see that it was young. The kitten spots were not completely faded from its coat and the cat's head and tail had not darkened into maturity.

"Curtiss Tappon, this has got to be a hallucination," he said to himself. "Been out here brooding too long. No cat can talk like that." Curt unconsciously ran his fingers through his hair. "You, you're doing that talking in my head?" he asked, feeling like a fool.

"Yess. I am call Sebastian." The cat's tail switched, and his eyes blazed. *"Listen Man, your horses fine. I need help! Pleasse!"*

"Easy, easy now, boy. Sebastian is it?" Curt asked, his hands extended before him as he backed away. "I believe you. Just let me wake up."

He hunkered down next to the still warm fire and stirred the coals. His mind was in a turmoil though his stony features showed no expression. Then in the distance he heard the loud bay of hounds on a scent, following a trail.

"They come for me."

It was then Curt made up his mind to help this unusual cat. He pointed, "Quick, run up that creek in the water as far as you can, then hide in the rocks. I'll see if I can steer them away."

Sebastian had barely disappeared when four noisy, snuffling hounds raced into the camp. They scattered his gear and further scared the already nervous horses. Close behind them came a party of three horsemen.

"That iss man who hurts me," Sebastian sent from where he lay hidden.

Curt straightened to his full 6'4" stance and pulled his Stetson down tight as the lead horseman rode in to his camp. The hackles rose on the back of his neck at the arrogance of the man before a word was spoken

"Morning, names Carmichael," the man clipped with an air of self-importance. "Haven't seen a stray mountain lion wandering around have you?"

"No," Curt answered with an expression of distaste on his face.

"Well my boy, the dogs have followed his trail all the way here. Are you sure haven't seen it?" Carmichael peered suspiciously at Curt.

"Look around *Mister* Carmichael. Do you see a cat?" Curt asked through clenched teeth as he swung his hand toward his camp. "And don't call me boy."

"No need to get hostile. Sorry about the mess. Seek!" he hollered at the dogs.

The hounds searched frantically up and down both sides of the fast running creek to no avail. Stymied, they sat down, tongues lolling.

"SEEK!" Carmichael bellowed, but they just looked at him. "Stupid dogs lost the trail again," he said to the men behind him. "Sorry to have troubled you. What did you say your name was?"

"I didn't," Curt snapped.

Carmichael gave him a searching look and shrugged.

As the men and animals moved out of sight, Curt felt the warmth of mind he was beginning to associate with Sebastian.

"Are gone?"

"Stay down Bass," Curt answered in like form. *"We have to make sure they don't come back. Can you hear me?"*

"Yess." came back the warm answer.

***

Several hours later Curt and Sebastian were headed southwest toward a ranch on the outskirts of the Apache Indian Reservation and the White Mountain Range. Curt had finally gotten Sebastian on the back of a very unappreciative packhorse in hopes of further breaking the cat's trail.

"You helped calm the packhorse didn't you?"

"Yes. I talked to Sadie. She felt better. Knew I wouldn't hurt her."

"I thought you couldn't talk to other animals."

"I think mind-speak is getting better." Sebastian answered with a mental shrug.

As they rode companionably through the September afternoon Curt said aloud, "Now my young friend, I think it's about time you told me what this hoorah is all about."

"Hard to say."

"Do the best you can."

"Was stolen from mother before eyes open. Was taken to big building with nasty smells and all kinds of hard flat places and things

that fall down and break. Put in cage. Would take me out and put pointy things into me. Made hurt and sick many days."

"That sounds like a laboratory."

"Yess, laboratory. Shrah was brought too after my eyes opened."

"Shrah? Who is Shrah?"

"Shrah a female like me. Did same nasty things to her. Sometimes make very hungry too, when wouldn't do what they say. No man but you have I tried the mind-think. Iss okay I talk to you?"

"Yes, of course, but why did you pick me?"

"Watched you many days. Felt very bad sadness in mind. Wanted to make feel better. Felt trust for you. Iss why I try mind-think."

"Were you and Shrah the only animals?"

"No, many others. But could not mind think to them, only Shrah."

"How did you get away?"

Watched door. Man not close it tight. They not know I can open cage, so got away many nights ago. Bad man follow with dogs. I find you."

Curt felt anger rise within him at the conclusion of Sebastian's story. It was not the helpless rage he held for the Destroyers, it was a clean directed anger. This injustice he could focus on. He knew he would help this animal no matter what the results might be.

"As soon as we get to the ranch I'll see what I can see do to help you and your friend," Curt said determinedly. "You keep close, but stay hidden," he warned. "I'll keep in touch."

***

Curt threw down his pen in frustration and leaned back in his chair. He now knew that Bioresearch Laboratory, a privately owned company, was working on a project using animals. No one outside the project, either knew anything or wouldn't tell what was involved. He'd tried contacting the lab by Visiphone but no one would take his call.

He had one choice left. He could call Colonel John Hadley USMC, United Space Marine Corps, head of Special Projects, his boss. It meant going through channels he'd rather not use.

He'd never actually met Colonel Hadley face to face. However he had worked on several off-world projects under his command. They usually worked as a combined cross section of military branches. Most involved seek and close down or destroy types. Actually they were really looking for any information they could find on the Destroyers.

Oh well. I might as well take the chance and try. In for a penny in for a pound as his Grandpa used to say. He opened the V-phone channel and coded in the number he knew was a secure line.

Within seconds an attractive woman answered. "Oh, hello, Curt." I thought you were on vacation. What's up?"

"I hate to bother everybody, Tanya, but I need to talk to the Colonel. Is he available?"

"What's this about Curt? He's pretty busy today."

"Tell him it's about the Bioreasearch Lab in New Mexico. It's really urgent."

The smile abruptly left Tanya's face. "Hold on Curt," she said abruptly.

To Curt's surprise the Colonel answered immediately. "What's this about Bioresearch, Curt?"

The Colonel was so abrupt and hostile that Tappon was startled. "Uh... Colonel, you know I'm with the intelligence section, detached. I'm on leave in Arizona. I was looking for some information on Bioresearch in New Mexico."

"WHY!"

Curt's eyes narrowed as he studied the stocky, silver-haired man carefully. The Colonel returned his look with piercing blue eyes. Curt knew from experience he could trust him. "Sir, can we have this line scrambled?"

Hadley noted the closed hard look on the face of the younger man, then seemed to relax. "Yes, of course. Give me a minute."

Five minutes later Hadley looked up. "We're in business. Now, what the hell is this all about son?"

Curt told the story of his meeting with Sebastian, and the run in with Carmichael. He hesitated, then went on to tell him of Sebastian's unique ability and why he had called him. "I've located the lab on the edge of Apache National Forest, outside of Glenellen, New Mexico.

"Hmm," Hadley mused. "This is highly irregular. My information is that it's only a research center on animal behavior. You say the cat is with you?"

"Yes, Sir."

"Alright. Since you're on leave, and your time is free right now, I'll assign you to go to Glenellen. Get me some proof about what's going out there, one way or another. Are you willing to do this on just my say so?"

"Yes, sir. That's what I want to do."

"Good. I suggest that you keep the cat with you since you can communicate with him. As soon as you get anything concrete, call me. I'll send my crew in for back up. You got that? Call me!"

"Yes, sir. I'll get on it first thing in the morning."

"I'll send you a jetcopter in the morning so you can get there quickly."

"Yes sir. Thank you, sir."

Curt signed off and leaned back with a sigh of relief. It felt good to know that he now had a purpose. Something he could fight against. *Bass?"* he sent out the thought. *"Did you get any of that? Are you out there?"*

"Yess, I am here. We go in morning?"

Curt just barely kept from jumping at the quick response, but he was learning. *"Yeah, Bass, we leave early. Good hunting."*

***

The jetcopter flew quietly over the hills and valleys of the Arizona wilderness. Curt's mind was still in turmoil over the events of the past few days. He felt a sense of awe whenever he looked at the cat dozing peacefully behind him. Curt stretched and ran his fingers through his hair.

*When you come right down to it. H*is expression softened for a moment. *I haven't felt this good in months, maybe years.*

He looked below and saw sunlight reflecting off a small lake. The pain almost overwhelmed him again as he remembered the swimming hole above the ranch where he and his family had spent lazy summer afternoons. The pond that was no longer there.

He shook his head, pushed the vision back inside again, and forced himself to return to the problem at hand.

How was he to get into the laboratory that Hadley had told him was well guarded? Especially without any credentials.

"I will help," came a soft thought.

Curt glanced back at the cat, and for the first time accepted the fact that he was not alone. *"I know you will, Bass."*

Curt and Sebastian reached Glenellen around noon, They landed at the small airport just outside of town. He had just stepped out of the copter, warning Sebastian to keep low, when he saw a familiar figure come out of the terminal building.

"Kira. Kira McCall," he hailed.

An attractive blonde-haired woman turned quickly in his direction. "Curt! What are you doing here? I'd have thought Glenellen the last place I'd find you. I haven't seen you since we closed up the project on Alturus."

"I'm back on temporary duty, checking out a project. How is the behavioral business?" he asked as he came up beside her.

"I work here now." Kira studied his face closely and noticed he still wore that hard look. "I've been assigned to Bioresearch to work with their lab animals. I haven't been there long." A frown marred her face. "From what I've seen—I'm sorry, Curt, but I can't discuss the project."

"I know, Kira, but that's the project I've been sent to investigate. I think you're just the person to answer some questions for me. Is there some place we can talk?"

"Danger!" Sebastian suddenly cut in. *"No come here!"*

Curt stiffened as he looked up and down the street. He slowly turned and came face to face with Carmichael.

"Well, Dr. McCall, who is your friend? I think we've met before," Carmichael looked Curt up and down with contempt.

"This is Lt. Curtis Tappon," Kira answered, not mentioning she had first met Curt as a patient.

"Hello, Carmichael. Just the man I wanted to see. I've been hoping to get a tour of that complex Kira has been telling me about. How about it?"

"Now what would you want to see a bunch of neurotic animals for? No, I think not. We're a specialized operation. Not set up for nosy tourists. Don't be late for work tomorrow, Dr. McCall," Carmichael smirked as he turned and left.

Curt and Kira just looked at each other. Curt made a quick decision. "Come with me. I have someone I think you'll want to meet."

As they approached the helicopter Bass poked his head out of the side door.

"Why, this is Sebastian," Kira exclaimed. "His disappearance has had the lab in an uproar ever since I've been here. Where did you find him? OH! So that's why you're here. I think you've some 'splainin' to do Curt Tappon."

Later, over dinner, Curt told Kira how he'd come to be there and what he needed to do, omitting his contact with Colonel Hadley. "So, that's why I've got to get into the lab," he finished. "Will you help me?"

"You know I will Curt, but isn't tonight awful short notice? We really don't have any plan. No." Kira mused. "I guess we should get it over with, before they realize why you're here."

"Good, we'll go in, say 0200?" Curt glanced at his watch. "We'll just have to plan as we go. I think we'd better get some rest first. I'll take you home, then find a motel room."

***

The moon had not yet risen when Curt, Kira, and Sebastian crept toward the well-guarded gate to the laboratory. They had parked Kira's copter-van about a half-mile down the road.

"How are we going to get past the guard? Kira whispered. "Even I can't just walk in."

"You distract him while Bass and I sneak up behind him. I'll knock him out before he can sound the alarm. The switch to the gate should be in the hut. You brought your keys right? Let's go."

Kira walked with an exaggerated limp toward the well-lit gate. The guard eyed her suspiciously as she approached. Behind her, just out of range of the lights, Curt and Sebastian quietly moved toward the hut.

"Out kind of late aren't you, doctor?" the guard asked as soon as he recognized her. "Are you hurt?"

"Yes. My copter broke down about a mile that way," Kira pointed toward the highway. "I tripped over a rock and sprained my ankle. I was hoping to use your phone."

The guard, suspicion allayed, peered toward the dark highway his back toward Curt, who by now was gliding silently around one side of the hut.

As he came up behind the guard Sebastian suddenly let out an ear splitting squall. The startled man stiffened just long enough for Curt to land a well-timed chop to the back of his neck. He went down without a sound.

"Why the screech, Bass?" Curt asked the cat as he pulled a zip-tie from his belt and secured the guard.

"To scare him," Sebastian answered with a seeming shrug. *"Could not, how you say, resist."*

Kira had to chuckle when Curt told her Sebastian's answer. They pulled the now rousing guard into the hut and sat him in the single chair.

Curt gave a quick look at the gate controls. "Uh-oh, we've got a problem, Kira. You don't by any chance know the gate combination, do you?"

"No, I'm afraid I don't. But, Mr. Julian here does," Kira supplied.

Curt turned to the guard, a menacing grin on his face. "I'll bet he wants to tell us too, or we'll sic the cat on him. Don't you Mr. Julian?"

The man watched with terror filled eyes as Sebastian slowly stalked toward him, his tail switching back and forth. "I'll tell. I'll tell. Keep him away from me."

"That's very smart of you, Mr. Julian. Guard Bass."

As soon as the guard told them the combination, Curt gagged him and left him in the hut. They slipped through the gate and closed it quietly. Warily, Curt and Kira, Sebastian trailing behind, set out toward the animal section of the lab using every shadow.

They were half way to the building when overhead they heard a screech and a rustle of wings. Kira let out a gasp, stopped short, and grabbed Curt's arm.

"It's okay. Must be an owl," he whispered.

"I'll protect you, Tall One." Sebastian told Curt.

"Thanks, just the same, but save the jokes for later, Bass. Let's move. Time is running short."

Curt carefully closed the door to the laboratory behind them. The smell of chemicals and close kept animals almost made him gag.

"I'll check the files," Kira whispered, indicating the computers to the left. "You check the animals and take the pictures we need."

Curt approached the cages of the now awakened animals. He looked closely at the sleek female mountain lion that Sebastian had just reached. As his eyes met hers, he felt a light curl of warmth, like a tail, wrap around the inside of his head.

"You came, friend. I thank you." Shrah purred.

Without thought Curt reached out and opened her cage. He began taking pictures and was amazed at the variety of animals, each with a male and female. He was quite impressed by a pair of river otters that kept reaching for him.

He heard a sudden gasp behind him. Turning quickly toward Kira he whispered, "How are you coming?'

"Curt, you won't believe this. I've found Sebastian and Shrah's records along with the others, but theirs is the thickest. Did you know that Carmichael has been using chemical DNA manipulation on them since they were babies? No wonder they have telepathy. He was going to train them as spies against Earth, to help the Destroyers if he could contact them. Here is a copy of his plans. Oh, Curt, this is awful!"

"Danger!" Shrah screamed into Curt's mind, just as the overhead light flipped on.

Kira and Curt spun around toward the door. The cats had disappeared.

"Well, well." Carmichael sneered. He stood in the doorway with a gun in his hand, the two men who had helped chase Sebastian behind him. "Fancy finding you here. And you're so early Dr. McCall. I appreciate you bringing Sebastian back Lieutenant. I suspected you knew where he was back in the mountains; especially after you showed up here. Did you think you were smart enough to stop my experiments? Don't move!" He waved the gun at Curt who had started toward him.

As the two men took hold of Kira and Curt's arms, chaos broke out in the form of two tawny furies. Glass and chemicals exploded onto the floor. Tables and stools flew. The other animals added to the chaos as they screamed. Sebastian roared, leaped at Carmichael, and batted the gun from his hand.

Shrah, spitting, slapped her claws into the leg of the man holding Kira and brought him down.

Curt took advantage of the surprise and gave the man behind him a swift elbow to the stomach, then dropped him with a chop to his neck. The man doubled over and Curt dove for the gun. As he came up with it he yelled, "Back off!" *"Guard!"* he sent to the cats.

Sebastian and Shrah backed warily away, hair on end, growling low in their throats.. The two men froze where they were and eyed the cats fearfully.

Carmichael used the opportunity and dove across the room at Curt. As they grappled for the gun, it went off, the bullet hitting the ceiling. Kira moved behind Carmichael and hit him over the head with a heavy microscope. He went down for the count.

Sebastian and Shrah stood with their paws on the backs of the two men on the floor, an air of smugness about them.

"Are you okay?" Kira asked. "You're bleeding."

"I'm okay," Curt panted and glanced at his arm. "It's just a scratch. By the way, that was good teamwork. Find some rope. We'll tie them up for the authorities."

Suddenly the door to the lab burst open. Two armed Marines ran through, followed by Colonel Hadley. After a quick look around, he entered, followed by more Marines. They were stopped short by a warning snarl from the two cats.

"It's okay. They're friends." Curt sent to the cats.

Hadley smiled at the look on Curt's face. "Well, it looks like you have things well in hand. Did you find the evidence we needed?"

"Yes, I think we've got enough to send this fellow away for long time." Curt nudged Carmichael with his toe. "But, how did you get here so quick? I didn't call you."

"I did," Kira volunteered. "But he didn't tell me you were working for him too." Kira gave the Colonel a critical look.

Unperturbed, Hadley asked, "Did you get any pictures?"

"Curt did."

"Good. Take over men and let's get this carrion out of here."

As the Marines went about their business, Curt looked around at the mess. He had just turned to leave when he spotted a familiar figure leaning against the door frame of the lab. His heart skipped a beat. His brother, Hawk, stood there grinning at him.

"Oh my God! You're safe!"

"Yep! We made it back." Hawk said. "Looks like I missed all the fun though."

"Didn't miss much."

"Come on, let's get that bleeding taken care of," Hawk grabbed Curt around the shoulders in a brotherly hug. "Good to see you bro. It's been awhile. Kira, you coming?"

Curt heard a soft mental call, as they walked out the door. *"Tall one. Tall one."*

"Where are you?" Curt sent when he realized the cats were not in the lab.

"Here. Outside. We go friend."

Curt stepped outside. He frowned when he saw the cats. "Go? Where will you go?"

"Do not know yet. Will find a place."

"I thank you, friend," Shrah purred into his mind. *"No be caged again."*

"Wait…" Curt said, but the cats disappeared into the night. His face turned stony as the strong feeling of pain and loss swept over him again. He stiffened as the warm feeling he associated with the cats left his mind and he felt the cold familiar wind of loneliness replace it, even with his brother standing next to him.

***

A few hours later Curt and Kira sat down to a well-earned breakfast. They had just finished discussing the events of the previous night, when Colonel Hadley came over to their table.

"May I join you?" he asked and sat down without waiting for an answer. "Well, my friends—

Curt snapped. "What happens to the cats now, Colonel? Do we just leave them loose out there to go wild again? They're not prepared to live that way, you know!

"Whoa, slow down, son. That's why I'm here. You two did an excellent job on such short notice. We've been trying to catch Carmichael ever since we suspected he was trying to contact the Destroyers. Rest assured, he never did you know. I'm surprised he left a copy of his plans in the files. He must have felt completely confident."

After a slight pause, Hadley continued. "I've got a proposition for you both." He looked at Curt. "How would you like to keep them?"

"Keep them? You mean Sebastian and Shrah? What would I do with them once I'm really back on duty?"

"That's what I came to talk to you about. Because of their unique ability, and that's just between us," Nelson looked pointedly at Curt and Kira. "I thought you and the cats would be a good undercover team. You'll be assigned directly and only to me permanently and trained on Mars. It also comes with a promotion Lt. Commander. What do you say?" He turned to Kira, "And you, how would you like to try working with the otters? I understand that they have similar abilities to the cats."

Curt became very thoughtful. He answered slowly. "I guess I could try it, if I can find them. They both took off for the mountains last night you know."

"I'd love it," Kira said with no hesitation.

Just then the familiar feeling of warmth entered Curt's mind and alongside it, a soft purr.

"We are here," Sebastian said.

Curt's hard face softened for a moment. It showed a mixture of surprise and wonder. *"Where…?"*He began.

"We decide to wait."

"You heard?"

"Yes, we go with you," Shrah purred.

"Okay, Colonel," Curt said. "The cats just said yes. We'll take you up on that offer. When do we leave?"

"Good." Hadley rose from his chair smiling. "You report to me as soon as you find the cats and finish you leave."

The Colonel and Kira saw Curt smile for the first time since they'd know him.

"Yes, that sounds great!"

All right. A feeling of release swept over him. The continuous background warmth and purr of the two cats in his mind helped soothe him and he felt a sense of peace.

The pain of loss for his family would never really leave him, he knew, but his world had finally come together. He would never feel that cold loneliness again. He rose silently from his chair and walked out into the sunlight to find his friends ready to face the world.

###

White Mountain Idyll (Part 1)

By

R.V. Neville

First Year, Day One

We'd been skimming along above the ground for a couple hours now. The sight of Earth rushing past 250 meters below the Hercules-class Bristol Hovercraft (Bumblebee) mesmerized me almost to the point where my eyes were glazing. For hours, the view of desert and burnt earth had been the same, punctuated by occasional swathes of buildings in various stages of decay.

We crossed the fifty-year-old Palo Verde meltdown site, and the Bumblebee had lifted much higher—200 meters more, according to the PSA agent—and we'd stayed far north of it. Then, a field of spread out houses had started. Massive old dwellings languishing across the flat-lands, with enormous shopping and auto malls, pointed out to us like prizes by the agent. Soon, they gave way to a hub of high-rises, skeletal office buildings and hotels in a graveyard of commerce.

They shimmered and shone in the extreme heat. Our pilots seemed to think a closer look would be fun, and even with the heatsink devices the Bumble was fitted with, the temperature rose. Sweat beaded in my hairline. The whole cabin of us frontiersmen and frontierswomen, which had merely funked before, began to reek. But no one complained; no one, not even the agent, said anything. We stared at the eyeless buildings as our craft circled the core. Jim touched my hand and I hugged our daughter closer to me.

As quickly as we had come upon the old city center we were away again and flying over more of the sprawling burbs. To my Menlo eyes, these long-abandoned houses looked squanderous in their consumption of land. That is, they would have, had they not been located in an uninhabitable meltdown zone.

Then, we were flying low over desert again, and my eyes returned to their aforementioned glazed state. So, when I felt Jim's hand grasp mine, and Dot's thin body grow rigid, it was a complete shock to see that we were aimed directly at a cliff face.

***

Our Pioneer Settlement Authority agent, the big fellow in the gold Nehru coat with hair to match, explained what to expect as we lifted off from Fresno Yosemite International Airport. The big craft rose straight up then wheeled away from the tarmac and gave us our first terrifying sight of the swamplands bordering solid land. From where we sat in the glass-bottomed belly of the thing, it looked as if we were perilously close to the roiling and sometimes bubbling waters of the bogs.

"You'll notice how close we stay to the surface, folks. Our typical cruising altitude is 250 meters, with capabilities of 500, but we hardly ever fly higher than 310 meters. Upper levels winds are just too unpredictable these days!" He said this cheerily, as if flying were an everyday occurrence for our sort. As the Bumblebee banked sharply to the south, I swallowed the bile rising in my throat.

So, our pendulous craft, the best one for the job of carrying numerous passengers in today's tumultuous climate, had buzzed south. Some people on board had even begun to relax by the time we reached our next port of call at Burbank Hoverport.

The Bumble had landed daintily, parting the morning mists on a dyke, pretty much all there was of the small hoverport. We perched there, high above two canals as the rest of our group boarded. By then, I had overcome the queasy feeling of free-fall, but had a renewed bout of vertigo as one of the frequent low-level quakes of the area shuddered through our craft.

Whatever, we first boarders had survived the last hour and a half, making us old hands. I felt a certain smugness as I watched the worried faces of our newer fellow frontiersmen. The agent began his speech as they filed in.

"Good morning all! As winners of the 2137 drawing for re-settlement of the upper Arizona Territory, you are lucky to be flying in a genuine Bristol Hovercraft! This Hercules-class craft is the workhorse of the line, designed for both comfort and capacity. When traveling at its peak speed of 180 kilometers per hour, there is absolutely no other craft as stable and trustworthy as the Bumblebee. Safe as houses, as they say. Harnesses everyone!"

"And you thought the breed of game-show host had faded out with the death of Television," my Jim muttered.

That made me giggle and any remaining tension from the earth tremors dissolved.

The agent went on, telling the new passengers all the same things he'd told us on our way to Burbank. He talked about the eight electric engines that were, "even now" being topped up via inductive charger plates embedded in the hoverport surface. They would give us enough power to lift above the mists blanketing most of Burghal California. Once we could get high enough, the multitudes of solar plates on the body of the Bumblebee and the heat-sinks would take over, providing a continuous feed of energy into the batteries contained within the craft. Yep, the same things, almost to the letter.

I tuned him out as I thought about what all this meant to us. There we were, a third of the future Snowflake Settlement crowded into a

Bumblebee. Twenty-six families, seventy-eight souls, new winners of the chance to escape the crowded California coast. We were being called on to resettle country that, half a century ago, had been evacuated due to the Palo Verde Generating Plant meltdown. The drawing had been a draw, so to speak, to anyone who wanted to find out what it's like to live out of sight of other houses. That's about all we were told by the authorities.

Homesteading wasn't for just everyone, of course. In this new territory, there were no conveniences like water and electricity and travellators. For some citizens, the idea of the absence of the ubiquitous cameras of Burghal California was unsettling, like having a blankie taken away. That, in a nutshell is why the lottery was relatively low in participants.

I'd be lying if said Jim and I didn't care about the loss of those luxuries. We had "discussed" the pros and cons of life in unknown circumstances for weeks before we ventured to purchase a ticket. Who was the more cautious? Maybe me. Probably me. Oh, come on, *definitely* me. I remember one night, when our conversation became extra heated, pointing out the possibility of "life" in this new place turning to death. The next morning, we saw three bodies that had fallen from a balcony in our arcology scraped up and packed away on gurneys. It was a reminder to us of the actual peril of living, and that particular argument ceased to have wings.

In the end, we agreed we were ready to try something new. Dot was the perfect age. At eight, she was nearly autonomous, but hadn't yet developed the crippling attitudes of pubescence. This meant, we were sure, we could transplant her, like a sweet dandelion, to our new home.

We longed to smell fresh air, not wait in queues for a sniff at the oxygen turbines once a day. Who cares if we had to walk or bicycle or find some other form of, so far, undisclosed transport to get from place to place. For there was only so much information the underground support groups could provide. Most of what *they* told us was hearsay and conjecture.

When I came back to the present, the agent was wrapping up his speech.

"Now, I've told you how these birds—er, bugs—ha, ha fly. It's time to explain our flight path to you...when you're all sitting...you want to get those harnesses done up, you know, you really do!"

Many of the newbies had ended up stuck in the front seats as most of the first group had retreated toward the back, as far as they could get from the large expanse of the glass bottom. That is *most* of our group had moved back. Jim and Dot and I had sat right up front. Dot had insisted: all eight fearless years of her had been captivated by the scenery. So, we stayed put on the front seats.

That gave me an opportunity to inspect our new compatriots.

They were certainly different from us. Mostly longer muscled, like long-distance runners, and all of them wore lighter clothing. Long-sleeved, of course. No one in their right nog would dream of exposing a millimeter more flesh than necessary now. At least, not when they had to be outdoors. They also smelled vaguely of a rich sour-sweet smell I later learned was garlic.

The hatch clanged shut, then made a reassuring sucking sound as the vacuum seal took effect. The last of the new passengers plopped into seats. The eight engines revved up and we lifted off. Again, my stomach fell away with the ground, but I was ready for the sensation this time.

Being so close to these newbies I couldn't help but observe their facial expressions. They were almost all terrified, some mingled with tiny sparks of uncertain delight as we climbed to cruising altitude.

Golden Man, as I was now thinking of him, started his talk again. "We'll be flying up the Sanberdoo Pass to the Mohave Desert and then due east. We'll pass over the Coloriver bed and then over the—." When the agent broke off like that, I craned round to look and saw him sheltering an ear with a soft groomed hand.

"Oh! Folks, we've had a change of flight plan! There's bad electrical storms over the Williams Mountain range, and we're being redirected across the lower route." He listened to his hand a little longer, and I swear I saw him blanch. He turned away. A moment later he turned his face forward again, and said in a bright shiny tone, "Lucky us, we're taking the scenic route!"

The Bumble had continued east along a wide valley, the damp mist clearing over an arid landscape in which small settlements lay half-buried in the earth. At 11:00 in the morning, no one was moving about who didn't absolutely have to. We saw perhaps three people hurrying between buildings, holding sun shields over their nogs; a score of battered looking droids conducting business in the streets.

In minutes, we had passed over Pasadena, then Sanberdoo, then arrived at Indio, or so Golden Man told us. I wouldn't know, just that the domes and exposed roofs of the troglopols were plentiful at the places he pointed out. After that, the barren desert lands took over, and the agent brought up the Palo Verde Plant.

He started conversationally enough, "You may have heard of the Palo Verde Generating Plant."

"Well, *duh,"* I commented, *sotto voce*, during the agent's dramatic pause. We had, of course, *heard* of it. Who hadn't?

"Love, we haven't all benefited from your education."

"But you've *heard* of it, yes?"

"Of course!"

"Well, *see?"*

Jim chuckled at me, which, as so often, did more to humble me than any amount of argument would. "Want to tell me about it?"

"It's considered the icon, or, uh poster boy, of the tipping point when everything went to pot."

"What do you mean?"

I rummaged around in my memory, "It was the site of the first major disaster that marked the point when the domino effect of environmental crises became evident to even the blindest politicians. Which coincidentally was also when the world finally agreed that 'we had a problem.'"

"So, you mean when the Pacific Rim's Ring of Fire blew…?"

"Yeah, it was the most tremendous of disasters connected with the earthquakes and tidal waves. Sort of notorious."

"Anything else?"

"That's pretty much all I know. There wasn't all that much other information on it. Just that the whole southwest from then -Arizona to western Texas had to be evacuated."

"Yowzah."

Golden Man supplemented my bare-bone facts, saying with a flourish, "Palo Verde Generating Plant was the largest nuclear plant in the old USA. When it was built it was the largest, and while it was in operation, it underwent several expansions, keeping it the largest."

I was feeling impressed, looking forward to seeing it, until he spoke again, his tone one of deepest gravity. "Right before it melted down, it was also the *oldest* plant in the country. It was a whole hundred years old and some say disaster was inevitable, what with the great quakes of Eighty-seven...fifty years past its decommissioning date…." He paused waiting until all eyes were turned on him.

"But don't worry folks! That was fifty years ago, and although the valley all around it is nowhere *near* habitable yet, it's safe enough to fly over." He gave a short laugh and his eyes rolled slightly in their sockets, the whites gleaming garishly against his dark skin.

Jim leaned in to me and whispered, "I smell fear."

I nodded, my eyes fixed on Golden Man.

We flew on.

He explained that as long as we kept an adequate altitude, the remaining radiation from the accident wouldn't harm us. Not a lot worse than a few dozen old-fashioned x-rays. Comforting words, but he still looked nervous to me.

"What about the protective dome? Won't that keep us safe?" Someone not far from me asked, his voice rising above the drone of the motors.

Golden Man lifted his hand partway to his ear, like a deaf man, listened a moment. "Uh, due to the extent of the damage over such a large site, and the strain put on the Emergent Construct Corp due to the considerable number of other situations occurring at the same time around the country, a dome was never built."

There was a stirring among the passengers. I heard it. Barely. Thinking of the words I'd heard to do with radiation: of the Pu239 and Cesium and SR90 that must still be floating around.

Golden Man was listening to his earbud again.

"Cheer up! This Bumblebee is equipped with best quality shielding. It will cut down seepage by 70%. Fellow travelers! Just think due to the severe storms to the north, we have the great chance to view a historic monument!"

After that, I realized Golden Man wasn't all-knowledgeable, at least not about the places we weren't scheduled to go. We were being listened in on. And he was fed the information we could know.

And, as it was, the dead generating station wasn't as scary as all that. The bones of the great city it had eaten were sobering. But the cliff we were heading straight toward? That's what was chilling me!

***

We rushed straight toward the sheer bluff, our speed never faltering. We were all caught in a terrible suspension of time as the moments before the inevitable crash seemed to stretch out, endless. Enough to think of the things I should have done.

Jim and Dot and I clutched at each other, and I felt Dot's body squeeze out from between us like a pea popping out of a pod when pressure is applied. I wanted to renew my grip, pull her back in but I felt frozen.

I became aware of a high, piercing wail that seemed to go on as long as our catastrophic zoom toward doom. It went on and on, and eventually, slightly annoyed my last moments were being so penetrated, I managed to tear my eyes away from the oncoming cliff.

As I looked around the cabin for the source of the sound, I realized everyone was making some sort of noise. But Golden Man sat on his high seat, his mouth yawning open as he too watched helplessly our onrushing fate. As if he felt my eyes on him, his hand went to the tiny mic on his jacket lapel, and the noise went from acute clarion to a level matching the rest of the company.

Abruptly, Dot's body moved away from me a little more, and my attention snapped back. She perched forward, a hand on each of our thighs. as if willing the cliff to meet us. The cliff came up all shades of gray and red and black. I squinted my eyes afraid to look, afraid not to look, turning my nog at the expected impact and then...we bounced. The craft, suspended by its air cushion, hovered.

The Bumblebee seemed to flip ninety degrees and suddenly skimmed *up* the side of the cliff, straight up toward the sky. Now our forward view through the big mullioned windows was of the blue-blue sky rolling with towering clouds, such as we never saw on the California coast.

Then again, suddenly we were at the top of the escarpment, popping above its rim like cork coming up from the bottom of a sink. The Bumble righted itself again, cutting our view of the sky in half, and we began to rise perpendicular to the top of the world.

Dot, who had been utterly silent while most of the rest of us had screamed, collapsed back into Jim and me, squealing.

"Let's do it again!" She drew breath and started to laugh.

"You knew that was going to happen," I accused.

In answer, she giggled some more. Finally, she said, "Yes, if you think about it, the only way for a hovercraft to climb as high as the cliff was, was to use it for pressure. Air currents will only get you so high."

I narrowed my eyes at my eight-year-old progeny, stunned at what she knew. "Did you learn that in school?"

"Aw, na Mom, they teach us about crop rotations in school and the basics of composting, you know that! I *inferred* it from what that man's been saying." She indicated Golden Man with her small chin.

"The word is 'no,' Dot, and he's the PSA agent."

"Tcht," Jim scolded me mildly, his face full of pride at our daughter's perspicacity. Good cop to my bad cop. That was alright. We had a plan to keep our daughter's head normal sized. You never knew who would spot genius and take her away from us.

Speaking of "that man," having regained control of himself, the agent made busy regaining control of the now buzzing cabin. "Settle down, settle down!" he said. His face sheened with a film of sweat, but he wore a comforting smile, and laughed weakly as if we had all fallen for a joke.

Slowly our company quieted.

"See? Look at the land below us, folks!"

We did, and where there had been dry brown desert before, now spread out a thick coating of *green.* Not the misty fuzzy green of our old home, nor the tropical shocking green we'd seen in Burbank, but a deep dark brooding green. It looked inviting, but at the same time I was aware of the small hairs rising at the back of my neck.

"Those, folks--" Golden Man's voice inflected a sort of verbal drum-roll, "--are the Ponderosa pines of legend. *They* are responsible for our ability to resettle this land so soon after the Palo Verde incident!"

Someone spoke up, "Is this where we're landing?"

"No, no, we have a bit more to travel. We wouldn't want to set down *here."*

"Why not?" The voice belonged to a quarrelsome-looking man, seated toward the back, his woman and a half-grown boy on either side of him. "Look how green. There's bound to be water here, and plenty of materials for building with."

"And it'll be cooler than that hell hole we just left," a woman across the cabin added.

"Yes, and it will be filled with altered beasts. There's wolves, bear, mountain lions...and wild turkeys the size of a small hoverbike. The winters are colder than you can imagine. And the pines? They cushioned the land beyond here from the effects of the radiation after Palo Verde. They are *hopping* with it still! No...."

He swiveled on his chair looking over us all, his face a cross between beneficence and scolding. "Pretty as this place does look, it's a death trap."

In the time it took for him to say this, the pines had thinned, and the land dropped lower. "See here?" We looked obediently. "See how the trees are sparser and we are skimming prairie? A few more kilometers and we'll pass Old Snowflake, then we'll be at the New."

I could hear a mild grumbling from the would-be forest dwellers, but otherwise the cabin was quiet. I watched the unrolling terrain.

The land wasn't prairie at all, as I recalled hearing of it in classes from my youth. The pines had given way to shorter wider spreading green trees. At first these formed a thick forest, but as we continued they became rarer and revealed brown and yellow grasslands crowding round them. Occasionally a ravine or dry river bed would emerge as we sped across. This land was way more interesting than the desert we had traveled over for so long.

"Approaching Old Snowflake!" The land rose slightly toward us and we flew on. "This is just one of many communities evacuated in 2087." Some of the same sort of houses we'd seen in the Valley cropped up, and then I saw a big blocky building perched on a short hill. It appeared to be a fortress, or possibly an old prison. We passed on over a storybook town, now crumbling. The climate in this place was not as kind to inanimate things, apparently, as the desert's had been.

"Was that it?" Someone sounded plaintive, while I thought of vermin and disease in those old buildings.

"Nope. Be patient. Your new home is minutes away!"

By now, the Bumble had slowed to little more than the speed of a hover-bike. *Excruciating!* I was as glued to the passing land as was Dot. The remaining smaller pines were long gone, but the other trees were thicker yet. The land rolled with only the shallowest pathways for water. Water, which here in our new "home" wasn't anywhere in evidence.

Like Dot, Jim leaned as far forward as his harness would allow, elbows on knees, studying the passing landscape. Around us, the cabin buzzed with the excited voices of the others. I didn't hear their words so much as their mood. Very few actually looked outside, as they burbled with relief.

Finally, as we passed over a wide dry watercourse, another hovercraft appeared in the distance. We seemed on a course toward each other. The Bumble's engines whirred up a higher pitch as she turned a slow arc, and we went between low hills into a shallow valley. Below us, another two hovercraft were already parked in a large flat area where several tents were erected. There were no buildings I could see from our suddenly low angle.

"Ah, I do believe we've arrived." Golden Man sounded mightily relieved.

The Bumblebee set gently down at almost the same time as the other craft. Inside our cabin, our fellow travelers cheered. One voice exclaimed, "First thing I'm going to do is kiss the ground!"

"Now, now, Everyone! I must ask you to remain seated until the engines have turned off. Once they do, you will be receiving instructions very soon." The cabin settled down a notch, although there was still a hum. "In the meantime, I would like to say it has been a pleasure flying with you."

"Ain't you coming with us?"

"Oh, no, sir. My job is to act as guide for people like you brave souls, going out to settle the frontiers."

"Aw, come on. How many of us can there be?" I knew that voice. It belonged to one of my neighbors in the Menlo Hills tenements, a thickset woman with a ten-year-old who used to scream like a banshee and run at Dot. "This is the first ever *I* heard of a thing like this."

"Ah Well. Since the semi-centenary anniversary, there have been several lotteries conducted by the various Constabularies. This is just one of them…."

The engines suddenly cut off, and for an instant the cabin was dead silent. Then it exploded with noise of harnesses being unclasped, people stretching, bags being shuffled, voices calling out. Golden Man added to the mayhem, bellowing for order. Eventually our crowd settled down again.

Distracted as I was by the goings on in the cabin, I kept glancing out the bow-windows. Our Bumble had landed very close to a long tent, and I noticed a slew of people dressed in Southwest Constabulary jumpsuits moving around busily. Then, I also got temporarily swept up in pre-departure preparations. It was Jim who touched me on the shoulder and said, "Look there."

The S.C.s had swiftly built out the long tent to meet our Bumble.

Then, the vacuum in the door released with that sucking sound. We all fell silent, craning to see what would happen next.

In the door stood a tall figure in a bright yellow hazmat suit, complete with double-filtered breathing apparatus. The figure said in an androgynous voice, "Leave all your baggage and follow me." And without another word spun round and descended the ramp.

I turned to look at Jim in shock. *Where in the blessed blue had we gone to?*

We were supposed to be pioneers, in a safe farming area, not battling unknown bacteria.

The last thing I heard from Golden Man was, "Don't you worry folks, your bags will be restored to you later."

Grumbling at having to leave the small bags, even if only temporarily, people lined up. The cabin slowly emptied from the front to the back, making us some of the first through the hatch. Instead of the great outdoors, we emerged into the long tunnel-like tent we'd seen the S.C.s building. Strong light filtered through the plastic walls, giving all the glow we needed to shuffle along its length.

The air changed from the funk of the Bumble's cabin to a sterile smell. Not the disinfectant I'd gagged on in school restrooms so long ago, but it was as if the air was simply *devoid* of smell. The people in front of us and behind us who had boarded at Burbank—the ones with the garlicky pong—they weren't half so ripe by the time we reached the flaps at the far end of the tunnel. I wondered what we northerners smelled like to them.

We came into a circular area half again as large as the Bumblebee's cabin had been. The hazmatted figure climbed onto a small stage and looked down on us, while other officials, dressed in olive green HazMat's, pushed us toward the stage, saying "Move along please, keep moving forward."

When the last of our fellow pioneers (*victims?*) had pushed through the flap into the new area, the figure on the stage began to speak. "Welcome, winners of the Southwest Constabulary first-ever lottery draw. I am Major Marietta Garner, your team leader for the next several days while we prepare you for your new life here."

Knowing the Major was female, I tried to hear feminine qualities in her voice, but it still sounded robotic to me. She continued.

"You have arrived at the site of New Snowflake. This area was once called Cedar Hills, but has now been deemed the appropriate place to erect the center for the new farming community you will be building here together.

"This will be your community room for the next days. You will meet here for all announcements, take your meals here, and you will be able to mingle with the other members of your Hovercraft party.

"We have much to do before your first meal and rest tonight, so for efficiency's sake we are dividing you into six sub-groups. Males Five to Twenty years, this is your section leader, Lieutenant Harvey. Please follow him." All the boys in the tent crossed to stand in front of the white-suited figure the major indicated.

"Males, Twenty-one to Fifty, your section leader is Lieutenant Orme." Jim pecked my cheek and moved away from me. Seeing how this was going to end up, I put my arm around Dot for a last hug before we were parted. The major had us all going our separate ways soon enough. Babies and toddlers stayed with their mums, so the group I was in (*Females Fifty-one Plus*) had half a dozen tinies. The rest were with the women in *Females Twenty-one to Fifty*.

Although our group had gained enough confidence to gripe at Golden Man about left luggage back in the Bumble, not one of us thought of arguing when someone in real authority told us what to do.

There were three flap exits on the other side of the community room, boys on the right, girls on the left. Each group was conducted through by the section leader we'd been assigned. Ours was a Lieutenant Eden. When we finally went through, we found ourselves in a narrow room with benches and not much else.

Eden said in a sweet mechanical voice that broached no funny business. "Strip down ladies and wait by your clothes." We did as we were told, and the L.T. came 'round to each of us. She had an olive hazmat following her around with a handheld device I'd never seen before. As they arrived at each of us, the olive hazmat used the device to install a number on each woman and her clothing. My number was 73. The olive hazmat—I had to believe there was an S.C. officer in there—she never spoke, just churned out numbers—held the device over my inner forearm and the number appeared an eerie glowing green which glimmered before settling down to a tattoo-like image. Then she turned and applied the same number to each item of my clothing.

"That'll fade in a few days, but will give you time to locate your clothes later." Eden said this to each of us as she made her way along.

When the last of us were branded, Eden opened the next flap and invited us through. Bending to try to avoid the touch of the tent flaps on our naked bodies, we walked onto a narrow raised metal slatted-floor. Clear plastic sheathed the sides braced out by stainless steel pipes. Shower nozzles switched on over our nogs and warm powerful jets blasted us from all sides. We were soaked through instantly.

"Keep moving, keep moving,"

We moved slowly, each hampered from speed by the woman ahead of her. I sort of liked the sensation of wetness and the massage of the jets, but some of the other women cried out or grumbled. Our little family was fastidious, taking a francobath every second night: a cup of sterilized water, cloth, and a good scrub. It seemed, however, that many of the group's women cleaned themselves much less often.

Reaching the portal at the far end, I found myself in another tunnel down which a strong—and by strong, I mean, tornado-like—air current blew. It was probably warm air, but after the heat of the water jets, I shivered and crossed my arms. Eden was already there, and said, "Seventy-three! Uncross your arms. That's right, you need to let the air-dry do its job."

I gritted my teeth and raised my arms in a parody of a cheer, not letting her see my irritation.

We were herded through a violet tinged tunnel. It seemed cold and eerie.

The next room glowed red as we came through. "Infrared, ladies! This will kill the last of the bugs!"

Then, it dawned on me. The Hazmat suits weren't to protect these people from the outside! Of course, they weren't. Hadn't I seen S.C.s outside erecting that tent in just a jumpsuit? They were to make sure they didn't pick up anything from *us!* For a moment, I felt incensed. Sure, we were a ragtag lot, many a load grubbier than ideal, but who did they think they were?

Then it double-dawned on me. We were being cleaned up before being introduced into the environment. Aha! *But why?*

***

The rest of the afternoon went on the same way. Once we "cooked" about ten minutes in the infrared, we sat on low stools while Eden and two olive HazMat's combed out our hair with very fine-tooth combs, and looked at our scalps with high mag glow lights. Of our twelve women and six children, two-thirds of us had our nogs shaved. I was lucky and got to keep my brown hair. Finally, after that we found ourselves in a room with more benches. Blue jumpsuits waited for each of us. We dressed and stepped into impossibly soft white boots.

I felt *amazing.* I'd never felt so clean or luxuriant. I'd have felt squanderous, if this weren't clearly approved of by the Southwest Constabulary. I looked around me at the faces of my new living mates. There were a few who looked like I felt and several more who looked to be in shock. Only a couple looked sour about things. I smiled to myself, sitting there on the bench, waiting for the next instructions.

As the last of us dressed, we were sent through the next flap which proved to bring us back to the community room, now set out with several long tables, benches down each side. No one sat at the tables. They milled about, finding their little Constabulary-approved families of three.

It was somehow harder to spot familiar faces with all of us dressed the same, and many of us shorn of our locks. When I saw Dot, perky in the blue jumpsuit and still possessed of her mob of dark gold curls, a little wave of pride ran over me. Jim found us a moment later. We hugged fiercely, but force of habit made us break apart quickly. Back in Menlo Hills, displays of affection could get you killed if the wrong person realized how attached you were. And *I* didn't feel all that comfortable here, yet.

A disembodied voice said, "When you've found your families, please take seats at the tables. Any table will do."

A few moments later, the Major pushed open the flat and her team followed her through to the small stage. No longer in the hazmat suit, she was still tall and imposing. Her dark hair was cropped short and her blue jumpsuit's arms were ringed with bright yellow. The Lieutenants, our section leaders, wore white rings on their arms. I tried to guess which of the women was Eden, and settled on a buxom blond who looked like she could throw down in a mat fight.

The disembodied voice now came out of Major Marietta's mouth. No longer disembodied. A rich alto, I found it likable. "Again, welcome, Pioneers. Having gotten initial cleaning out of the way, I think you'll find yourselves more comfortable. Cleaning was necessary to ensure you are pristine subjects when you enter the outside atmosphere."

"You will be served dinner as soon as I am finished with this announcement. Then you will be shown your assigned bunks for the night. I am sure this afternoon's proceeding were tiring for most of you and possibly a little stressful.

"Tomorrow we will conduct various tests, and soon you will be able to take your first steps into your new home. Thank you for your attention."

With that, she left the stage and Olives, now out of HazMat's and into green jumpsuits, started to arrive with dishes of food. More food than I remember ever seeing! A platter that had contained Textured Vegetable Protein sausage rolls reached me empty, and an Olive was at my side with a new platter piled high. I looked up to say thank you. With a start, I realized the Olives were droids. It hadn't been apparent when they were inside hazmat suits.

We chattered and stuffed ourselves as we had almost never done before. Feeling a camaraderie with people who only this morning had been mostly strangers, I briefly contemplated the leveling effect of these clothes...and of shaved nogs. Only our basic physiologies set us apart from the southern berghals. In a few days, we'd meet the pioneers who had come in on the other two hovercraft. Today, this was most certainly enough.

When we finished eating we were split again into groups, this time of sets of families. Lucky me, I got Eden again as section leader. Her voice without the filter of the hazmat mask proved to be super-sweet and girly.

Our section of four families were led through a maze of tunnels, ending up in a large tent divided into sleeping pods. Each pod was set up with three cots. "Latrines that way. There's a shower room, too. Lights out in fifteen minutes. Glow sticks in your pods for night time trips." Eden's mouth opened wide in a lioness yawn. "Night all. Breakfast at 0600. Sleep well."

She left, and we chose a pod. We found bottles of water and soft blankets. We did our weird little routine, Jim's idea, of swishing water in our mouths Tonight, we rubbed our teeth and gums with our fingers.

"Maybe we'll get our stuff back tomorrow," he said. I knew he was longing for the small brushes we usually used in our mouths. Dot, who had said very little since dinner, was asleep by the time we'd tucked her in.

Jim and I looked at each other, wanting to talk about our day, afraid of waking Dot, knowing the fabric that divided our pods was thin. We settled on an embrace and lingering kiss. The lights dimmed, and Jim, who could sleep in a hurricane, was breathing regularly.

Well fed, clean, and warm, I lay on my back in my cot. Jim's hand touched mine, and I thought, as I drifted, how lucky we were. How bright our future looked. Soon we'd be in this brave new land where we could stand anywhere and see open country, not arcologies. Where neighbors were friends and support, not competition.

But I still didn't really understand why we had to be *so* clean? Weren't we just farmers opening up land that had been fallow for half a century or more? Ah well, we'd see soon enough. For now, it was enough to know we were blessed….

White Mountain Idyll (Part 2)

By

R.V. Neville

First Year, Day Four

At 5:30 Reveille rang throught the camp. Being March, it was still dark outside. I peeled myself from the sleeping bag like a bad-tempered interrupted caterpillar-butterfly thing, *incremeta interrupta. No... right...I know that's impossible. There's no half-ways: you're either a caterpillar or a butterfly. The point is, I was feeling grumpy.*

It was the fourth day of our new life as frontiers-men and -women and -children. So far, we hadn't stepped foot outside the tent city the Southwest Constabulary had knocked together for us on our arrival. Since our hovercraft had come into land, I hadn't got even a glimpse of the great outdoors. We didn't know anything more about the landscape that was our new home. We hadn't even met the families flown in on the other two Bumblebees. What had been going on was we had been poked, prodded, sampled and tested sufficient to make a Martian proud.

As I shrugged into the bright blue jumpsuit the SC had issued us and pulled on the soft white boots, I grumbled to myself. The shininess of being clean, well-fed, well-clothed, and warm had nearly, although not quite, worn off. (*There's nothing quite like being clean after years of having to struggle to maintain the most basic hygiene. And I hope you never have to find that out for yourselves.*)

I knew I wanted outside to start our *real life.*

I shuffled toward the latrines and Dot raced passed me throwing back a, "Good morning, Mum!"

Nothing wrong in her life, I noted.

She had taken to the program at Camp New Snowflake seamlessly. The children of South Burghal California provided plentiful new friends and new games; she even seemed to enjoy the endless rounds of testing they were putting us through. Her tests, of course, were disguised as games, so that was understandable.

But her enthusiasm, as ever, encouraged me, and I pulled myself together enough to say, "Good morning," to one of our pod squad mates who was on the same trajectory as I. I got a comradely, if bleary nod, from her, and felt cheered.

Dot was already coming out as I got to the latrine flap. I was ready to grill her on her ablutions when she showed me her clear eyes and clean hands, palms and backs. She headed back to the pod.

Inside the latrine, were four composting toilets, each enclosed in their own private tent. I used one and then enjoyed, for the umpteenth time, the sensation of warm running liquid as I washed my hands and face.

I left the latrines, and went back to our pod, feeling resolved to face the day.

I'd better get Jim up. I hadn't noticed him lying in when I crawled out, but then, between the dark and my own attitude, I hadn't noticed much of anything.

Daylight, in typical high desert fashion, hadn't tarried in lighting the interior of the tents and the inside of our pod was bright. Our belongings, which had been released to us after "purification" the day before were heaped in a corner, waiting, like I was, for our new life to begin. Dot had thrown her cot together, and rushed off. I wondered if the comb and her hair would meet today. The muddle of cloth that was my sleeping bag lay as I had left it, but there was no Jim in the next cot. In fact, his side was unusually neat for him.

Intrigued, I made my cot, smoothed Jim's and Dot's over. Then, I took a little of the precious almond oil I'd brought with me from Menlo Hills, and dabbed my face. Finally, I brushed my hair, and, in the company of the Dickmans from the next pod, headed for the community room.

As we pushed through the flaps into community room B for our morning briefing, I realized something was different. Breakfast smells floated around, strong and enticing. Usually, we got breakfast only once the briefing was over. Today, people were heading for their breakfast places. Dot sat, an eating implement propped upright in each hand on the table in front of her, like a hungry child caricature. I smiled, and made my way to our table.

When I arrived, she broke off from her in-depth conversation with the boy next to her and said, "Hi, Mumma!" She was trying out every word for "mother" she had heard from her new friends.

"Hello, Child. What brings you here?"

"Starvatious-ness!!" She banged her cutlery once on the table in emphasis, and looked at me amusement and audaciousness flickering in her pupils.

I didn't chide her for her behavior, just opened my eyes a fraction wider. She had the good grace to laugh once and set her tools down. She smiled her megawatt smile and said, "Where's Jim?"

"You haven't seen him?" A stab of alarm hit me. To lose contact with your mate in the Hills was a really, really bad occurrence. No one there went out on the archology without telling their nearest and dearest exactly where they were going and for how long. But here, in this enclosed society there should be nothing to fear. After all, we were in Camp New Snowflake. I sat down.

"Nope, not since he left at five." A beat. "Couple of SC's came to the pod and got him." She seemed utterly unperturbed. The other kid studied our interchange with interest.

"Never mind, honey," the kid's mother leaned across the table toward me. "I expect he got called up for scout duty."

"Scout duty?"

"Least that's what I heard from my friend in Pod Squad Three." Funny how the term we'd coined for our groups of sleeping pods had spread. "Her hubby went out really early this morning, as well."

Why didn't he tell me? My mind screamed this at me. My face and mouth said, "Really? How exciting."

Dot, who can read minds, I am sure of it, replied, "He said he didn't want to wake you, 'cause you've been tossing and turning so much."

I looked at her, grateful and appraising. A veritable mine of information she is, if you just know what spade to use. "What else did he tell you?"

"That's it. And he sent you this." She blew a kiss across the table.

I smiled, feeling warmed.

"But I thought he'd be back by now."

Food appeared, care of the Olives, and we passed along the various delicious morsels. It was good basic staple food, such as in the old days was considered nothing fancy. Pancakes, breads, heaps of TVP sausages. To drink we had coffee, tea, and water. To us at the table, it was still like proverbial manna.

Hoping for Jim's soon return, hoping I wasn't being squanderous, I heaped his plate with food. Just when I thought there was nothing for it but to start eating without him, a commotion at the door made me glance up and Jim and two other men strode through the flap. He appeared to be keeping in a great glee. Relief must have shone all over my face, because he looked at me, that knowing sparkle in his eyes, and increased his already long stride an iota.

"Morning beautiful," he slid onto the bench beside me and squeezed my waist. Exchanging nods with our near eating neighbors, he finished his look-round at Dot, "Matrix." They shared their old-fashioned joke with grins and he attacked his meal.

Finally, I could eat. I breathed in the delicious smells of the food and went to work, pondering how surprisingly quickly, in this new friendlier environment, small displays of affection had returned to our everyday intercourse.

"Do you know why there was no briefing this morning?"

"Probably because they weren't finished with us yet." He stuffed half a pancake in his mouth, managing to talk around the food without sounding blocked.

"Tell," I urged in an undertone.

"All will be revealed soon enough," he swallowed and grinned at me.

"You're beginning to sound like them," I grumbled, half serious.

"You are the eternal skeptic, aren't you?" He gave me a quick peck and returned to his food.

Suddenly, another scent reached my nose. One I had hardly ever smelled in the last thirty years. Could it be? Yes! A droid for each table emerged from the scullery area bearing a platter. On it, were hen's eggs, fried in oil! One per person.

Such lavishness. I softened toward our tenders a little.

When the tables were cleared of breakfast's debris, we lingered at the tables, uncertain of what would come next.

We heard Major Marietta's before we saw her. I never really got why she performed that odd bit of theater before each briefing, but she never seemed to grow tired of it. In every other way she was the most *defacto of persons.*

"Good morning! I hope you liked your treat today." She stepped out onto the stage, tall and commanding, "We would have had them at a meal sooner, but it took a few days for the chickens to settle in before they would lay again. I expect that will happen again when we split them up to go to their new homes with you."

A murmur went up around the tables. By now, people knew better than to actually talk when the major was giving a briefing. Her laser stare had quelled the biggest mouths in the room, already. They did, however, have a way of making noises in their throats when excited. Our commandant waited until it was quiet again.

"First let me say, you've been very patient over the last few days while we completed our evaluations. You'll be happy to know that each and every one of you is now deemed suitable material to go forth and bring bounty out of this land." She beamed at us a moment, her face cracking a near-smile.

"Today, will see a change in our activities. My people have worked through the night, droid and constable alike, re-configuring the main tents to hold all three delegations as one." She was referring to the families from the three hovercraft. "Delegations" seemed a fancy word for us lottery winners, but I guessed that was as succinct a word as any. A buzz of approval went up.

"Without further chit chat, meet your new fellow pioneers." The major nodded and the long-side tent walls fell away. We were suddenly the central group facing the stage. The other two groups of tables bordered it on two of its other sides. View screens were being wheeled away and the major was now in the center of a live group of 228 people.

Silence.

I think we were stunned to finally see the other people who would be our most trusted circle—*our only circle of friends and neighbors.* I'm not sure we had any idea of what that meant.

***

We sat at our tables, looking each other over. I felt trapped by the long bench I sat on between Jim and another pioneer. Even though it would have only taken the lifting of my body, pressing palms to table and the pivoting on one leg to bring the other over and behind the bench, where I could pull the other leg free, to stand and go greet these others. But like someone gripped by sleep paralysis, I could not act. I'm not even sure if I could get as far as the wish to act. It appeared the feeling gripped us all, as no one moved.

What I could feel was shock at how much like us these people from the far-flung reaches of the Southwest Constabulary were. I knew some came from even further south than the group we met at Burbank. Some of them came from the furthest north reaches of the SC. But they all had the same latte colored skin. Smooth heads or hair in all the possible textures and shades of brown we had. The jumpsuits hid body shapes to some degree. Oh, I could see some were short or tall, slim or more robustly built, just like our people, but I found I was disinterested in trying to find differences between us. I realized I was looking for the same-nesses.

Then, a small child from the other side of the room slithered off his bench, avoided his parents' reach and toddled toward the next group of tables. He waddled straight to a slightly built man and lifted his arms. "Grumps!"

The little man smiled and held out his hands, and the spell was broken. The baby's parents hurried over, saying, "He misses his grandad."

"Well, thank you," the man said to the child as he gathered it in on an arm. "This is my family." He indicated another man and a pretty girl of about seven years.

Meanwhile others crossed the room. I finally broke my inertia, swung out from my bench, and approached another table.

We mingled.

In the course of twenty minutes, I found out where the other two

Bumbles had brought their passengers from.

One hovercraft had started in the Old Mexico Mountains and swung all the way up through the Albuquerque Badlands. That meant lots of farmers, some miners, and people with experience of the altitude here. The other came from the new coastal lands in the northern most parts of the SC. Once known as the Northwest Territories, they had merged with the Southwest Constabulary after a series of much belated aftershocks (forty years after the Implosion) in the old Ring of Fire. The rumblings had flooded every acre land reclaimed in the previous four decades. At that point all hope of resettling Portland or Seattle had been abandoned, and the NWT had crumbled. Living behind fortress-like seawalls, their arcologies were usually damp and chilly. Much worse than our Menlo Hills ones had been. They were mostly fishermen, netting the farmed shellfish and wetfish in the tidal farms. A dangerous profession.

About the time I thought I was getting a handle on where everyone was from, something made me become aware of the general surroundings again. Some people were still sitting at their tables like buoys, but others had approached them coaxing them from their moorings in what they had come to know. It looked as if not a single person wasn't getting to know their new comrades. The major was gone from the stage. She had left us to our own devices, which made feel more relaxed. I was about to turn back to my convo when I saw her come back through a flap. She mounted the stage again.

"Alright, alright," the mic squealed like they sometimes do when a person first speaks into one. That brought the room back to her.

"Alright. I'm glad to see you aren't shy. We won't need to spend time on introductory games. Instead, we'll carry on with business. Please, just sit down where you are."

We did so, separated from our recently developed tribe, everyone scattered among new allies.

"You probably noticed some of your dear ones coming into

breakfast late. We got them up early today for an introductory course to their first jobs in New Snowflake. No time to lose."

"New Scouts, come up here please." Jim and seven other men went up on the stage. "These men, and yes, they are all men and I'll tell you why in a moment; these men were all chosen because our tests revealed they are the most curious of you all, together with having logistical skills coupled with sound judgment." I felt a prickle of irritation and glanced around at the others, spotting one or two women who seemed to feel the same as I. Major Marietta seemed to be expecting that reaction.

"Let me assure you, some of the females scored higher in all three of these categories, but don't have the physical strength for what Scouting may entail. The land out there is rough and unexplored. There could be instances where brute strength is the fourth but temporarily most important attribute for our explorers."

Brother. But I had to admit, as I had no idea what sort of emergencies could come up in the field—especially as I had not seen outside since we landed—I would have to defer my opinion on the matter, at least for now.

"We've been drilling these men all morning on their new duties. They will be responsible, together with four of my lieutenants, for seeking out suitable homesteads for each family."

Jim and I caught each other's glance and I hoped he could read the depth of my confidence in him.

"The Scouts will be assigned hoverbikes, and in pairs, under the lieutenants' supervision, will take a compass direction each day for as long as it takes to identify the seventy-eight homesteads needed to house all our families. Once, at least that number of homesteads are noted, and all Scouts have had opportunity to tour and stake out all four quadrants surrounding New Snowflake, families will have a chance to choose theirs."

A roar of approval went up from our crowd. I felt suddenly light as air, knowing we would be out of this tent city soon!

She held up her hand and the roar stopped. It made me think of an old comedy routine I'd seen before television failed. Something where a world leader played with his ability to make a crowd stop cheering then pick up their cheering again simply by lifting his hand and letting it fall again. I smiled.

"We estimate the Scouts will be finished with this mission in about eight days. In addition to Scout duties, they will be trained in the care, repair, and general maintenance of the bikes. This will be an important knowledge base in your future, as we will be leaving you with one hoverbike per three families. These will be your main implements of transport other than your legs, so the men responsible for the welfare of those bikes will be very important to your settlement, indeed. In addition, as there can be only one hoverbike per three families, we expect settlers to take that into account when choosing their homesteads. Scouts, you may return to your seats."

The men clambered down and Jim came back to my side.

"Any questions so far?"

"What do you mean about 'taking it into account,'" called a light voice.

"On the whole, you want to be within easy reach of each other. It would be ill-advised, for example, for any one family to play hermit and hide themselves half a day's march away from the others."

"Why only one hoverbike per three families?"

"What's your number?"

The man looked confused, then said "Uh, 123, Ma'am."

"Pioneer 123, please understand, the Southwest Constabulary has not only offered you a chance to make new inroads into a forgotten territory, but are providing you with tools. You must appreciate, you are not just being dropped off here to fend for yourselves, but are being given tremendous assets with which to begin your community. Hoverbikes, like solar generators and water pumps are not in plentiful supply anywhere in the world."

The next person raised her hand, instead of just calling out.

"Yes," the Major stared at the broad bald woman, who hesitated before speaking. "You have a question?"

"You said 'leaving.'"

"Yes, we are leaving. Of course."

"All of you?" A different plaintive voice cried out.

"The Southwest Constabulary has limited resources. My team is primarily a peacekeeping corp. You are a settlement of 234 individuals in a landscape free of overcrowding and crime. You will be left with the gift of self-determination as regards your own government, including laws of punishment for any incursions of it."

The rest of the occupants of the room seemed stunned, while the flicker of an epiphany lit up in me. "Ohhh," I breathed.

"Shhh," Jim said. He was listening, intent, as the Major resumed.

"Of course, all the tests we have been conducting had an objective. We have determined recommended specialties for each of you. While the scouts are beginning their first day with instruction in basic hovercraft maintenance, you will all be assigned to various learning environments to further your natural skill-sets."

That buzz of approval started up again.

"Let's get started, shall we? Scouts, go with your team leaders, now. You want to be ready to make a start surveying as soon as possible." Jim and his fellow trainees rose from their places and followed four white banded SC's from the room. I watched Jim go, his supple body, lithe and catlike, until the exit flap covered him.

The Major was talking again, "For simplicity's sake, we will divide into our First-day Groups. Please find your leaders…."

As I made my way to the spot where Eden stood, I glanced around and found Dot on the other side of the room already at a table with her group. She looked keenly interested in the other youngsters around her. I didn't even try to catch her eye. *We're among friends here,* I reminded myself.

We Females Fifty-one Plus took seats at a group of tables over which Eden and two lieutenants I didn't recognize presided. A few of the humans I thought of as sergeants, as opposed to the Olives who were all droids, stood nearby. With the addition of the other two hovercraft groups, each bunch now looked unwieldy to me. It wasn't long 'til I found out that wasn't going to be an issue, however.

The major continued, "We are going to divide you now into camp job groups. Some of these jobs will be permanent, and some are temporary while you are in camp. For example, once you have found your homesteads, childminding will disappear, as homeschooling will become the norm. I'm going to turn the job assignments over to Lieutenant Chavez, here."

A handsome White-ring holding a tablet in front of him stepped up beside Major Marietta and said in a lusty voice, "Will the following please step this way: Lizzie Boynton, Natalia Starcross, Lotus Lightchaser, Brian Golya, Stewart Loster, Cindy Avila, Boris Wyler, Victor Ali. Childcare."

Three of the women with smalls left our tables to stand with others by the stage. They were met by a different lieutenant. I strained to hear what was being said, but the megaphone voiced lieutenant was still calling names, clanging across my auditory field.

I satisfied myself with listening for my own name to be called.

As our crowd of thirty-six women slowly got whittled down, I listened carefully for my name. There were only eight of us left. The jobs already called ranged from cleaners to cooks to carpenters. As Major Marietta had said, some were temporary camp postings, some were more permanent jobs meant to serve the community. Most of the jobs included training where needed. I guessed those called on as mechanics and carpenters might have some pre-knowledge of the fields.

Finally, all names were called, and still I sat on the bench. Eden and the other two LT's had moved away from the station with newly formed work-groups. I concluded they thought I was unemployable. In Menlo Hills I'd been a street cleaner. It was a dirty, menial job, but it gave me a legal reason to be out on the arcology, where I could see what there was to be seen. I wasn't one for sitting at home, as so many others were forced to do. I had felt lucky to have the work.

Let's face it, not much call for street cleaners in the countryside. I hated the idea of idleness. But I may have done this to myself. I hadn't exactly completed the many, many tests over the last few days to the best of my abilities.

Sitting by myself at the empty tables I was preparing for a pity party slash self-recrimination fest, when someone threw a leg over the bench and sat down facing me.

It was the major. "What do you think of all this?"

"Well, I have been wondering why you sent us back to our seemingly redundant first-day groups for this division of labor. The groups could have been formed with us sitting any old haphazard way in the room." I thought for a nanosecond. "Or, for that matter from our normal eating places."

Marietta chuckled. "Interesting response. It was a convenient way to allow all of you to see that the division of labor is fairly made. Men and women receiving like jobs, etc. Helps to avoid grumbling."

"Fair enough," I said. I ducked my head a little, avoiding her eyes.

"What I was originally asking, though, is what do you make of our setup here? Organization, efficiency, etc.?"

"Why would you want my opinion?" *Why ever would you want my opinion, my suspicious mind insisted.*

"I am doing a small survey for future planning, asking the common migrant what he or she experiences."

I said nothing, mulling that answer over.

"Please, humor me and answer the question."

"Okay. Physically, you have made us exceedingly comfortable. Most of us have more food, sleep, and security here than we ever imagined possible." I warmed to my subject. "Your organization seems excellent, although how efficient it is is questionable. It seems you are lavishing a great number of resources and staff on us. Human staff to pioneers alone must be at a ratio of, oh, one to five people. Factor in the droids, and it seems like you have one staff member per every two of us." I snapped my big trap closed. Too much!

"Thank you," *the major looked like the cat who had found the cream, as the old saying went. I had never actually seen a cat who had got cream, all cats in Menlo Hills being feral and considered vermin, but if anyone looked like that, Major Marietta did at this very moment.*

My stomach seemed to fall away from me, as a feeling of dread welled up.

"You know, Pioneer 73, your evaluations present you as something of a... mystery. Your knowledge tests indicate you are neither more educated nor less than others of your group, or for that matter than any of the groups here. In other words, basic levels of writing, reading, and trigonometry as related to agricultural and other resource gathering occupations are at standard levels. Your historical knowledge seems to be standard. Nothing special."

Am I supposed to respond to this in some way? I just ducked my head again, feeling like a serf. A serf with a number. I thought those were meant to go away in a few days. I couldn't help glancing at my inner forearm.

She saw me doing it, and said, "Don't mind me 73. I don't have time to learn everyone's name. And it also has been recommended that we don't, given we will be leaving you here. Our mind healers feel it will be easier all the way around for people not to get too personal with each other."

"I see." I tried to sound impartial, but the way I said it sounded cold, even to me.

"Now, where was I? Oh yes, on the other hand, your spatial cognizance, logistical analysis, and emotional balance tests put you far above the others. In fact, all the *un-fakeable determination processes we put you through did that."* She leaned back as if to appraise me.

I felt as if a hole were being burnt through me.

She seemed perfectly happy to let that happen for a while.

In the silence, I lifted my eyes to her and stared back stolidly.

"You know, we need to find a pioneer capable of taking on the administrative duties of the settlement. He or she will be responsible for putting together a governing body of representatives from your factions, drafting rules and regulations for the future of New Snowflake, and preparing the settlement for development as a viable community." She fell silent again.

Finally, I said, "Alright."

"We think that person should be you. You have the general makeup of a leader. You only seem to lack in knowledge. As to that, you will have access the libraries we will leave you with."

I looked at her wide-eyed. That wasn't what I had been expecting at all. Stunned.

"What do you think?"

I don't know, can't you see I'm busy looking at you wide-eyed?

She waited.

"Uh...that would be a challenge and an...honor, but I thought I came here to be with my family, to farm."

"Depending on how you govern your fledgling community, this could easily be a temporary posting, until such time as you, and whoever you choose to help you, have developed a code and rules by which to live."

"What do you mean about developing a code and rules?" I sensed a trap of some sort. There was only one code I knew of in the Southwest Constabulary.

"A good question...well, part of your freedoms of starting in this wide-open place, will be your opportunity to self-govern."

"That sounds interesting." I was beginning to warm to the idea of such a thing. Forgotten was this morning's angst over not having been outside. I could see the light at the end of the tent tunnel, and was feeling intrigued and excited.

"Not just your opportunity, understand, but your responsibility and a requirement to your survival."

"I understand."

"So, Number 73, do we have a settlement governor in you?"

***

At dinner that night, we were all back at our usual tables. The talk was animated, everyone telling stories of how they spent their days. No matter what camp jobs they had been given, each of our pioneers had experienced a learning curve. And that was a good thing.

I contemplated how much more alive my companions looked than only a few days ago. The body movement, the exercise of the mind seemed to bring these people to life. I thought, watching them, education on things a little outside normal everyday experience is *good.*

It was the first time in many years I'd seen people glow. In a good way. (There were the ferals in San Jose who glowed, but that was an entirely different situation.) I didn't know how long I would be "in charge" of the settlement, but if I could, I would find ways to encourage the expansion of these people.

Jim and Dot were gabbling like the rest. I listened intently to their stories of hoverbike driving and maintenance and of new friends and a game with an actual ball one of the lieutenants introduced.

"So, did you go outside, then Jim?"

"Ha ha, love, keep your knickers on. We just drove around the interior of the maintenance tent. It wasn't much, but enough to teach us to steer the things. Most of our time was spent on daily maintenance. Tomorrow, we'll start on periodic maintenance, then after that they said they're going to choose three of us to learn serious repairs."

"When do you go out on your first actual...reconnaissance?" I didn't know whether to call it a mapping exercise or search or what, so I settled for the military term.

"Once we all get how to change the laser points every hundred hours, they said we're going on our first tour. The day after that we should be good to go."

I smiled back at Jim, warmed by his enthusiasm.

He grinned, shot with a moment of telepathy, and my next question, "End of the week, maybe?"

We turned our attention back to the rest of the table. Whenever anyone asked how I had spent my day, I diverted the conversation. After only a couple of counter-queries, the askers forgot I hadn't answered and continued to talk about themselves.

I could tell Jim noticed this, but he bided his time.

***

Later, when we were alone in our pod, our exhausted Dot already sleeping soundly, we lay face to face, propped up on elbows and talked.

"So, my darlin', just what were you up to today? What job did they offer you?"

I snorted softly, not sure it had been an "offer" so much as a command.

"Well?"

"They want me to be governor of the Settlement." Trying to look casual, I rolled on my back and crossed my hands behind my head.

"What! That's great news!" Jim's Austro-american accent veered to the Australian when he got excited. His parents had been visiting San Francisco when the Pacific Ring blew, and they had been trapped on the West Coast permanently. "What happened. Did they call your name and title, or what?"

"Ha, the major approached me privately after everyone else was assigned jobs. A little psychology at work *there"*

"You mean, because you were left at your station all alone?"

"Uh, yeah. Suggest by singling out a person they're not good enough to do anything else, then offer them a job they daren't refuse."

"Love, you were a refuse collector a week ago."

I felt a grin splitting my face. "I was, wasn't I?"

"Great training for being a government official."

"Stranger things have happened...." I rolled back to face him, warming to my subject, "And it really could be said to be a good foundation for government work. I've been out on the streets working alongside our people. Like James I, I've seen how the base...the foundation of society operates and I've learned how to survive the machinations of bureaucracy from the belly of the beast."

"No idea what you're talking about, but, too true, you sound like a politician already." He nuzzled my neck and a flopped back again, stifling a giggle.

We both looked over toward Dot, but she hadn't budged.

"So, what did Major Marietta say to you?"

"She told me my knowledge tests were about the same as everyone else's here but that I tested high in almost everything else."

Jim stopped nuzzling. He was paying close attention.

"Yeah, and she seemed to make a point of saying the ones I tested high in were the ones it would be impossible to fake."

"Strewth!"

"I thought I was found out!" I let a little of the pent-up anxiety escape in my tone of voice.

"But you weren't...."

"Strangely enough, no. They seem more intent on finding someone to leave the welfare of the settlement with."

"What would they do if they did suss it out?"

"Punish me? Maybe I'd be taken back to the City, never to see my family again?"I hazarded.

"Well, we seem safe enough, if you're going to be in charge here."

"There's other stuff. Have you been called by your name by any of the SC?"

"Nope, just Pioneer 47."

"Mmmm. The Major says they're ordered not to use our names. It makes me think of laboratory rats."

Jim just looked at me. Even in the dark, I could tell his trim black left eyebrow was quirked up. I could feel it.

"I'm *serious* Jim. Maybe they plan to keep us in these tents forever." I shivered at the thought feeling tight.

Jim gathered me to him and stroked my hair, "Okay, Luv. I know. And you may well be right. In two days' time, we've been promised our first excursion. Let's see how that goes."

I nodded, my face buried in his chest. It was a little hard to breathe with my nose squished to the side, but I didn't want to break the feeling of being cherished.

White Mountain Idyll (Part 3)

By

R.V. Neville

First Year, Day Six

Another restless night. This time punctuated with a startled awakening and a sensation of immense constraint.

No wonder.

My bedding was wrapped so tight around me I could take only shallow breaths.

I untangled myself and rearranged my body, back flat, then started to think about the previous day.

Major Marietta and I had been closeted in her cluttered office, her command center, for hours discussing the different governing strategies for newborn settlements. When I say "discussing," I mean, I sat quietly while she lectured on historic civilizations, and then left me for two hours with a set of vids on the subject. That was the morning.

The afternoon was taken up by lists. They consisted of what would be taken, what would be left behind in the settlement for our permanent use, what would be collected when the SC came on a "visit" forty-five days after they pulled out.

"But don't worry, we're here for at least another week."

The major went back to the lists, acquainting me with the function of every item being left behind.

"So," she had said at the end of the day, "We'll be expecting you all to have made other arrangements within the initial forty-five-day period. We'll want our temporary housing back by then. Do you understand?"

"That will be inevitable," I'd said, breaking my long silence. The major had asked few questions of me throughout the day, seeming to prefer I listened, so I'd complied.

"Inevitable?"

"With the construction materials you're leaving for us, people will lose little time setting themselves up in their homesteads."

The major nodded at this. I thought I detected a "we'll see" expression in her face, but as Jim so often reminds me, I am prone to over-analyzing everything. Reliving it now, I made another promise to myself to keep my language simpler.

I yawned and felt my brain unclench.

***

When I woke again, the pod bathed in a buttery sun light. Jim and Dot were gone, and I realized I'd slept through reveille. As I rushed to get ready for breakfast, I noticed I felt surprisingly rested. I had the fizziness in my throat I get when I'm excited. *Today, we'd be going outside!*

The major had promised. It was marred only by the fact I didn't know more than that. Although the major had laid the moniker of "camp governor" on me, that position seemed a private thing between the two of us: I was no more privy to the details of the orientation itinerary than I had been before she assigned me. *Ah well, plenty of time.*

I caught up with Jim and Dot at breakfast.

He bolted his food. "We have a final preparation meeting this morning, getting our kit together for the day, inspecting the hoverbikes, and then we're off!"

"Can I come with you?" Dot pleaded. She was practically

bouncing in her seat.

"Ah Matrix, you know we've got to do this on our own. Especially today. I want to make sure it's safe out there for you first."

She looked crestfallen for all of thirty seconds, then beaming a smile at her dad, she started talking to the girl sitting beside her about *their* day's opportunities.

"Crisis overcome," I said to Jim.

He chuckled. "She's a wonder."

"Thanks for letting me sleep in. Do you know which direction you'll go today?"

"We 'won' our sectors by lottery. The sectors radiate out from camp in wedges. I got east."

"Who do you ride out with?"

"A chap from the old NWT. He's been fishing along the tidal pools they have up there for years. So, he's strong and agile. They weren't pulling anyone's leg when they said those are two necessary talents for hoverbike wrangling."

"What's he like, other than strong and agile?"

"Don't really know, yet. I'll report in this evening Madam Governor."

"Shhh. You know she hasn't announced anything yet," I hissed.

Jim's eyes gleamed with amusement as he shoved a last pancake in his mouth. "Gotta go."

As her father went out one of the entry flaps, Dot glanced up from her conversation at me. She seemed to appraise me for my state of mind.

"I'm okay, Dot."

"I'm going with Quiera to the open group, k?"

"Sure. See you at the midday meeting."

Dot came around the table and threw her arms about my neck, pecking me on the cheek, brief as a lightning flash. Then, she was away again. *Phew! I'm going to have to get creative when we start lessons again if I'm going to hold her attention.*

Then, it occurred to me. There may be other options. Formal schooling sessions, perhaps? With a variety of subjects. Very old fashioned. How would the others take to that, when training solely in their technical subjects was the norm? I wished I had someone to talk things like this over with. (Besides Jim. Jim was great, but his time and his mind were consumed with hoverbikes, mapping, exploring.)

The major had said I could choose an assistant…but we were right back to the position that I had to have the job officially, first. I returned to my breakfast, lost in thought. Afterwards, lingering at our usual table, mug cupped in my hands, I tried to concentrate on the general conversation, but my mind kept picking at the frayed edge of the things I didn't know.

The previous day, Major M had replaced early morning and evening briefings with a single midday one. She hadn't yet said anything to the settlement about self-government…or about me. I knew I should prod her about that, but was satisfied using the time to listen, trying to see through to the core of what she said. I was about 93% convinced that she was on the up and up, and 7% suspicious, which, for me, was extreme acceptance.

When not meeting with the major, I spent my time listening to the people around me. If anyone wondered what my role was, dipping in and out of classes, they didn't ask me. So intent in their own affairs, the seemed oblivious to my presence. Which was good.

Sounds corny, but I wanted to gauge the heartbeat of this…this organism we were evolving into. Not just the heartbeat, but the pulse, the respiratory rate, and all its other vital signs. I was aware the job I was being asked to do could mean the success or failure of this settlement.

The major had never pressured me about that, which surprised me. She wasn't exactly subtle, and I'd be surprised if she were trying to spare my nerves.

This train of thought led me down new darker paths. *Is my overweening pride telling me I'm important when she really chose me because I'm* not *the clever person she says I am, but because I can be molded to do her bidding? Am I just a cipher?*

I shook my nog, dispelling these thoughts, resolving be more proactive in my training. I was familiar with most of the material we'd covered, but my cautious self held those cards close to my chest. If the major thought I was an uneducated savant, so much the better. I realized, though, I needed more useful information than I was getting at this IV-drip rate.

I emitted a sigh, accepted another cup of chicory root "coffee," and turned my mind back to the conversation going on around me. As time for classes drew near, people were drifting from one table to another, and ours was now populated with the water treatment group. With fifteen minutes left to go before classes started, they were already discussing their previous day's lesson. A good sign of their engagement!

Satisfied this small group, at least, was on the right track to taking part in a successful community, I headed for the major's CC.

***

The major spent the first hour lecturing me on infrastructure. After she'd dissected the components of community framework, she wound up with, "And that's why we're concentrating on group skills. This way, there will always be several people in the settlement who can change a tire, for example, or mend a plastics remolder."

I nodded. *Have I really let her waste all that time on something so obvious?*

"But then, you know that don't you Pioneer 73? I suspect you know a great deal about the things we've been working on. Don't quite know *how*…." She left that thought dangling, but I didn't take the bait.

"A lifetime of watching what my neighbors do, Major. When

you're a trash collector, you have the chance."

"I think you might be surprised by the depths of ignorance most of your fellow settlers swim around in."

"Maybe not. As a people, we're kept on a fairly narrow track. I mean, we are taught what we need to know to perform only in the fields chosen for us."

The major looked at me for a moment eyes slightly narrowed, then nodded to herself. "The SoCo finds it works well as things are now, with its citizens excelling at the jobs they're assigned. It avoids unnecessary longing after things they can never achieve. Do you have a different opinion?"

"I don't exactly have an opinion," I lied. "But I was wondering about expanding education here a little further. Perhaps teaching subjects our people don't normally get to experience."

"And for a farmworker to know about history, for example…how would that assist her in her daily tasks?"

"It could give her knowledge of what things have been tried before, and an idea how to overcome obstacles to a reaping a good harvest."

"That's a big 'could,' 73."

"Or, more specifically, a good grasp at mathematics could help with sow-rate calculations and fertilizer spreading. You've said yourself, we won't have the infrastructure *here* that is available on the arcologies."

"True enough, but who would you get to spread your education?"

"If we could keep access to the archives on old forms of education when you leave, we could get something started."

"Mmm... Have some ideas written up by the end of the week and we'll see what sort of progress you make by the time the forty-five days is up."

"Thank you, Major."

"And if you *do* get permission to run this type of school you desire, you must understand that the basic curriculum takes precedence at all times. The tests we ran over the last week, were designed to identify best job assignments *with* the lack of our normal infrastructure in mind. On balance, it is unlikely you will get permission, but I will put the request across if you are showing progress here."

"I understand."

The major put her hand to her earbud, then she rose and rolled her shoulders, "The scouts are about to start out on their first excursion. This seems to be as good a time as any to introduce everyone to the environment."

***

I trailed behind the major's loping stride through the maze of tent corridors, trying not to skip with excitement. Outdoors was waiting *and* I'd get to wave off Jim on his first trip to look for our future homestead. Of course, they were recording *all* the feasible homestead sites, but I couldn't help but feel an advantage in being married to one of the surveyors.

I was puffing gently be the time we reached the doors through which we'd entered nearly a week before. Four of her lieutenants were already waiting. Major Marietta adjusted her jumpsuit, straightening its already crisp lines, then looked me in the eye.

"Ready?"

"Yes."

"Get up here then." She faced forward again, and two of the lieutenants opened the double doors.

I stepped up beside her. Olives handed us each a wide brimmed hat and shaded glasses. We entered the airlock passage together, and then through the last two doors sealing us in from the land.

Then, we were outside, sunlight notching the lumens up by about a thousand-fold. Despite the dark glasses and hat, I squinted and ducked my nog. After a few moments, I opened my eyes again slowly. Our old home had been enveloped in a permanent overcast, which had protected us from the worst of the sun's rays. Here, there was a bright blue sky overhead.

"Don't worry, this isn't the lower desert. You won't cook in moments. Just always wear nog-gear here, and *always* put on the glasses when you go out between sunrise and sunset.

I nodded. As we walked, I stared around our encampment. We had emerged into a wide dusty courtyard in the shelter of our tent city. Three huge tents were set up in long rectangles the biggest bridging the distance between the two shorter which ran parallel to each other. The doors we'd come through were set in one of the ends of a shorter side, and we were the only ones in sight.

"Surprised?" Major Marietta regarded me, lips quirked.

"Yes, it's so big! And…from moving around in it the last few days, I would have guessed that it was L-shaped, but there's that whole other leg to it."

"That's the workshop, storerooms, and livestock containment area. You'll see them shortly. Good spatial perception," she added over her shoulder to Lieutenant Soleri. He made a note on a pad.

We stopped in the center of the courtyard next to a communications tower, all sparse metal and bio-plastic poles and angles. A breeze blew up as we came to a rest and even through my hemeossistant jumpsuit, it felt chill.

Half a score of Olives, which had moved out with us, walked along the long side of the main tent. They stooped and began to hoist on ropes so that the tent walls rolled up, revealing the translucent skin that allowed light in most areas of the complex. Silhouettes of people appeared behind it. The Olives rolled up the skin as well, and I could see the whole camp was gathered, facing onto the courtyard. Only slim chains draped between bollards separated them from us. That, and their natural fear of direct sunlight. They all wore the dark glasses.

I looked for Dot, but she saw me first, and shouted, "Mum! Hi, Mum!" I spotted her midway along the group, kneeling on the floor at the front with the other children. She waved her arm energetically as she called. I waved back.

A wide door, about three quarters of the way along the workshop wing, rolled up and the scouts emerged, the soft swishing of the hoverbikes murmuring clear across the bright landscape. They rode toward us in pairs, a lieutenant bracketing each six-bike column. The bands on the LT'a arms flashed blinding white in the sun. As they approached, the columns split away from each other, one line forming a circle to our left which kept time until the other column came 'round behind us. The two columns ended up in formation, facing each other between us and the rest of the pioneers.

The crowd broke into applause and hoots, and the scouts nodded and smirked their thanks. I joined in the clapping, biting back a laugh of pleasure.

The major leaned toward me, "The formation drill is important to the scouts' ability to handle their bikes in tight quarters, and it is the closest thing we have to a parade today."

"I thought it was great!" My eyes had settled on Jim.

I was talking to myself, though, as Major Marietta had turned to Lieutenant Chavez to accept her megaphone. She took several steps forward leaving the rest of us where we were. As she raised the horn to her lips, the hoots fizzled out. "Good morning, Pioneers. Welcome to the great outdoors!"

Another cheer.

"We're here to wish our scouts good luck and happy hunting. But first, and we need your attention as well, Scouts, I want to introduce you to someone who will be fulfilling a very important role in your lives.

"She has tested highest amongst you for no specific skillset, but shows great general competence. This makes her a Renaissance woman, and a Renaissance woman is exactly what you need here at Camp New Snowflake. I have confidence that she will be able to organize you and guide you through the complex trials and tribulations of forming a new community."

It may have been my imagination, but the faces of my fellow pioneers seemed to be looking past the major to where I stood. The darkened lenses of their glasses gave them the inscrutable look of a horde of insects. I shut my eyes, trying to wipe the image away.

"Pioneer 73 has been working with me since job assignments began, and she shows a good grasp of the concepts necessary to build and maintain a successful colony." I opened my eyes in time to see Major Marietta motioning me forward with rapid hand movements.

I moved up beside her and she said, "Please welcome your new Colony Governor."

The crowd stood silent. I hadn't expected to feel so nervous. My stomach descended several floors below its normal level. *Are they rejecting me without even knowing me?*

Sharp cracking noises, like gunshots, rang through the clear high air, only a few at first, then, gathered momentum, until the noise was recognizable as scattered applause. Apparently, my usual fellow diners thought enough of me to welcome me in my new position. Jim and Dot, of course were clapping loudly, and I felt gratified that others joined in.

"Say something," Marietta handed me the megaphone.

"Hello," I paused. The smart chip in the megaphone, not recognizing my voice pattern, sent it veering off into a high-pitched scream.

After a chorus of nervous laughter, while people covered their ears, I was rewarded with a healthy, "Hello."

The fact that they responded, made me feel a little braver. I opened my mouth to continue, but the major, who had had her hand cupped over her earbud during the interchange, took the megaphone back and said, "That's good, that's great, no more time right now everyone. We need to get our scouts on their way, and there's much to be done this afternoon. Our cooks and kitchen staff will be making their first meal tonight with the help of the service droids, preparing you for when we withdraw. For now, you should go back to your morning activities. I'm cancelling the midday meeting, as convened just now. Any questions?"

When none came, an Olive stepped forward. It stood to attention and a fanfare played, apparently out of it. I suddenly realized where the morning reveilles came from. There were some titters from the ground where a group of children sat, and I felt like joining in. The major spoke again.

"Scouts, you've been provided with knowledge of mapping, emergency repairs to hoverbikes, and a packed lunch for your first tour. You have the assistance of four of the Southwest Constabulary's highly trained lieutenants. I look forward to your report later. Good hunting to you in your first day out, Scouts."

With those words, Major Marietta put her hand in the air and revolved it once. The motion was repeated by the lead bikers, and they peeled away from their formation, three bikers heading off in each of the four directions of the compass. Another burst of cold breeze ushered them away.

My eyes followed Jim's receding figure. We hadn't had time even to nod to each other, and I watched him go with a mixture of envy and sudden loneliness. Since we'd met eighteen years before, we'd never been separated by more than an arcology's span.

But then, my gaze took in the wider aspect of the low bowl of land the tent city was situated in and I forgot self-pity. The valley we were in felt friendly. It was sheltered by a wide black mesa on one side and low hills and ridges on its other sides. The threads of an ancient road, once paved, ran east to west. Hollows led out of the valley in different directions making it a natural focal point.

Our tents were built on a low mound near the center of the valley, the land rolling gently away in golden grass waves, and up again to the ridges. A few ramshackle old buildings lay scattered about the land. Most of them were so far gone as to be only materials caches, but one, a long low stick-built close to the old road, looked likely repairable. *Hmm, community center?*

I turned to watch Jim and his companions as they hovered east along the ancient trail. They were already cresting the ridge. I stifled a desire to call out to them, and turned back to the crowd. They were already dispersing, and the Olives were rolling the translucent tent sides down.

The major was absorbed in her earbud again. After a time, she said, "Yes Sir, we'll be on standby." She signed off, then saw me.

"Nothing to worry about right now, 73. Let's get back to the office, and I want you to make a start going over the education archives you requested, so I can pass it on to HQ. By the way, make sure you live up to what I said about you just now." Her voice edged toward strained, and I inspected her demeanor, but it seemed as confident and authoritative as always. We set off for the tent again.

Despite the disquiet her tone roused in me, I felt pleased she was willing to put forward my request, and wondered if I should solicit for more. When we arrived at her CC, she handed me an old-fashioned clipboard and pen and told me to go in the adjoining room to make my list. I complied and she dropped the tent flap between us.

As I booted up the pc, I could hear her giving orders to the single lieutenant who'd followed us back. I started looking through the records, and for a while there was scholarly silence.

Lost in concentration, considering whether I could ask for the curriculum of the long-defunct Pomona College's social studies department without raising suspicions, I became aware of voices in the

CC. From the sounds of it all eight of the lieutenants still in camp were speaking, pretty much at the same time. Voices rode up briefly then descended to quieter but urgent tones.

I raised my nog trying to catch the drift, but only made out a few phrases: "*too early, bad timing, survive.*" Otherwise, it just sounded like mush from where I sat. *She's going to have to tell me what's going on sooner or later.*

I forced myself to return to work, but I soon admitted that weeding out crucial files was a mammoth task. *What I* should *do is figure out what I* don't *need.* I sighed. *I'd so much prefer to just to keep the "sum of all human knowledge." It wasn't like they don't have copies.*

I tried to guess what would be most important to a tiny spot of humanity, growing their own culture in the White Mountains. There were the obvious things like day-to-day survival skills, but what about when we developed our community, growing our own food and remolding our own bio-plastics, creating our own energy, making our own clothes, then what? Would we actually *need* our people to know about grander ideas? Well, in my mind, the answer was an obvious and resounding "Yes," but was it responsible of me to include arts, culture, and the record of human inspirations and aspirations in my application, if doing so might endanger its success?

The major's voice broke into my thoughts as it rose above the others in the CC, "All right! There will be no further discussion of this matter. Any decisions about the matter do not lie within *our* purview. You are to return to your duties until we get further word of developments. Proceed as usual. Dismissed."

The CC emptied with shuffling footsteps and some mumbled, "Ma'am's," Moments later, the heavy flap swung up and Major M strode in. "How are you coming on that, 73?"

"There's quite a lot of data I would like to request…and I'm having some difficulty knowing where to stop."

"Well, well, you can come back to that later this afternoon. For now, you'll be lunching with me today, then we'll tour the works tent. I'm stepping up your training."

***

Lunch was awkward. Major Marietta seemed to chew her thoughts along with her food. The desire in me to ask about the squally meeting with her subordinates grew with each silent minute. I couldn't think of anything to say that wouldn't be an intrusion on the grounds of her fortress-like introspection.

Finally, when our plates were cleared, I ventured, "Major, if you don't need me for a few minutes, I would like to relieve myself."

"Yes, of course, 73. Just get back here straight away. We'll be taking that tour immediately."

As I walked to the latrines in my pod section, I wondered why she'd ordered my presence at the recent meal if she had nothing to say to me. *Unless, she was afraid I'd spread gossip about that meeting.* I allowed myself to feel rankled for a moment, supposing she distrusted my discretion, but then, I shrugged it off. *Maybe she wants to make our afternoon startup quicker.* I hoped Dot was keeping herself out of trouble.

When I returned, the major was ready for me, but instead of setting off as she'd said, she tapped the table, indicating where I should sit.

"I expect you were aware I called a meeting of my senior staff before lunch." She paused, uncharacteristically waiting for my answer.

"Yes, I was."

"And how much did you hear?"

"Nothing beyond random words and phrases. And your dismissal."

"So. You didn't get the drift of the meeting at all?"

"Only that something was 'too soon'...and the word 'survival' stood out. That was all really, Major."

Looking at the patch of table in front of her, the major took a deep breath, "Seventy-three, there are reports of heightened seismic activity in the far south of our region. The activity has generated concern that the long-silent Popo Volcano at New Tenochtitlan could blow. I have been put on notice that the evolving situation *could* require the attendance of all personnel. It's too early to be sure, but I think you should be aware that things here could change."

"I see…you mean you would be withdrawing all support of this project?"

"Conceivably. Word of this only came through when we were on the parade ground. Be assured, we will continue with training and tuning, right up until we're ordered to pull out. And each specialist group has at least one individual who has experience of the subject."

My mind ricocheted from feelings of abandonment to the opportunity for a negotiating platform. She seemed to take my silence for agreement, and started to rise.

"How soon will you get word?"

"We should know within forty-eight hours, one way or another. Let's walk. You need to at least *see* the workshop wing, this afternoon."

Her sense of urgency infected me, and we started the long trek through Camp Snowflake. As we walked, her tone turned conversational, "You know, this area was called 'Cedar Hills' at one point. The droids found a sign out by the old east west road, buried under several inches of dirt."

"But you chose the name 'Snowflake?'"

"Well, I didn't. It was the Conception Committee that chose the name. I imagine they thought the promise of snow has a more positive ring to it. Also, Snowflake was at one time an important governmental seat in the region. So, there's a sense of history there."

All things that no one's going to care about if we can't feed ourselves. I pushed back on the self-doubt. "Interesting to see someone has time for that sort of cogitation."

"Their job. We all have jobs to do."

Never had the major sounded more like a cog in the wheel. I began to appreciate her as something less and something more than the interim leader of this undertaking. She was, *of course,* reporting to her superiors. Working for them. Doing their bidding. For the first time, I wondered how much autonomy she had in decision making here.

When we arrived at the end tent, we entered the food prep areas first. Kitchen, pantries, and dishwashing areas were heavily populated with Olives and pioneers alike.

"They're being trained in the preparation of fresh foods from scratch, as you won't have access to the manufactories. At least to start with, all your produce will go back directly into your community. If things work out well, you may have the opportunity to trade with the rest of SoCo."

"So…the way we've been eating since we got here doesn't stop when you leave?" I could hear the incredulousness in my own voice.

"Assuming you can grow it, you can eat it. You'll be left with the remaining stores we brought here, of course, to help you get by until you are in production. And there are certain crops you will find it impossible to grow, I think. This climate can be difficult, I understand."

We moved past the dinner prep stations, where quite a lot of chopping was going on, to one where the half dozen people and two Olives were clustered around big glass jars which had just emerged from a steaming metal pot.

"This is the 'canning' station. We had to do a lot of digging in the archives to discover how to use this, but our planners wanted to give you skills you could duplicate without heavy use of technology, as energy will be in short supply, at least to start. This is a simple method of preserving certain fresh plant products. A jar of sliced pears, for example, will last months when prepared properly. You should read up on it."

I most certainly would, wanting to know how to achieve this miracle of preservation when we had our own place. For an instant, I wished I'd been assigned such a job detail, instead of as the overseer of all this, but then my sense of duty kicked in and I settled down.

"Come this way, 73," the major said, stirring me out of my reverie.

We left the food prep area and walked down a long corridor on the far side of the tent from the central courtyard. When we emerged into a huge section of tent, there was an earthy smell I wasn't used to. Major Marietta looked at my face, and she came close to smiling

"Animal dung," she said.

"The smell?"

"Uh-huh."

The wall on the far end of the tent was rolled up to allow that pungent odor to escape, and I thought I rather liked it, though glad it wasn't trapped in the great room with us.

"The eggs we had at breakfast are from these birds."

"Hens! And cocks." I felt a grin spread across my face. I'd seen them once before, as a small child. They were making a din: chortling, clucking, hissing, with an occasional screech. I wanted to stand and watch their scratching and pecking behavior, but the major tramped along to a different set of enclosures. The smell there was more pungent.

"And these, do you know what these are?"

I looked at the multicolored hairy-skinned, short-legged beasts. There was about a dozen per pen. Some rootled around in piles of rough brown grasses. A couple were lying in the dust, rubbing their skin into it. Two tussled over a short scrap of vegetable matter, pulling from opposite ends. "Swine?"

"Close, they're pigs. Rare…and rather valuable. We've drawn these groups from the four different genetic pools available in SoCo. It will be your community's responsibility to breed and increase their numbers. Historically, they were very useful animals. Now, only limited numbers are available for certain members of the authority."

I nodded, mesmerized by the piggy interactions.

"One more set of animals."

We walked along the pens, and I asked, "Why are there no humans in here? I've only seen Olives—er, the droids."

She stopped and looked a me. "I wanted to get everyone started on their specialties first. Every family will need to care for their animals, depending on how *you* organize the pig breeding program. There are enough chickens for all the families to start a flock, of course, but a shortage of pig stock. That will be your first duty. Olives, hmm?" This time, the major smirked, turned on her heel and led the way round the end of the bank of pens.

I was already trying to guess what the final variety of farm animal would be. As far as I knew most others were extinct. What I saw stunned me. Dozens of pens, each inhabited by a *dog*. I'd never seen so many in one place.

When I'd been on the run as a thirty-year-old, they usually hunted in hordes on the outskirts of settled areas. I'd been chased by plenty of packs. The sight of these animals, lying quietly at the bottoms of their cages, staring at me, made my insides feel like water.

"What are they for?" I couldn't help my upper lip lifting in something close to a snarl.

"Ah, don't worry, they're not for *eating*. Some cultures did that before the Ring of Fire, but the practice died with fallout. A few deaths from radiation poisoning was all it took."

"Yeah. But, then, what are they *for?"* I muffled the panic as best I could.

"They're for protection, 73. These dogs have been specially bred to protect their human handlers. Some of the predators inhabiting this area are not to be taken lightly."

"So, these aren't wild dogs?"

"That's right. They've been bred and trained to be obedient, quiet servants. Second generation removed from the wild dogs captured for the project. The SoCo has been planning this experimental colony for quite some time."

They looked identical to me, enormous, all brown and black, with unblinking flinty eyes. Every dog stared at me, and I stared back.

"Want to go closer?"

I shuffled a few inches.

"They're behind the wire, 73, and they're docile—except when there's a threat. What is it with you?"

"I was chased—attacked by wild dogs once. A long time ago, but seeing all these dogs. It was a shock." Feeling foolish, I took a real step forward, a silly big one as if I were playing a childhood game, like 'Mother May I.' Their eyes followed me.

"I can't imagine what you were doing outside your arcology. Did they come on a farm you were working on?"

Lying about working on a farm, and especially about its perimeters being breached by a pack of wild dogs, would only cause trouble, so I just shook my head.

Evidently, she didn't want to pursue the subject either, as she heaved a sigh. "Is this going to be a problem?"

I took a deep breath. "No, of course not. They just surprised me."

"Good. We need to keep moving. It's already getting late and we still have the workshops to tour. Come along."

She strode back toward the corridor door, and I followed, relieved she'd dropped the wild dog subject. When we reached the door though, she had one more thing to say. "Tomorrow, you'll have a chance to look at the lists of some candidates for your assistant. Once chosen, perhaps you can assign that person dog oversight. Save you from it."

"Oh, they're alright. I'll cope, but it will be good to have some help."

We visited the remolding shop next and saw the machine, a medium sized model, in action producing new blanks from the bioplastic being fed it by some pioneers. "Normally, the remolder would just be used to directly create needed objects, but you'll be in charge of planning a schedule for small parts when you're ready to start building."

"This is our only machine?"

"Yes, it's an older model, but quite reliable. Your people have been getting instruction on repairing it, and I believe three of the workers here are already experienced in its operation."

"What about a 3D printer?"

The major hesitated before answering. "We'll see how you progress. Printers are expensive items and rare, but I'll put in a request for one when the colony is ready to make good use of it."

The next two workshops were small and less busy. A lieutenant in each was demonstrating the care of hand tools to pioneers. Finally, we came to the hoverbike shop. It was empty, except for an Olive, which was cleaning a workbench. It was another spacious room, big enough to allow a single biker practice riding in it. Workbenches and lockers lined two walls and parking harnesses hung from the ceiling against the third side. On the fourth wall, a table with mapping equipment stood a little way from the rollup door I'd seen in the morning.

The major pointed to the harnesses. "Case in point, you'll be able to use the remolder to produce harnesses for each of the new homesteads for when they have their turn at the hoverbike…or however you set that up." Again, I had the niggling feeling we were being left to our own devices as some sort of experiment.

After inspecting the workbenches, we loitered by the mapping table and I asked, "Do you know when the scouts will return?"

Major Marietta looked down at her tablet. "Anytime now."

As if on cue, the Olive left what it was doing and went to the rollup door. It unlatched some bolts and hoisted. Three quarters of the scouts were waiting outside.

"Why we hurried," she smiled, apparently pleased with the perfect timing.

Nine hoverbikes, their riders dusty and windswept filed slowly into the big room. Jim wasn't among them, but before the bikes were fully clipped into their harnesses, he and his two companions arrived.

When he saw me, he gave me a tired, but ear-spanning, grin.

The men finished stowing their bikes and removed their outer gear, the major waiting calmly. The lieutenant who ran the department came over quickly and snapped a salute.

"Report."

"My team headed south, Ma'am. Once we skirted the big mesa we found a wide valley crisscrossed with numerous old watercourses, which have, in their time wreaked havoc on transportation and living conditions. With the climate settling some, this area *may* be worth settling, although…further exploration recommended."

The major grunted and turned to the next lieutenant to approach. He told a slightly different story of higher ground to the west, but cautioned that anything built there might catch wind damage. While the lieutenants reported to their leader, I watched the other scouts, the ones I would be left with when the SC's moved out, as they gathered 'round the mapping table.

One of each scouting pair held a dark grey device about the length of a forearm and width of a palm. While the unencumbered men cleared the table top of compasses, rulers, and styli, someone touched a corner and a crude embedded area map flickered alight. I only knew it was a map from the unmistakable outline of our encampment. My interest grew by tenfold. One of the scouts carrying the device offered an end to his team-mate and, holding it across the width of the table, they walked it along its length. A small area on just left of center came alive with contour lines and box-like renderings.

I moved a little closer, delight making my head feel light. Jim's gentle laugh made me look up. "Great, isn't it?"

"This is what you've been doing other than just racing around on hoverbikes?"

"Yep."

"How does it work?"

"Just a minute, and watch closely." It was his and his partner's turn next. They held the wand between them, a thumb on a button at each end. The button triggered a red light to shine on the interactive top and start filling in the detail of the area on the map.

"Wow!"

"So much knowledge taken for granted fifty years ago has been lost," Jim said.

"So much of *everything* we took for granted fifty years ago was lost when the satellites failed," the major's voice amended, causing me to start. I'd forgotten her in the pleasure of the moment.

"We do things a more basic way. This device," the lead lieutenant took one of the wands and showed it to me, "has two modes. Carried on the handlebars of the hoverbike it automatically records elevation, which are what these lines here show. Then, when a ruin, or other some other interesting anomaly is spotted, the driver stops and records it here." He showed me a keypad on the top of the wand.

I looked again at the map. Now that all four teams had finished scanning it with their wands, it showed narrow bands of detail radiating spoke-like from the center, where before it had been white or crude.

"And this will give us a true understanding of the lay of the land. We can see where it appears best for farming, building, and where those before us chose to build."

"True, it will show a historical record of sites favored by the last inhabitants of the region, but you shouldn't put too much credence in that. *They* didn't have to work with the environmental conditions we have to consider."

"That's correct. Many seem to have built in unthinkable places by today's standards. See here, here and here on the map? Those would be swept away in the sort of flooding the big storms bring in. Like everywhere else, the climate is more violent now." The major nodded at the scout who'd spoken up.

We looked over the small amount of information the map now contained, which was 100% more than it had had a few minutes before, and discussed what we could see.

"Tomorrow, we'll concentrate on filling in detail around camp, before going out further." When the lead lieutenant said that, I imagined the scouts plying back and forth on their hoverbikes like combine harvesters.

"How wide a picture do the wands make?"

"Six meters wide."

Not bad.

"Okay Scouts, you're dismissed. Get some rest, and you'll start again in the morning. Seventy-three, why don't you take the rest of the evening off. We'll get busy ourselves tomorrow."

Jim and I headed for the showers. Along the way he painted a word picture of what he'd seen out there: of wide valleys still brown in the chill spring air, the forests of cedar and pinon pines.... I felt happy, excited, thoughts of being lab rats miles away from my mind.

***

That night, I slept peacefully for the first time since our arrival.

Sometime before midnight, however, I was hauled up out of happy oblivion by a hand on my shoulder, shaking me.

"Pioneer 73, wake up." It was Lieutenant Eden.

"What's wrong, LT?"

"The Major sent me for you."

Bleared with sleep, I squinted at her. She looked only marginally more awake than I did. I rose and followed her to the Major's office.

"Seventy-three," she greeted me when we arrived. The rest of the lieutenants were already there. They all looked torn from sleep. A clock display read 23:47. "The volcano I told you about? It blew, and it set off a reaction along the entire Mexican axis. We're needed down there."

"*All* of you?"

"Afraid so, 73. The refugee situation in the Tenochtitlan arcology group will be dire. We're pulling out in the morning."

I felt an immediate sharp sense of compassion for the people of Mexico, but a sharper sense of concern for the people she was leaving me in charge of. "And, you think our group is far enough ahead in training for that to work?"

"Mostly. As I told you, every training group has at least one member who's experienced in the activity. You are bright, and I'm leaving you the pc's and all the archives, even the ones we spoke about earlier today"

That's a bonus. "There won't be any problem with your superiors? I mean, I thought you had to put in a request."

"Needs must. I'm also leaving you six of the AI units."

"Six?" That was six more than I had expected.

"They should be good for a long run, but if they malfunction, you should just switch them off. We will try to be back within the forty-five days. We have quite a lot of work now, 73. Your best course is to go back to sleep and be fresh in the morning."

"Isn't there more I should know?"

"There doubtless is, but we have to plan our withdrawal and approach to the axis area. Lieutenant Eden will be back for you in four and a half hours."

And that was that: I was dismissed.

Back in the pod, I lay in my cot planning, and then worrying the bone of that plan.

I wasn't fearful whether I could do the job (my studies had made me ideal for such circumstances in my former life); the question was, would I be allowed to? The Southern Constabularies residents were used to doing as ordered, of course, and the major had told them I was in charge, so perhaps I wouldn't have reveal my past to the other pioneers.

One thing was for certain, I had to face the fact that, if required and for the good of the settlement, I would have to tell them if push came to shove.

Did I mention I slept peacefully for two hours that night? It was the last time in a long time.

(To be continued ...)

White Mountain Ornament

By

DEUM

When it comes to Christmas ornaments, I am a traditionalist. I've never decorated a tree all in one color nor bought a season's worth of all new holiday baubles. Each year my tree is trimmed with trinkets that have historic or sentimental value. I still have a collection of thrift store ornaments from the mid-80's when I was in nursing college, bedecking my very own "first tree away from home". So annually I adorn my tree with a rag tag collection of memories of warmth and stories of my life and my loved ones. Among this collection of tender moments there is one item I place on my tree each year with tears of wonder in my eyes. It was a gift from a complete stranger.

The story of this Christmas gift begins on a hot July afternoon in the early 1990's. I was working as an ER nurse in a small hospital in east central Arizona. Our trauma team was horrified when a distraught father rushed into the ambulance bay door with his unconscious six-year-old son in his arms. Even as we hastened to begin life saving measures, the father sobbed out the story of his "fun day on the tractor" gone tragically wrong.

In a few short sentences Dad described teaching the boy about the controls, letting the child watch while he moved some earth. At the end of the lesson, he turned briefly away from his son. He had no idea that his son chose that moment to lean out so far that he fell with a yelp. Before Dad could stop the tractor the boy's head was crushed beneath its tires.

Our team worked desperately to keep the lad alive with this severe head injury. Every minute counted as we waited for the emergency transport plane to arrive and fly him to a neurologic center in Phoenix. The youngster left our care more stable than when he arrived, but it was still touch and go. As often happened in our tiny ER in those days, we had no follow up to learn if the child lived or died.

Fast forward to December of that year. Another understaffed busy afternoon with team tempers running short. In the middle of the bustle our unit clerk declared "some lady" was in the waiting room asking for four of us by name. The lady said she wasn't sick but wouldn't say what she wanted. I was declared the least busy and sent to find out. I bit my tongue, took a deep breath, and said a prayer for patience in the face of this interruption. I had one goal as I hurried to the waiting room: keep this short!

The woman was small and nondescript. She held a wire coat hanger that had four "clothespin angels" dangling from it. I looked at the pins clumsily decorated with fabric, paper and fake hair. My first thought was *Oh, no! Not another person trying to sell us crafts! These are ridiculous!* I steeled myself to tell her vendors were not welcome at the hospital and send her away.

Then she called me by name. "Are you Dawn?" When I nodded, her tears began to flow. She quickly shared her story in a small voice. She was the mother of the little boy on the tractor. She made these ornaments for the trauma team that worked on her son that day back in July because we were her "angels". She wanted us to know. Her boy had not only survived, but was home and doing well enough to start school again after the Christmas break. Soon my cheeks were wet, too.

My eyes brim full every year as I recall that woman and her kindness. She took the time to remind her son's care team that we made a difference in her family's life. I hang that homespun clothespin ornament every year as a grand symbol that I have had the privilege to touch and be touched by angels.

###

The Writing Lesson

By

Nico Crowkiller-Scherr

There is nothing worse then a pixie strung out on a sugar ride.

I woke early to bright blue skies on the first day of fall, kissed my sleeping husband, Steve, and dressed.

Rays of sunshine greeted me through my kitchen window to the contentment of my fourteen-year-old black cat, Baloo. He stretched on the side table while my other three swirled around my legs and talked to me about their food needs.

Once my motherly duty to a pack of cats was fulfilled I made toast, spreading it with blackberry preserves, then slicing a sliver for Sprite and poured my black gold into my mug. I knew the essence of the coffee would wake Sprite from her nightly repose.

I took the eye dropper from its place in the coffee mug which had a picture of Tinkerbell to place in my pocket and started for the library.

Sprite didn't disappoint. She burst from the door of her pixie hut on the shelf above my writing chair when I set down the plate on the end table.

Stretching and yawning, she shone with the sheer beauty of her aura. Today her auburn hair was pulled up in a pony tail allowing the curls to fall down her back to her iridescent blue wings. Her emerald eyes sparkled at the sight of my coffee mug.

"Give us some gold, Love." She squeaked in her Irish brogue

while she held the child's miniature tea cup she claimed from my childhood set in her small hands.

I dipped the dropper in my mug and delivered three drops of coffee into her cup.

“There's a, Love,” she smiled blowing across it to take a sip.

“There's toast and preserves.” I offered when I noted the devil-may-care look in her eye when my youngest cat, Eli, walked in.

“Have the beasts been fed?” Sprite inquired, watching the cat hop to the child's bookshelf and begin to clean himself.

“Yes, and you may have the fur after I brush him.” I took my seat in the chair as she blushed at the pleasure the fur would give her.

Flitting down she settled her five-inch frame on the tomato pin cushion she pilfered from the sewing supplies five years ago when she came into Steve's and my life. She took her sliver of toast to first sniff then examine the preserves.

“Blackberry.” I stated, sipping my coffee.

Sprite bit into it with razor-sharp teeth and chewed. Emitting a squeal of delight, she licked her lips. “Cracking good, Bear.”

I looked at the outfit she wore today. It was one of my favorites. A deep blue mini skirt with a shimmering gauze pink halter top that didn't interfere with her wings. During cold days she wore vests or cloaks made of the fur from my kitties. Eli, being half Persian she coveted his long fur. She had two vests that were her prizes. A white one that came from our only female cat, Oct, and one she'd made the first springtime she'd lived with us. That one came from our Husky/wolf who'd passed away last winter. I caught her sometimes dazed, looking at his photo. She, like the rest of us, missed Duke.

She finished her toast then drank her coffee, then took flight to the shelf where my writer's books set.

“Dictionary, thesaurus?” she quipped, hands on her hips.

“My dictionary is under my chair and the thesaurus is next to *On*

Writing."

Sprite buzzed past me to perch on my shoulder. "Well then, are we ready?"

I opened book two to *The Six Mile Creek Chronicles* to where I had been rewriting a scene.

She tisked at me tapping a finger against her chin. "That character needs something. He's too cold. He's one sided."

"He's a hit man, Sprite. He's also a lesser character." I tried to explain.

"He has a bairn though. Family. What would your mentor say? She'd want a little more life to him. Where's your *Dynamic Characters* book?" Sprite left my shoulder to look on the shelf.

"Next to my grammar book. Here, I'll get it." I leaned over to take the book out. I turned to the chapter on background to read. "Your right, Sprite. He's too one-dimensional. Let's see what I can pull from my depiction papers."

I reached up to the second shelf to take my notebook down. Opened to the pages on villains. I found Sydney Abbot and discovered that indeed I had something I could mention about his coldness. The loss of his wife and son in child birth.

That problem solved, we moved onto the next.

Reading over my spelling, Sprite was aghast.

"Ye claim to speak the King's English. Yet, at times I can't understand a bloody word ye say." she huffed, folding her arms across her tiny chest as she hovered in front of my face.

"That's because she's from K and A in Philly. You can't understand her accent." Steve put his two cents worth in when he came through the hallway of the trailer to get his coffee.

"And pray tell who taught ye to speak yar Baltemoreese? What knave names a football team after a big nasty bird? And do not be getting me started on yar so-called football. Rugby is by and far the better sport!" Sprite thrust her hands to her hips glaring at his back when he entered the kitchen, then turned to me.

"Well, he did buy me the dictionary." I laughed at her shaking her head.

Sprite simply could not comprehend the American slang language or the fact that I so brutally cut my words and spell things out the way they sound to me.

"Spelling test... I want ye to take a spelling test each Friday. A list of yar most misspelled words. I know ye can not spell 'against'. Every time ye have Tommie lean on something it's misspelled."

"Sprite, do you want more coffee?" Steve called entering the library.

"Aye, I knew thar was a reason we keep the Lad around. Now yar talking me language." She fluttered to the end table to pick up her mug just as Tiggers, our Tabby, made the jump for the arm of the chair.

The collision sent an explosion of pixie words out of Sprite along with a shower of her magic. She regained her balance, looking at the cat then into her mug.

"Not a drop spilled. Mr. Cat! Might I remind ye that that is me eating area. It would do both us well if ye'd kindly clean yar paws after you've spent yar time in the litter box." She twitched her nose and patted him on the head, then took her mug to Steve who then picked up the dropper and put three drops of his coffee in her mug.

"Y'all alright, Sprite?" He watched her pluck a cat hair from her skirt.

Sprite inspected it then flew to her little bag that hung from the shelf. Setting down her coffee she placed the multicolored hair in her bag marked with Tiggers' name, then picked up her mug to fly back to Steve.

"Never better, Love. Would ye be willing to do that thing with yar phone? Ye know the magic... Find Bear a spelling book?" She sipped her coffee, "Ooh! It has sugar..." She licked her lips and I watched as the sweetness hit her like a candy bar with a hyperactive child.

Sprite started to flit from place to place. A whirlwind around the room as she knocked books down and crashed into shelves. Finally, Steve plucked her gently from the air.

"I'll get Bear a spelling book."

She shuddered from head to foot as he deposited her on her tomato cushion,

I ate my toast while the sugar wore off of Sprite.

As I said, there's nothing so bad as having a pixie strung out on a sugar ride. They have body spasms and their minds, already active to begin with, spiral into uncontrollable thoughts, then once the sugar is gone they sink into sleep.

So here she laid curled up with Tiggs and snoring, Thus ended my writing lesson for the day.

###

About the Authors

Orina Hodgson has loved the written word since she was a small girl. Connecting with self and others through scripted expression comes naturally to her. Whether telling a story, writing poetry, journaling, or preparing instruction she flourishes in reaching her intended audience. Her world is okay if paper and pen or keyboard are close at hand.

Myra Larsen is a native of Arkansas, having lived in Arizona for most of the years after 1963. She lives in Show Low with her husband, Ernie. As a mother of three children she created on-the-spot oral stories for them. She has published articles in newspapers. She is working on the authorized biography of Robert Yellowhair, Navajo artist and co-authoring a book with a local amateur archaeologist.

TDL fell in love with this area when traveling through Arizona. She now has time to write and ponder life's wonders. Living "out east" has opened her heart and mind. She hopes you enjoy her first attempt at writing a story.

DEUM writes and gardens on the eastern Arizona Colorado Plateau. Her professional publications include the essay A Call to Nursing which won honorable mention in the compilation: *21 Peaceful Nurses*.Through her work with the Cedar Hills Writing Group, DEUM is finding her voice writing fiction and memoir.

As a toddler, **RV Neville** lived on the Lowell Observatory campus in Flagstaff with her parents (of course.) That was where she was first exposed to the wonder of the stars, and also caught her lifelong love of Northern Arizona. She’s been writing since she was twelve.

Jonathan S. Pembroke is a lifelong fan of fantasy and science fiction. A military veteran, he and his wife Lisa settled near Snowflake to be close to family. His first novel, *Pilgrimage to Skara* is available on Amazon for Kindle. He tweets at odd intervals and posts to his blog, the Flint Hatchet, at http:// flinthatchet. wordpress. com , which is not safe for reading by anyone.

Kaye (Milton) Phelps is a native Michigander who has also lived in Oregon and Illinois. She is semi-retired from a career in medical records. She has been married to her husband Paul for thirty-eight years and together raised two adopted sons and have three grandchildren. Kaye helped a friend move to east-central Arizona and fell in love with the country, moving there in 2015. She and Paul trail ride and breed Appaloosa horses and share their home with five cats and two dogs. Kaye has written some technical articles. These are her first fiction stories.

Kendra Rogers taught junior high school science and is now retired living with family in the White Mountains.

Nico Crowkiller Scherr is originally from Philadelphia, PA. She lives off the grid with her husband, Stephen, of thirty-five years, who is an inventor and a musician, along with four diverse, headstrong cats and a lovable husky hound. She is the unpublished author of the *Six Mile Creek Chronicles*.

Paula F. Winskye began writing stories at age 12, but did not publish her first novel until 2003. In 2017, she released her 18th, the first Randy McKay mystery, *Rewriting History*. Best known for her Tony Wagner mystery series, Winskye has also published a middle grade novel, four romances, and four volumes of the Collins family saga. A native of North Dakota, she & her husband John live near Snowflake. Learn more at www. winskyebooks. com .

Conni de Wolfe has been writing since the 1970s. In between spurts of imagination, she worked various jobs and raised four children. She has published poems and has written impromtu verses for other people and occasions. She enjoys reading books, bowling, the outdoors, and camping. Her greatest joy is getting together with family and friends.

Trish Zaabel draws on personal experiences for her ideas. She grew up on a dairy farm in Wisconsin. Although Trish was used to living in a rural area, nothing could prepare her for the challenges presented by living remote and off the grid. Trish wrote for her school newspaper while attending the University of Wisconsin-River Falls. She also was published several times in *Arizona Horse Connection.* She lives on 80 acres outside Concho with her husband, a dog, a cat, and 12 horses.